SHINY LITTLE THINGS

LINDA SHANTZ

ALSO BY LINDA SHANTZ

The Good Things Come Series:

Bright, Broken Things (a prequel)

Good Things Come (Book 1)

All The Little Things (Book 2)

All Good Things (Book 3)

This Good Thing (Book 4)

Merry Little Things (Book 5)

All The Best Things (Book 6)

Horse of the Year (Book 7)

Shiny Little Things (Book 8)

Good Things Come Series: Books 1-3 Box Set

Good Things Come Collection: Books 1-5 Box Set

Good Things Come Series: Books 4-6 Box Set

Buy direct from the author:

https://bit.ly/LindaShantzDirect

For updates and bonus chapters, sign up for Linda's newsletter at

https://www.lindashantz.com/writes

For everyone who wanted Faye and Will to get their happily ever after...

And in loving memory of Sampson, who inspired much of Gus's character.

A NOTE TO THE READER

Shiny Little Things takes place after the body of *All The Best Things*, but before its epilogue. It runs concurrent to *Horse Of The Year*.

The Good Things Come Series is set in Canada, and the main characters are Canadian. Canadians use a hybrid of British and American spelling. Sorry, it's just how we roll!

In 2023, following the death of Queen Elizabeth II in September 2022, the Queen's Plate returned to being called the King's Plate to reflect the new British Monarch, King Charles III, but this story happens before the change came into effect.

CHAPTER
ONE

"Ooh, shiny."

Emilie placed a hand on Faye's forearm, and Faye followed her friend reluctantly to the jewellery store, glancing at her phone. They didn't have time for window shopping, not really, but there was no point in deterring Emilie. Faye could spare a few moments to humour her friend.

The display windows facing into the mall's main aisle were filled with beautiful things, and Faye peered cautiously over Emilie's shoulder. Emilie and her boyfriend hadn't even been together for six months yet and she was already gushing over engagement rings. Faye had been with Will for over two years, and they avoided the 'm' word as if it were the most dreaded outcome on earth.

"I love that one. Isn't it exquisite?" Emilie pointed to a brilliant diamond with offset sapphires and a white gold band. "But I adore the classic simplicity of this one."

The stones were pretty, sure. And if someone gave Faye one to wear, she'd do so for the pure beauty alone, if not for what it symbolized. Except Faye had stopped wearing her rings a few months into taking over the café she operated. She worried about misplacing them, having to remove them as she worked flour and crumbled butter into scones, so now they stayed safely in her mother's old box on top of her dresser. She had to remind herself to put them on these days, for those rare occasions she went out.

"Which one do you like?" Emilie persisted.

Faye sighed and played along. Who was she to tarnish the joy of a young woman still feeling the glow of new love? It wasn't Emilie's fault that lustre had worn off Faye's relationship with Will.

She ran her gaze over the various sets wondering how a girl would choose, and couldn't help drifting to the price tag on each one. As much as she admitted — before Will — she'd dreamed, on occasion, of a man who would lavish her with expensive gifts — who didn't? — Faye would never understand why someone would spend that kind of money on a trinket. Some of these rings cost more than her car had, and she'd bet she got a lot more mileage out of the car than these rings would see. Her used Toyota Corolla might be rusting out with a vengeance, but that engine would go on forever.

Nonetheless, one snagged her eyes and Faye couldn't pull them away. It was gorgeous, a simple but flowing design, the rose gold setting accenting a white gold band. The round diamond was modest, but intricately cut so it almost looked like a tiny dahlia.

"That one," she said, pressing her finger to the glass, the heat and oils of the pad leaving a ghost of a print on its smooth surface when she withdrew it. A strange warmth encased her heart, an odd, momentary thing. Did she like the idea? Did some deep part of her long for what it represented, when her head denied it?

Faye forced the sentiment away and turned to Emilie, letting a smile play on her lips. "Your turn."

Emilie scanned the display, a finger resting on her lips, and wandered to the next case, then back to the first one, and tapped her nail against the transparent barrier opposite the simple solitaire she'd commented on earlier.

"That one."

Emilie's boyfriend, Tim, was a professional hockey player. A rookie, but still, he could probably afford one of the larger stones, and just might be the kind of guy who would go for one — like it would be his introverted way to show her how much he loved her — but it didn't surprise Faye that Emilie opted for something more practical. That was Emilie. The only thing she splurged on was expensive coffee and pastry. Even her horse had only cost a dollar.

Speaking of... "I need caffeine and sugar," Faye said. "You in?"

Emilie's head snapped from the rings, back to reality. "Absolutely."

Faye glanced at her phone again as they settled at one of the sticky tables in the food court. They were going to run right smack into Toronto rush hour traffic on the drive home. No avoiding it now, so they might as well relax.

There had been a time, not that long ago, when a Christmas shopping trip to the city would have been a highlight for Faye, but right now all that flooded her mind, leaving a prickly residue of resentment, was that this would be her last day off from the café until December twenty-fifth, and she could think of better ways of spending it than dealing with crowds of harried parents dragging crying kids, overtired salespeople, and tinned holiday music. This is what online shopping was for.

But it was her little tradition with Emilie, and they'd

missed the previous year because last December, Emilie's life had been the insanely busy one. And spending time with Emilie was always fun, though Faye could have had just as much fun without leaving the comfort of the small town of King City where they both lived.

I must be getting old.

"What do we have left to do?" Faye asked as she nibbled a cranberry white chocolate square. She made a copycat for her own shop — it hadn't been hard to figure out the recipe — and her version was better.

Emilie had opted to pack both the sugar and caffeine into her beverage, an industrial-sized gingerbread latte. "I just have one more thing. I'll go back to that little kiosk by the department store for one of those nice toques for Nate. Just to rub it in at Christmas that he hasn't gone to Florida yet." Emilie's sister and brother-in-law usually headed south for the winter early in December with the racehorses they worked with. This year, they'd promised to stay until after the holiday. "What about you?"

"I might grab one for Dean, too — then he'll be done," Faye said, sipping her cappuccino. It also wasn't as good as the ones she made at her Triple Shot Café, but would do its part for her mid-afternoon pick-me-up.

It was a relief when they finally agreed they were finished and trekked to the parking lot laden with their purchases. The mall was so busy, even on a weekday; they'd had to park far from the entrance. What would it be like two weeks from now? Faye shuddered to think. At least they were ahead of the last-minute madness.

Emilie's Honda Civic blended in with the rest of the vehicles — it didn't look very red right now with its layer of brown road slush. Snowflakes falling in slow motion from the grey sky tried to lend a festive atmosphere — a thin layer accumulating on the windshield — but it wasn't quite doing the job for Faye.

As soon as Emilie left the highway forty minutes later — traffic could have been a lot worse — Faye felt her blood pressure drop. There was more snow up here and though the highway had been clear, the ploughs hadn't been out yet on the rural roads. The farm would be pretty with a blanket of white, the vision of it making Faye eager to get home and take her dog for a walk, to decompress.

Yes, I really am getting old.

Emilie pulled up to the café, set in a small strip mall. Faye's Corolla waited loyally under a cosy blanket of white. She'd need more than a swish of the wiper blades to clear her windshield.

"Call me if you need help with anything," Emilie said as Faye transferred her bags from one car to the other.

Emilie's words were merely a nicety. This was one of the busiest times of the year for her friend, as the racing season wound down. When Emilie wasn't at her physiotherapist job or riding, she was helping with the local Thoroughbred retirement group, ensuring all the racehorses had somewhere safe to go. Things would slow down for her in the week leading up to Christmas though, and Faye would gladly call on her then as her own life got a thousand times more hectic.

"Thanks, Em. I will." Faye smiled with a small wave before swinging the door shut and watched as Emilie drove the short jaunt down the road to the physio clinic for her evening shift.

The "closed" sign was flipped on the door of the Triple Shot Café, but Faye unlocked it and slipped in, just to give it a walk-through and prepare a couple of things to make tomorrow morning easier. Everything was dark, the only sound the hum of the large refrigerator in the kitchen. She flipped on the kitchen lights, finishing her tasks before retracing her steps through the front of the shop in the dim light from the parking lot. Once she'd locked up, she shuffled to the car, letting it warm up while she brushed off the snow, then headed home.

When she reached the farmhouse Gus waited for her, his fluffy Golden Retriever ears flopping as he bounced on his forepaws. Faye stomped the snow from her boots inside the back door. She wouldn't deceive herself — it wasn't so much her arrival as what came next that made Gus so happy.

Faye changed out of her shopping clothes into sweats and sweaters, dragged on her less-fashionable long, puffy coat, and tugged a knit hat down to cover her ears, now that she didn't care what her hair looked like. The crisp air would clear her mind of the building pressure in her life.

It was a beautiful evening. Nights like this she didn't mind winter so much. And Faye was looking forward to a break from the business once the rush was over — a quiet Christmas after working long hours to make the holiday better for others. By then she wouldn't care if she ate takeout, though she wasn't sure how Will and her older brother Dean would feel about that. She was closing for three whole days, a respite before the demands of New Year's, and she couldn't wait to just sit around reading a good book with a glass of wine, letting Dean talk her into a game of Scrabble while Will picked his guitar in the corner. Then, after New Year's, with any luck, January would be relatively quiet. A time for plotting and planning the months ahead. A time to rejuvenate.

Autumn had been unusually cold, the ground frozen before the first snowfall. The guys were excited because the farm's pond was already solid, planning an open-air hockey game whenever they could get their schedules to mesh. Faye wasn't a sports person — never had been — but there was something charming about a group of grown men reliving their child-hoods on an outdoor rink. Of course, the women in their ranks

— other than Faye — would not be content to cheer and sip hot chocolate on the sidelines like she would. Emilie and her sister, Faye's best friend Liv, were scrambling through old boxes in their garage for skates that hadn't seen action since they'd left Montreal.

A shovel rested against the old willow tree that hung over the pond and Faye picked it up and shimmied down to the frozen surface, two inches of fresh powder giving it a uniform cover. Shuffling carefully, she pushed the sharp edge through the fluff to the firmness of the ice beneath and began clearing. This much she could do. It would be her contribution. Well, that and being in charge of refreshments, as always. Gus the Golden alternated between sniffing rabbit tracks and bounding up to bite the shovel.

Gus didn't mind that they weren't out for long, racing to his food bowl as soon as they were in the house again, looking expectantly from the stainless steel dish to Faye and back again while she removed her outerwear. Dogs were lucky, not needing all the gear to have fun outdoors. Her face flushed and burned as it warmed and she poured herself a glass of water after doling out his dinner.

Other than the sound of Gus snarfing up the last of his kibble, the house was silent. Her brother, Dean — with whom she'd shared the old Victorian home since he'd returned to care for her when she was fifteen, after their parents' death — was out, and Will was staying in the city tonight. Faye wasn't hungry and carefully contemplated what to do with this precious pocket of time.

Left with that strange combination of warmth and chill after her walk, she decided on a bath — a rare indulgence these days — and climbed the steps to her room, determined to cherish every moment and every thing: the foaming water, the quiet space, the solitude. A little taste of paradise.

There was nothing fancy about the bathroom, but one thing she loved most about this old farmhouse was its vintage tub. Cranking the hot water so the room was soon steaming, she poured in bath oil and suds, the mere smell of the combination relaxing. With her hair piled on her head, Faye slowly inched her way into the scalding depths, setting her skin on fire.

Bliss.

She loved the boneless, drowsy feeling the bath left her with when she climbed out; the knowledge she could pat herself dry, slip into flannel PJs, crawl into bed, and give in to sleep. Before she turned off the light, though, the bouquet caught her eye. It always did.

The flowers were dried now, almost a year later, dust clinging to the petals. It wasn't as if she could clean them. And it wasn't as if she could throw them out. She wished the desiccated bunch was only a sweet reminder of her friend Liv's special day: the beautiful beach wedding. Instead, it was a taunt. An insinuation. But as much as tossing them in the garbage the way Liv had fast-pitched the fresh flowers at Faye after the ceremony would feel so good, it would also seem disrespectful — both to Liv, and what the flowers stood for.

Faye didn't disapprove of marriage; she'd just never pictured herself in a white dress, standing in front of friends making a public profession of her feelings for someone. That said, she'd never pictured Liv doing it either. To be fair, it hadn't, nor would it ever have been Liv's idea, but she'd gone through with it just the same — and Faye hadn't heard a peep of regret.

Faye would bide her time, and it would pass. The "When are you and Will getting married?" questions would taper off. She loved Will; didn't want to be with anyone else. But she didn't need to wear the white dress or have the big party to prove her commitment. All that money would be better used for something else. Investing in the business. Or a new vehicle, when the day came her faithful old Toyota needed to be retired.

Faye had never had a lot of money. She'd learned how to be a smart shopper so she had nice clothes. Nice-ish things, so she could be stylish without going broke. It made no sense to spend that kind of cash on a show any more than it did on the shiny ring. It wasn't as if it guaranteed the success of a relationship. No matter the expense of the wedding, a couple's odds were still fifty-fifty. Most of those folks who put on those lavish events probably would have been better off doing something lower key and investing the rest in a savings account to pay for couples' therapy — or lawyer's fees — when things went sideways.

She could have married rich. Could still, if that's what she wanted. Finding a rich man in the racehorse world was like shooting fish in a barrel. She had the skills and assets. But money could only do so much. Faye had seen it come and go in her life, but one thing endured. Love.

And lack of love wasn't the problem with her and Will. They were happy. They could go on like this indefinitely. And why not? There was nothing wrong with it.

Was there?

CHAPTER
TWO

The piano dropped out abruptly, Nate's fingers falling from the keys as he frowned. "You were kind of flat there."

Will stilled the guitar strings with a thump, glowering. "Pretty sure that was you."

Except it was him, not Nate. Not the chord he'd just struck — but everything about him. He was flat. There was no denying it.

The music they were practicing didn't help. Will was sure Nate would wholeheartedly agree — for different reasons — but there was no avoiding this session for either of them. Last year, the Christmas carol night at Triple Shot Café had been a hit, the only complaint being that Nate hadn't been part of it. This year, Nate was staying, when he was usually in Florida within forty-eight hours of the racing season ending.

They had two weeks to sound like they meant it.

"Let's try it again," Nate suggested, adding with a wry twist of his lips, "Maybe this time we can infuse some actual *joy* into it?"

"'Infuse some joy?' You might be asking a lot there, bud." But Nate had a point. "Joy To The World" was supposed to be, well, joyful, right?

Christmas music made Will melancholy. It brought back contrasting visions of the holidays. One was quiet, organized — controlled — but a bit cold. A bit stressful. A bit lonely. The other was noisy, verging on chaotic — yet filled with all the warmth and comfort that had been lacking in his own home. Looking back, he was sure there'd been stress in Nate's family, too, but the kid version of Will had never noticed it.

As a child, growing up down the same street from each other in Calgary, he'd envied Nate at this time of year. And maybe Nate had envied him, too. Because Will had the fancy gifts — and what kid didn't want those? But Nate had the lively family, and Will had always been jealous of that.

After another joyless go at "Joy to the World," Will suggested, "I think it's time to move on to something different."

Maybe he'd find what was lacking by the time the carol night rolled around. Either way, he and Nate would pull it off; put on the show the patrons were expecting. They were both good at performing under pressure.

His mind drifted back to the past. Some years with his mother and father had been okay. Will woke to a filled stocking, then twitched through breakfast in anticipation for what came next: the mountain of gifts. He always received an abundance of presents, because both his parents had good jobs, and he was the only child. Now, Will could see they'd been overcompensating for careers that interfered with the more old fashioned, single-income family life the Millers had.

Christmas Day afternoon Will would get together with Nate and compare notes. It wasn't a competition, but if it had been — *he who has the most toys wins* — Will would have been the victor, hands down. It had always made him uncomfort-able. Funny that now it was the other way around. Nate was the guy making money hand over fist — and not entirely at ease with it — and Will was working in a restaurant, living in a loft in downtown Toronto with a curtained-off corner for a bedroom.

"We've got to come up with some non-traditional songs," Nate said, his aversion to overplayed holiday tunes seeping to the surface.

"What did you have in mind?" Will asked. "Because 'Peace On Earth/Little Drummer Boy' is now just as overplayed as everything else."

"Do you remember the first time we did that together?" Nate grinned. "At the high school holiday thing? We were a hit."

A broad smile spread over Will's face. "We were not wanting for dates at dances after that."

"Overplayed or not, I think we have to do it. It's a classic."

And probably one of the few modern songs Nate could tolerate.

"All right." Will gave in. "What else?"

Other years, no amount of excess made up for the truth: his parents' jobs came first. Will's mom got called to the hospital, because sometimes babies liked to arrive on Christmas Day. The irony wasn't lost on Will that as an obste-trician, his mom spent the holiday just as often with other peoples' kids as she did her own son. He and his father might watch the NFL football game, if there was one, because that was some male bonding right there, wasn't it? Sometimes they went to a movie. They'd pick up Chinese takeout on the way home and watch another film on TV. Will would try to be happy just hanging out with his dad, when really he wished he was a few doors down with Nate's family, part of the big holiday dinner happening there — messy, but filled with love.

After Will's dad left his mom, he got his wish.

Because then, when Will's mom was called into work, Nate's mother invited him over. Will was sure Connie Miller felt sorry for him. Even her husband, Reid, who came off as kind of gruff, never let Will feel anything less than welcome. He tried to let himself pretend he was the fourth brother, but Christmas Day was always a reminder that holidays were for family. He could wish all he wanted, but this one was not his.

Will had no doubt Nate loved him like a brother. Possibly even loved him more than Nate had loved his real brother, who had betrayed him — though that was a complicated thing. But music couldn't help but take Will back, and this year the memories seemed to hit just a bit harder. Maybe because of this — spending time with Nate, still his best friend after all these years, hashing out holiday classics, something they hadn't done since they were teenagers. Will hoped nothing ever came between him and Nate, though putting together a setlist for this night at the café might threaten to.

"I'm thinking Joni Mitchell's 'River,'" Nate said.

Will groaned. "'River' is depressing. How is that Christmas music?"

"It's such a beautiful song, though."

"What else?" Will prompted.

"'A Fairytale of New York?'"

"I don't think —" This was deteriorating quickly.

"'I Will Be Hating You For Christmas?'"

So, maybe part of Nate's dislike for this music was the fact his ex back in Calgary had broken up with him during the holidays, because even though Nate was over that, all happily married and, *whatever*, the sour association apparently lingered.

"No. Just... no, Miller."

"All right. I'm going to have to do some more research. But let's try to squeeze in as many actual carols as we can, okay? Carols I can deal with. They make me think of my mom." Nate's expression softened.

Will could still picture the last Christmas he'd spent with the Millers, Nate at the piano in the living room, singing carols with Connie. Will loved his mom — she was beautiful and generous and ambitious — but he wasn't going to lie, there had been times he'd wished he had a mother like Nate's. Lots of times.

"We just failed, miserably, at 'Joy to the World,'" he reminded.

"That was you, remember?" Nate grinned.

Sometimes Nate could be really annoying.

A staccato rap came at the door, and Will was glad for the interruption. He lifted the guitar strap over his head and set the instrument down carefully. "Back in a sec."

His neighbour, Lara, a short woman with a blonde bob wearing a maroon business suit, waited in the hallway, clutching a pretty grey tabby with white markings.

Will beamed, holding out his hands in welcome "There's my girl."

Lara deposited the cat in his arms and Will tucked the tabby into his chest, stroking her automatically. The cat started purring, motor running so loud he had to laugh.

"There's no question she likes you more than she likes me," Lara said, handing over a tote bag with the cat's belongings. *Maybe because you're away so much she's with me most of the time?* "Thank you so much. I don't know what I'd do without you."

"It's my pleasure," Will assured her. "See you when you get back."

Will closed the door, cooing with a terrible fake French accent, "Come in, come in, *cherie*. Make yourself at home." He set the cat on the floor and carried the tote bag to the kitchen. The tabby sat where he'd placed her, tail switching as she looked around. Then she rose and sauntered over to Nate.

"Mandarin!" Nate exclaimed as she butted her head against his leg and he scooped her into his lap. Her name was Clementine, but far be it from Nate to ever call an animal by its proper moniker. Not that Will was innocent — she was "Lemon" to him.

Unlike Nate, Will hadn't had pets growing up. Lemon wasn't his, but she was the closest he'd come. It surprised him how attached he'd become to the little thing. He loved the companionship, even if his agreement with Lara to take care of the cat while Lara was on business trips sometimes kept him in the city more often than he might have liked. Faye never complained. She was busy enough at the café, and Will was careful about not infringing on her independence. He didn't want to overstay his welcome at the farmhouse in King City.

Sure, last Christmas he and Faye had joked about him moving in with her and her brother, Dean, after Will had given up his high-pressure job at one of Toronto's most popular fine dining establishments. But it had only been that — joking. Obviously, because they'd never taken the discussion further.

"Looks like she's packed on a few pounds," Nate said.

"Meh, it's the holidays," Will said. "Lara spoils her because she feels guilty, I think. A few times when I've had her for a couple of weeks I've been able to get her trimmer, but she just puts the weight back on." He covered the open can of wet cat food with a snap-on blue lid and set it in the fridge, then found Lemon's water bowl and filled it. Lemon hopped from Nate's lap and wandered over to Will's feet where she plunked herself in front of him with a sultry *meow*. Will looked down at her green eyes. "I can understand how easy it is to give in to her, though. I mean, that face! How can you deny it?"

Nate smirked. "I can't even get you to bring out some of your pastries, but the cat gets whatever she wants."

"Yup. But I'm doing you a favour. Your job relies on your ability to stay trim."

"Didn't you just say it was the holidays? This close to the end of the season, everyone's tacking overweight. I'd just be fitting in."

"Or not fitting in," Will quipped. He didn't know how Nate did it, watching his weight like a supermodel so he could ride racehorses, but he made a lot of money doing it, so it was probably worth it. Will pulled a plastic container from the fridge and from it took two small petits fours. "Seems like we're on a break, anyway. You've got to try these. I'll make some tea to go with them."

Nate laughed as he took a seat at the kitchen table. "Once it was beer and potato chips, now it's tea and pastry. How far we've come."

"In the right direction, though?" Will asked. "I'm not sure."

"Some ways yes, some ways no."

Will served chocolate-peppermint tea — how did they make chocolate tea? — and joined Nate at the table, wrapping his fingers around his steaming cup. Nate reached for one of the sweets with something resembling reverence for such an indulgence, and bit in.

"You two have any plans for your anniversary?" Will asked between mouthfuls. A year had passed since Nate and Liv's Florida beach wedding, a year of the question, *so when are you and Faye getting married?* Like logically they were next in line — when the concept seemed too grown-up to a guy like him who was still trying to make up for a childhood that part of him felt he'd never had.

"We're going to wait until we get to Florida to celebrate. Just makes sense, with everything happening before Christmas," Nate said.

Will nodded. At least Nate was busy enough with his own life not to be among those pushing Will to pop the question. "Gotta hand it to you," he said. "You followed through."

Nate glanced at his cup of tea like he still didn't believe this is what they were drinking, then took a sip. "So what's up with you and Faye these days?"

Too busy not to push, up until now, apparently.

"Faye doesn't want to get married."

Nate paused, the last, tiny, bite of the petits four poised in mid air, his eyebrow quirked. "You sure about that?'

Sure? Well — yeah. Faye wasn't that girl. Besides, if Will were going to propose — he wasn't — it would *not* be at Christmas. Possibly because of Nate's own experience. If it went wrong, and Faye said no, Will might hate the holiday for real.

Nate still eyeballed him. "If you believe that, you're a little deluded."

Will didn't like that look. It was a reminder his best friend had dated Faye before Will had even met her; that Nate still knew things Will didn't, especially if he was saying something like that, when Will had been quite confident in his position. He didn't want to think about the probability that, had things been different, Faye might very well have married Nate. It was a reminder that maybe it wasn't that Faye didn't want to get married. Maybe it was that Faye didn't want to marry him.

"Just leave us alone. We're fine the way we are," he grumbled.

"Whatever you say." Nate rose, taking his dishes to the sink before sauntering back to the keyboard.

Nate was wrong.

Because if Will asked, and Faye turned him down, that would be it. It would be over. And he wasn't ready for it to end.

CHAPTER

THREE

"I'll finish up here, Faye. Get home."

"Thank you, Lucy." It was a rare thing for Faye to manage leaving the café before daylight faded, so she would take advantage of an offer like that when she could. "I don't want to put pressure on you, but you might be solely responsible for maintaining my sanity right now."

Lucy scowled and waved her off, ducking her head as she resumed wiping the counters. Faye lifted her coat from the rack next to her desk, hanging the apron in its place, then waved silently at Lucy and sneaked out before she had a chance to notice *just one more thing* she should do, feeling guilty as the door jangled closed behind her.

By the time she reached the farmhouse, the temperature had dropped with the setting sun. Chili bubbled in the slow cooker on the kitchen counter, the smell of rich spices intermingling with that of wood smoke. Dean lifted a hand in greeting from the couch as Faye scooted past, the crackling of the cheery fire in contrast to the news anchors sharing the day's doom and gloom on the television.

Faye went through the usual motions of piling on warm clothes, returning downstairs where Gus waited patiently for his walk. She had no doubt he'd been out with Dean, but the excursion was just as much for her health as his.

Big, fat, flakes descended from the darkening sky, Faye focusing on the quiet stillness around the farm, the horses tucked in for the evening. Night fell so quickly these days, but she tried to look ahead to the approaching solstice, when the trend would reverse, the daylight hours increasing. Her stroll with Gus wasn't as long as she would have liked; it rarely was, but it was better than nothing.

She'd only just removed her outer clothes, Gus gobbling his dinner, when she heard the slow crunch of tires on gravel and the familiar rumble of Will's Camaro. A flash of headlights lit the window briefly before extinguishing. Gus abandoned his empty bowl and barged over as Will entered. Faye felt her shoulders tighten, and scolded herself for the disquiet creeping up her neck.

"Snow's started," he said, as if the clumps he was stamping from his boots and the dusting he brushed from his coat didn't tell Faye that it was falling more heavily than it had been when she'd been out. He hung his coat on a hook and kicked off his boots, leaving them on the rubber tray next to hers to catch the melting white stuff.

"Great." Faye frowned as she stirred the contents of the Crock-Pot. "I guess I'll be getting up even earlier to be at the café on time."

Will set a paper bag and a loaf of fresh bread on the counter before he came over, wrapping an arm around her from behind and kissing her neck. His cool skin added to the shiver it sent down her spine. "Don't wake me up."

She elbowed him. "If you're going to be like that, you can just go back down to the city."

"You don't mean that," he said, his tone feigning hurt.

No, she didn't. She was just in a mood, and he was far too chipper. "You're right. I don't." She turned around, finding a smile, and stretched up, kissing him lightly. "Hungry?"

"Always," he murmured, his arms keeping her there, pulling her against him.

Faye leaned her head back and sighed. It was too easy to set aside her frustration when his hands were on her. An awkward cough interrupted them, and she pushed Will away with a saucy grin before rearranging her expression and turning to her brother, standing in the doorway between the kitchen and living room.

"Ready for dinner?" she asked.

Dean's expression was a combination of, *you two are cute, but would you get a room?* And, "I could eat." Food was a priority for the two men in her life. Three, counting Gus.

She served up bowls of chili and Will carried them to the table. Faye followed with the bread and wine, passing Will the loaf before filling their glasses as he cut slices from the baguette.

"How'd things go today?" Dean asked once they were all seated.

"Fine," Faye said. At least Dean was interested, while Will was diving into his bowl like he wasn't around food all day at work. "I put an ad up on a couple of job sites. Lucy's an angel, but I feel bad relying on her so much. I miss Sylvie. I should have had you talk to her about the rewards of giving up a Master's degree in favour of less admirable pursuits."

It had been wonderful to have Sylvie's help for most of the year — an arrangement that had worked for both of them. It gave Faye a desperately needed extra set of hands, and Sylvie something casual to do while supporting her parents as her mother went through cancer treatment. But with Sylvie's mom

— thankfully — in remission, Sylvie had returned to academics in September.

Dean smiled, his expression a clear display of his immunity to Faye's sarcasm. He'd been pursuing a Masters himself before he'd come back to take over training their father's racehorses after Ed Taylor's death. "She's almost done, isn't she?"

Faye couldn't remember, and it irked her that Will never took these clues, like *hey, imagine if* you *helped me run the café* you *made happen — two years ago?*

When Faye learned Lucy intended to sell her bakery business to care for her ailing mother, Faye had crunched the numbers to see if she could pull it off. Though Lucy was infamous for her grumpiness, her butter tarts were worth the discomfort of dealing with the woman. In the midst of a quarter-life crisis, it seemed like just the thing to give Faye's life purpose. She'd needed something to get her over breaking up with the guy she never should have fallen for in the first place — Nate Miller. Never mind that she met Will because of Nate. That could have happened without the heartbreak.

Will had both restaurant business smarts and pastry-making skills Faye knew would be handy if she pulled off the takeover. And, he'd done it. Worked out the deal, accepted an infusion of cash from his doctor mother, and rallied their friends to invest, making up the difference. They all wanted Lucy's butter tart legacy to continue. Will helped transform the plain hole-in-the-wall into something extra special... then left her to manage it, when Faye had thought they'd run it together.

At first she'd chalked it up to the demands of his fancy restaurant job in the city. But when he'd finally quit that job at Christmas last year, nothing had changed. She'd joked that now he'd be around. *All. The. Time.* Assumptions had been made, at least on her part. She'd thought he'd move in, and help her make Lucy's — which they'd renamed the Triple Shot Café — even better.

But maybe he'd taken her joking to mean she didn't want that — when it was exactly what she wanted. She wanted him by her side at the café. She wanted him here, every night.

Instead, a year later, things were just the same. He stayed over two or three times a week. Most weeks, she spent a night in the city. Faye had convinced herself he must like the freedom of having his own place. He was a city boy, after all. The farm was fun to visit but he'd never really suggested he'd want to live here — which was exactly how she felt about the city.

"You'll find someone," Dean said, confident in things that didn't really affect him.

Faye thought she had. Found someone. She stifled a sigh, and reached for her wine.

"Are you two coming for closing day?" Dean asked. The final day of Ontario's Thoroughbred racing season was nearly here.

Faye glanced at Will. He didn't look at her as he said, "That's Sunday, right? I've got a catering gig. Sorry."

Faye pressed her lips together as he went back to devoting all his attention to his bowl. It wasn't as if his declaration was a surprise. They hadn't been out together since... when? She responded, "Lucy said she'd cover me." *Again.* "How was your day, Will? How are things going for music night?"

He snapped his head up, worry creasing his forehead before he tamed his expression. "Good. Coming along." He reached for a slice of bread and buttered it.

Faye's eyebrows crept up. *You'd better not mess up this one thing I ask you to do.* And it wasn't even for her, really. A portion of the proceeds the café made from the event went to Emilie's pet project, a retired racehorse charity.

"Hard to believe this time last year I was still working that nightmare job at Mysticus, isn't it? It was bad enough at the best of times, but before the holidays?" Will shuddered.

Faye stared at him. The abrupt shift in topic felt a lot like a deflection.

She couldn't blame him for not missing the pressure of holiday madness. She was feeling it at the café right now, after all. Just another sign that he liked his easy job at the casual dining restaurant he'd taken after leaving Mysticus. It gave him time for his music and for making those delectable pastries. Helping her at the café would be one too many things. He wasn't one of those driven guys. It wasn't as if he'd ever had to make money to survive. His parents might have split up, but his mother, at least, was always there to fall back on if Will needed something.

It was hard not to envy his laidback life. On the one side, Faye had her brother, and Liv and Nate, with their crazy race-horse lives. On the other was Will, all chill with his bit of this and that to pay the bills. Comfortable in his bachelor life. He didn't want responsibilities weighing him down.

Will and Dean started talking about the hockey game that night. Now that Emilie's boyfriend, Tim, was playing for Toronto's NHL team, Faye did pay more attention, but tonight she tuned it out. It was her cue to clear the table. But when she started, Will rose and put a hand on her shoulder.

"Let me do that. Go put your feet up." He took the dishes from her and kissed her on top of the head.

Faye stood, lost for a moment, and then smiled. "Thank you." It was another offer she wasn't going to turn down. She couldn't stay mad at him. In two years, he'd never stopped being thoughtful.

Climbing the stairs, she pictured her three boys downstairs in front of the TV. Dean and Will poised on the edge of the chesterfield's cushions, intent on the game; Gus going from sleeping in front of the fire to jumping to his feet along with them when a goal was scored. She should probably be with them, watching Tim play. Maybe she'd go back down in a few minutes, after she'd changed.

You should talk to him, Faye.

It had been nearly a year since Nate and Liv's wedding. Since Liv had so pointedly tossed her that bouquet — the one that collected dust on the bookshelf in her room. It might as well have been hanging over her, the way it stirred a pot of emotions. *Are you happy with this? Truly? Is Will? Or is this it?*

On the one hand, Faye couldn't imagine life now without him. On the other, was there something wrong with her — with them — that she didn't want to get married?

They needed to have a conversation, but now, with Dean here, was not the time. Dean steered clear of conflict. Never offered relationship advice.

After closing day, when the racing season finished, Dean would take off for his almost-annual vacation. When Dean was gone, she and Will could have that discussion. Figure out what — if anything — came next.

When she woke the next morning, Will was in bed beside her. Faye hadn't stirred when he'd joined her, and now — because, hearing the creak of Dean going downstairs, she knew it was nearly time for her to get up as well — Will didn't budge, his breathing slow and steady. Faye resisted the temptation to whack him with her pillow for sleeping so soundly, because that would be childish, but it irked her as she crept to the bathroom. She stared at her reflection in the mirror, and thought it again.

Is this it?

FOUR

Last night's game had ended in a shootout, so it had been late when Will crawled into bed, Faye already sound asleep — and she was long gone by the time Will woke. Dean was probably hurting this morning, because he didn't have the luxury of sleeping in, while, by the time Will rose, the sun poured through the gap in the curtains, warming the room.

The house was quiet, the only sounds the creak of the stairs as he descended, and the distant hum of a tractor somewhere on the farm. Only Gus waited for him, curled up against the back door, his tail thumping.

"Hey buddy," Will said, dumping out the half-inch of cold coffee in the bottom of the pot and making a fresh one.

While he waited for it to brew, he pulled out a box of cereal and dumped some in a bowl, doused it with milk, then scarfed it down as he gazed out the window over the sink. Everything was clean and bright, freshly dressed with two more inches of snow. Will hoped it had stopped before Faye had driven to the shop.

The coffee maker sputtered and gurgled with its final drips. Someone really needed to put that poor old machine out of its misery and find a replacement. Will had a shift at the restaurant later this afternoon, and Lemon, his part-time cat, was expecting him, so he'd stop for a proper cup at Triple Shot on his way downtown. He poured himself a mug, then continued to stare at the perfect picture scene outside.

From the first time Will had set foot on this farm, it had taken him back to his grandfather's ranch in the Alberta foothills, where he'd spent some of the happiest times of his childhood — cattle grazing in expansive grassy pastures, the horses living alongside them distant relatives of the sleek, energetic Thoroughbreds born and nurtured here. But the underlying sense was the same: long days of hard but rewarding work; bales of hay and big tractors. A life far from the constant strain of the city. Will loved it.

When he'd first met Faye, after the Queen's Plate party, he'd intended to steer clear of her. Not that he wasn't interested, but she was Nate's ex, and it seemed like a bad idea. Will wasn't going to lie, though; when Nate had asked if he wanted to help unload some hay wagons for the Taylors, he hadn't agreed for the sake of nostalgia. He wanted to see Faye again.

He'd had so much fun that afternoon. Faye had pushed first, after the Plate. But working himself into a sweat, covered in hay dust and riding the exhilarating satisfaction of physical labour, his common sense had given way — and he'd pushed back.

Or, more accurately, picked her up and tossed her into the pond. Will would never forget her face, and had no idea how he'd gotten away without payback for the stunt.

Winter was a different vibe, vibrant horses in a sleepy landscape. Not quite as welcoming as it was in summer, but the peacefulness of it all still drew him. The pond was frozen, the snow cleared from its surface. After growing up spending winters skiing in the Rockies, the hills around here weren't worth talking about, but an outdoor rink was an outdoor rink. Apparently when Faye and Dean had been young, they'd skated on this pond regularly and her brothers had played hockey with the neighbourhood kids. But the neighbourhood had changed — not in small part because Faye's parents and middle brother, Shawn, had died. The unspeakable tragedy lingered around every corner of the farm, but it didn't feel like an upsetting thing to Will. It was pockets of fond memories, a present of perseverance, and a future that posed the question: what next?

Will rinsed out his mug and set it in the dishwasher, then rubbed his hands together. "Want to go out, bud? Let's go."

Gus sprang to his feet, his golden plume of a tail waving as he danced in anticipation. Will tugged on his jacket and boots and pushed open the door. The sun reflecting off the snow was so bright he grabbed his sunglasses from the car before they set off.

He swung into the main barn and grabbed a pitchfork as Gus went from stall to stall, hoovering up under the feed tubs of messy horses. A voice chirping, "Santa Claus is Coming To Town" along with Mariah Carey drifted from the other end of the building. Stacy, the farm's live-in manager, poked her head out of a stall as Will slipped alongside the manure spreader parked in the aisle. He entered the stall opposite her and started picking.

"Thanks, Will!"

Will started asking about her holiday plans so she wouldn't start singing again. Stacy didn't have a bad voice, but he'd had enough of the incessant holiday music and it wasn't as if he could ask her to turn it off. Conversation pushed the Christmas tunes mercifully to the background.

Stacy was faster than him, but always seemed to appreciate the help and the company. Once the barn was done Will called Gus and left Stacy to dump the spreader and finish her other chores. Gus galloped toward him, shavings sticking to his silky coat, a big grin on his face.

Will paused at the pond, the huge willow that provided shade in the summer a lonely skeleton against the deep blue winter sky. Was it wrong he could picture the next generation on that pond, teaching them to skate, teaching them to play hockey? Except Dean didn't seem to have any interest in carrying on their branch of the Taylor name, and Will couldn't shake the feeling that Faye didn't see him as anything more than her part-time boyfriend.

But whose fault was that, really?

He'd worried at first he might be Faye's rebound after Nate. It was argument number two against getting involved with her in the first place. They'd broken up briefly at Christmas their first year together, when he'd asked her to come to Calgary with him. He hadn't been thinking, but meeting his mom back then was probably too much, too soon. He should have known he'd freak her out.

They'd smoothed things over in January, though, and he no longer worried he was her rebound. They'd just fallen into a rut. And maybe proposing wasn't the answer, but he *could* do better. He'd win her over, all over again — it might take some work to convince her she still needed him.

Gus romped ahead through the field as they made a loop around the perimeter. Maybe he'd get Faye cross-country skis for Christmas. They could do it together. Something different, away from their jobs. She wasn't much for sports, but she walked. It was pretty flat here; she could learn to ski.

Ending up back at the pond, Will leaned against the tree trunk and scanned for the dog. Gus was stuck on some scent along the fence line — but before Will had to call him, the Golden came tearing back in a whoosh of flying snow and hair, stopping short of the ice.

"It's never as big as I remember it."

Will slid his gaze from the dog. He'd been so absorbed; he hadn't heard Dean come up. Was it that time already?

"Things like that never are, are they?" he responded. "Except the mountains out west. I think they get bigger the older I get."

"Ah, won't be long now," Dean said, a smile spreading over his face.

"I don't want to hear about it." Will missed those mountains. It was different for Dean — he'd be a visitor, heading out there on a skiing vacation next week — but Will was completely jealous. "You'd better say hi to them for me. How long are you gone for?"

"A week."

"A week is good. You'll be back for our music night at the café."

Dean just nodded.

Will's eyes travelled to the ice again. Gus stood on the bank, staring too, as if he were wishing it were water so he could launch in, like he did in the summer. That dog was in the pond from May until October. Wet, stinky Golden, for months on end.

He glanced at Dean. "Think we can get a game together this year?" Will was determined to revive the tradition of a Christmastime game on the pond.

"Sounds like a great plan," Dean said. "Keep me posted."

They walked back toward the house, Gus shoving his nose in the snow then bounding to catch up. The dog's energy, the crisp air, the respite from metropolitan sidewalks filled with people —

all of it flushed the sludge that leached into his joint spaces in the city and made him sluggish. It had left him just a little out of synch with Faye; one of those things you saw in the rear view mirror and thought, *when did that happen?* He would set things right.

Will screeched to a halt. "Dean — what's that?"

The big, rusty chunk of metal on wheels was backed off to the side in the brush, snow clinging to its roof and fenders, dried-out weeds spiking thickly around it.

"I'm sorry. What?" Dean looked around, like there should be a wild animal or unique bird. Definitely something more appealing than a heap of steel that had been left to die.

"That." Will nodded in its direction.

Dean's brows furrowed. "That? That's a horse trailer. A very old, two-horse, bumper pull trailer that hasn't been road-worthy for many, many years."

"Is it yours?"

Dean still looked perplexed, then nodded. "It's been on the farm for as long as I can remember. I might even be able to recall when we still used it. Before one of my dad's banner years, when he bought a new rig."

Will climbed through the weeds and tramped around the derelict trailer. Ideas began bouncing around his head like a pinball. Forget cross-country skis. He needed to give Faye an amazing gift this year, and this one was going to be epic.

"Can I buy it from you?"

Dean chuckled. "Buy it? You can have it. It's an eyesore. I've been in denial about that thing for years. I should have taken it for scrap long ago. Just promise me you won't put a horse on it."

Will stifled a laugh. "No worries there, man. Is it safe to pull? Without a horse on it."

"Depends on what you mean by safe," Dean said. "It might

not fall apart, but if you get pulled over, I had nothing to do with this. You're on your own."

"Deal." Will grinned and Dean grasped his outstretched hand. "Now I have a favour to ask."

"What's that?"

"Can I borrow your truck?"

Dean shrugged. "Care to share what you're going to do with it?"

"Not until I'm sure I can bring the vision to life. And don't say anything to Faye, okay?" Now — what was the name of that guy with the shop they'd taken Nate's Mustang to? Will pulled his phone from his pocket and headed for his car. "Thanks, man. Catch you later!"

CHAPTER
FIVE

Dean was already cradling his first cup of coffee when Faye stumbled into the kitchen. Even the dog knew not to greet her until she was girded with one of her own. The toxic brew hit her brain, making everything clearer — which wasn't altogether a good thing.

The darkness didn't help her state of mind. These days it took so much longer to get light in the morning and the sun set far too early in the evening, so most days she was heading to work before the sun was up, and coming home after it had ducked below the horizon. This time of year counting the days till the solstice was just as important as checking off the squares on the calendar until Christmas.

It was so wrong that she now rose at the same time as the racetrackers — and, unlike them, there was no end to her season. The racing meet wrapped up this Sunday, and didn't resume until April. Faye tried to take a day off every week, while Dean and Liv and Nate did not — though being self-employed, a day off wasn't always a day off — but there would be none of that for Faye from now until the holiday.

Will had stayed in the city last night, so at least she didn't have the added withdrawal of leaving him, face smushed into the pillow, all cosy and scruffy and rumpled. It might be easier to get out of bed when he was absent, but she undeniably missed him. She closed her eyes and dreamed of Christmas morning, when she'd finally be able to snuggle up with him and sleep until well past dawn.

"Why did you let me do this?" she muttered at her brother over her cup once there was enough caffeine in her system to be remotely civil. The counter she leaned on was the only other thing keeping her upright.

"Do what?" Dean asked, dropping two pieces of bread into the toaster.

"Take on Lucy's." *Buy a café, they said. It'll be fun, they said.*

His eyebrows twitched, a slant to his lips. "You never asked me, as I recall."

Well, there was that. Faye changed the subject. "Ready for the season to be over?"

Dean nodded, a wistful look gracing his features. "Looking forward to hitting the slopes."

It's what he did every year after the racing season at Woodbine was over. Last December had been the only time Faye could recall him missing his annual vacation. She hadn't been sure he'd want to go to Liv's wedding in Florida, but in the end friendship had trumped his feelings of unrequited love. Dean had kept them to himself for too long and when he'd revealed them — at the racetrack's biggest social event last year of all things — all it had done was make everyone uncomfortable. Thankfully, it had all smoothed over, because the lives of their group of friends were still intertwined. They needed each other.

For a man she'd lived with for nearly thirteen years — Faye wasn't counting the ones before Dean had left for university, because she barely remembered him then — her brother was a bit of a mystery. She knew he went skiing with friends. Whether those friends were male, female or otherwise? That part she didn't ask. If he'd ever had a girlfriend, Faye didn't know about it. There was enough of an age difference between them — eight years — it felt like none of her business. They stayed out of each other's personal relationships, though Dean had given a subtle endorsement for Will early on. Faye hoped he wasn't holding back from finding a girlfriend because of her. She hoped she wasn't holding back from more, with Will, because of him.

It made her wonder. They'd inherited this farm; shared this house since their parents' death. How would it work, if they both had spouses? Kids? Could they all live here? It wasn't that big; had felt cramped when they were growing up, with just *one* family.

Golden slices sprang from the toaster, and Dean transferred them to a plate. "The last couple of weeks have been nice, though," he said, slathering the toast with peanut butter. "Having Nate and Liv around makes it a breeze for everyone."

"That's because they're both bored. Too much time on their hands since their horses left for Florida."

Nate was staying until the end of the season because as a jockey, he needed to be there for his career. Liv, who trained for her father's Triple Stripe Stables, was staying for Nate, leaving her assistant trainer to handle things in the Sunshine State until she and Nate went down. The decision still surprised Faye. Things hadn't always been like that. Her friend was fiercely independent.

Dean grinned. "Liv, especially, has been a bit, shall we say…"

"Twitchy?" Faye suggested. Liv did not deal well with either inactivity or transfer of responsibility, though her assistant, Jo St-Laurent, was completely capable of managing things on her own — even if she was training some new staff this time around. Previous years, the crew from Woodbine had gone south with the Triple Stripe racehorses, so it was basically the same show, except with palm trees and trips to the beach in the afternoons.

Faye would give a lot to be on a beach right now. She sighed and set her cup in the sink.

"I'm off," she said, heading for the coat rack. "Have a good day."

At least it hadn't snowed more overnight. She started her car, willing it to warm up faster than it ever possibly could. Okay, yes, she loved the Corolla, but times like this it would be nice to have one with a heated steering wheel and heated seats. She backed out and puttered down the driveway, knowing the chill she felt would finally lose its edge right about when she pulled up to the café.

The older she got, the more she enjoyed spending time alone, so as much as getting up early wasn't Faye's favourite thing, once she was in the café doing prep, it was the best time of her day. She opened the doors early for locals who commuted to work in the city, a steady stream of regulars stopping in, most of them just for coffee.

Lucy, the original owner of the shop, had been helping for a few hours each day recently. Faye didn't know what she'd do without the older woman right now. She had to find someone to help, missing the full time set of hands Emilie's friend Sylvie had provided until the end of the summer when she'd gone back to school. It wasn't fair to ask Lucy to come more often, even if that would be the perfect solution. Lucy had given up the business to care for her aging mother and though her mother's health had stabilized, she still needed Lucy's assistance more than Faye did.

Once the morning rush came, Faye didn't have time to think about it; she just acted, ticking along to keep up with everything. It seemed before she knew it, she was glancing up to see Liv pushing inside, setting the bell hanging on the door jangling.

"Hey," Faye said, dragging her hands over her apron and smiling. "Where's your other half?"

"Racing today, remember?" Liv said, drying off booted feet on the doormat before coming over.

That was right. Nate would be riding this afternoon so he'd still be at Woodbine. "I've lost track of what day of the week it is. Sorry."

"Dean's sticking around to watch so he said he'd drive Nate home."

"Nice. Thanks for popping by. Time for a cappuccino?" Faye visualized her to-do list for the day. She might actually be able to sit down with her friend. Liv had managed to get here before the lunch rush.

"Thank you," Liv said. "No, wait —"

Faye quirked an eyebrow as she stopped before reaching for the espresso. "What?"

"Show me how to do that. It shouldn't be too difficult. I know how to work the one you gave us as a wedding gift. Walk me through it."

Faye stepped back. "Okay. But... why?"

"Because I'm tired of you waiting on me when I'm here. You do that all day for everyone else."

Faye shrugged and did as she was told. It wasn't rocket science. Even if it had been, Liv probably had a higher IQ than anyone she knew — even Dean — so she'd get it.

"See?" Liv said, grinning as they sat at one of the tables once coffees and treats were in place. "Now I can do something for you."

"What have you got up your sleeve?" Faye narrowed her gaze over her cup and saucer as she lifted it to her lips. She nodded appreciatively at the perfect way the steamed milk balanced the bitter espresso.

Liv picked up a brownie. "Nate's parents are coming for Christmas."

Faye recognized the underlying anxiety that came with Liv's remark. She raised an eyebrow — not at the information, but at Liv's unease. "Why is that a problem? You get along with his parents." She had heard Reid and Connie Miller were going through a rough patch. Was it just that? At least they were both coming.

"I know, but Connie is such a great cook. She does the whole thing for Christmas dinner." Liv waved her hands around. "I can't pull that off."

The woman could manage a stable of Thoroughbreds, risk her neck riding them, and was smarter than anyone Faye knew, but the thought of preparing a meal was cause for a potential meltdown. Faye snagged Liv's eyes. It wasn't often she had to talk her friend down anymore.

"First, I'm sure she's not expecting you to do anything extravagant. Second, Nate can cook, so why are you worried? Put him to work. Especially as it's his family. Third, if one and two don't satisfy you, do what someone else in your position would do: hire a professional. There are places that will make you whatever you need. You pick everything up and reheat it. Presto! Dinner is served."

Liv looked back cautiously. "That's why I'm here."

Faye laughed. "Because you don't know how to use Google, so you want me to point you in the right direction?"

"No. I want to hire you."

Faye sighed. "Liv."

How did she say no to her best friend? It wasn't that Faye

didn't like all the people who would be at that dinner. She did, very much. Connie was lovely. Her husband was reserved, but polite. Emilie and Tim were the cutest couple she knew. But taking on that job would obliterate the peaceful day Faye was so looking forward to for herself.

"Please?"

Liv's tone niggled at her and Faye groaned. "Fine. I'll help you. But you're not hiring me. All I'm doing is directing you. Assisting in the delegation. All right?"

"Yes. I think. Maybe."

"The good news is you have lots of warning. It will all work out, trust me." Faye dove in, seamlessly taking charge despite her reluctance. "You know Connie is reasonable. She'll just be so happy to be with her boys and their girls. You could serve her dry toast and she wouldn't notice. And Reid doesn't strike me as the high-maintenance type. Maybe I can loan you Dean so he'll have someone to talk to."

Liv almost choked on the sip of cappuccino she'd just taken, her lips tight together as she swallowed it, and her laughter.

"It is rather convenient for their boys to have married sisters, isn't it?" Faye noted.

Tim and Emilie weren't even engaged yet, but it was only a matter of time. Of course, that's what everyone had said about her and Will last winter. Emilie's excitement over the rings at the mall strongly suggested Faye was right to be suspicious.

Also, Liv did not correct her. "True."

Faye played with the handle of her now-empty cup. "Your biggest job will be keeping Connie from trying to jump in. She's like you, but with domestic stuff."

Liv grinned. "Being compared to Connie, even in that small way, is the nicest compliment." Her affection for her mother-in-law shone in her eyes.

Liv had won the lottery with that one. While Faye adored Liv's mom Anne, that mother-daughter relationship had always been moderately contentious, especially since Liv had dropped out of veterinary school to pursue a career in horse racing. Faye tried not to think how her own holiday would be, as always, motherless.

Spending Christmas Eve with Liv's family after they'd first met, as kind a gesture as it had always been, had always been difficult for Faye. The evening never passed without remembering that it would only ever be her and Dean. Even if she did marry Will, he had no brothers or sisters; no cousins, and he wasn't particularly close to his divorced parents. She wondered if the grief would ever wear off. Over the years it had changed, shifted. She'd adapted — but it seemed as if it would always be a part of her.

"I'll make it up to you," Liv promised.

"How?"

Liv scooped up their empty dishes and headed for the kitchen, Faye following her friend suspiciously. "What are you doing?"

"Helping. You may not trust me to bake, but I can clean up. And make a mean cappuccino. Am I right?"

Faye laughed. "Yes. That one was quite acceptable."

Liv was good at putting things away and tidying, only needing to ask Faye where items belonged. It really did help, allowing Faye to take care of other tasks, popping out as needed to serve customers. Liv stayed through the lunch rush, until another lull hit, and Faye finally chased her out.

"We'll have to sit down sometime soon and come up with a menu. Can you clear your schedule for that?" If Faye did things right, she could set everything up beforehand for the dinner at Liv's and not have it consume her entire Christmas Day.

"You're the busy one right now, Faye." Liv shrugged into

her coat. "Just tell me when. Come up with a few potential dates and get back to me."

Faye hugged her. "Look at you, not avoiding hard things."

"Ha ha," Liv said. "*That* will not be the hard thing."

Liv gave a little wave as she pushed through the door. For the first time in hours, it was just Faye in the shop again. She inhaled, taking a moment to regroup, recalibrate, before heading into the kitchen again.

On top of her stack of notes was the holiday edition of the *Food & Drink* magazine. It was full of expensive ads for alcohol and glossy photos with recipes and tips for entertaining. One ad stopped her.

The only limit is your imagination.

Faye ran her hand over the smooth surface of the page and fingered the edge. Blue sky, blue water, a boat, a group of friends holding tumblers. She didn't even care what the ad was for. Despite the image it left her with, the thing was, when it came down to it, she didn't want much.

She didn't want to stress about money, so she needed the café to hold its own, but didn't expect to ever retire to a world of luxury. What she did want was time. For herself, for her friends, for walks with her dog.

For Will.

Except, she wasn't entirely sure Will wanted the same.

CHAPTER
SIX

The loft always felt empty when Lemon went back to her person – Lara had picked the cat up at eleven. All Will's belongings, including his collection of instruments, took up space, but didn't fill the small flat with anything close to what one tiny feline brought when she stayed over. He was glad he had the trailer project to distract him from her absence.

Dean had told him this afternoon was good to borrow the truck. He'd called the guy with the body shop they'd taken Nate's Mustang to for an overhaul this past summer and gotten the okay to bring the trailer over. Will locked the door behind him and trotted down the stairwell. Once he was in his Chevy, he turned the key and let it warm up as he swiped open his phone and dialled, the phone ringing in his ear. It didn't take long for Nate to pick up.

"Hey," Nate said. "What's up?"

"What are you doing right now?"

"Why?" It didn't sound as if Nate was trying to hide his suspicion at all.

"I've acquired a trailer," Will said.

There was a beat of silence before Nate said, "I'm sorry, what? Why?"

"Dean's old horse trailer, yeah."

"Again — why? I'm pretty sure it should have been scrap years ago."

"I'm going to fix it up. You know, instead of a food truck, I'm going to use a trailer. You can help, seeing as you're going to be around."

"Liv and I are flying down to Florida next week after the season's over to check on the horses."

"For how long?"

"Dunno. A couple of days, if everything is going okay."

"That still leaves lots of days."

Nate sighed. "And where are we going to do this?"

We. That was what Will wanted to hear. "In Gil's shop. You know, the guy who fixed up the Mustang for you."

"I see."

"Don't worry. He'll do most of the work. We'll just do something token, like help paint it, then finish off the inside once I figure out what it's going to be."

"Good. You had me worried for a second there." Nate chuckled. "How are you going to move it?"

"Dean's letting me borrow his truck. The sooner we get it over there, the sooner we can start."

"We? You need my help to move it?"

"Where's your sense of adventure?"

"Fine. I'll head over."

"I'm still in the city. Give me an hour."

Will hung up. The plan was coming together, his image for the trailer forming pixel by pixel inside in his head, and he started a list of things he'd need for the transformation.

When he reached the farmhouse, Dean's black pickup was

there. Will pulled in beside him and got out of his car, hopping up the steps to the deck.

"Hey Dean!" he called as he pushed through the door, rubbing Gus's head automatically. "Where are you?"

"Office," came the answer.

Will was glad Faye wasn't home, both so he could get the trailer out of here without her seeing and because he didn't really need to take off his boots, right? It was just snow anyway. It would melt and dry before she got back tonight. He peeked in the office door. Dean was at the computer, watching horse races from somewhere.

"Okay if I borrow the truck now? Nate's coming over to lend a hand."

"Sure." Dean reached for a set of keys sitting on the desk then turned, tossing them to Will.

Will snapped them from the air and closed his fingers around them. "And if Faye asks what happened to it, just tell her you took it for scrap, okay?"

Dean laughed. "She won't notice. But all right."

"Great. Thanks again, Dean."

Will was halfway to the back door when Dean's voice reached him. "Wait, Will."

He ambled back. "What's up?"

"I forgot to tell you I don't have a ball hitch the right size for that trailer anymore. I got rid of a lot of stuff a while back. Maybe call Kerrie at Triple Stripe?"

Will nodded, even though Dean's attention had returned to the computer monitor. He gave Gus a good-bye pat and called Nate —who just happened to know exactly where Kerrie, their farm manager, kept the hitches— and texted back when he located the correct size. Obviously this project was meant to be.

There was some digging involved to facilitate the trailer's extraction from its bed of weeds and snow, but Will had it done by the time Nate arrived. He was pretty sure there would have been more grumbling had Nate needed to shovel. Nate slipped the ball mount into the receiver on Dean's truck and secured it with the pin, then guided Will as he backed up, lining up the ball and coupler. It dropped into place with a satisfying thunk.

Will hopped out of the cab to help but Nate was already cranking up the stand and snapping the safety chains in place.

"You almost look like you know what you're doing." Will grinned and removed the wheel chocks. He'd needed to loosen them with the shovel to free them from the ice.

"So, what's the grand plan?" Nate asked as Will cautiously drove down the country sideroad away from the house. The trailer had creaked and groaned so much as they wrenched it from its resting place, Will had been afraid the tongue would break right off. "What's it going to be?"

"A mobile espresso bar," Will announced proudly. "What do you think?"

"I think it'd be great if they let you drive it around the race-track, but that's not going to happen," Nate said.

"Once again, you're only thinking of yourself."

Nate grinned. "Sorry. It's a cool idea. But how much of a demand do you think there is for such a thing?"

"People use food trucks for all sorts of things now. I'll just have to spread the word. It'll be all about the marketing." Which wasn't exactly Will's area of expertise, but he'd figure it out.

They pulled up in front of a cinder block building painted slate grey, and climbed out of the pickup. The body shop was cold, if not as cold as outside. An old car sat in the farthest bay, surrounded by a random mess of tools and parts. The closest bay had a landscape trailer that looked to be in decent shape, probably here for maintenance. Will knocked on the office door.

"Yep. Come in," came the voice on the other side.

Will poked his head in. "Hey Gil. What do you want us to do with it?"

"Middle bay's empty. You can pull it in there."

The shop was set up so that there were large garage doors for each bay on both sides, making it easy — no backing up required. Will just drove up, waited while Nate blocked and unhitched the trailer, then drove out. Nate had the garage doors rolled down by the time Will got back.

"What've we got here?" Gil emerged from the warmth of the office, rubbing his bare hands together. They were brown and cracked, probably permanently stained with grease. "Let's have a look."

Gil crawled under the trailer to assess the frame, even though it was just warm enough in the garage for the snow packed in the wheel wells to start melting with steady drips onto the oil-stained concrete floor. When Will helped him open up the ramp, chunks of rusted metal crumbling away. Gil lifted the old mats, still crusted with the remains of dried-out shavings, and peered at the boards under them.

"We won't really know until we get into it," he said. "But it doesn't look too bad. Lots of surface rust. Floor needs some work. You're not using it for horses though, right?"

"Right. It just has to handle a couple of people standing in it," Will said.

Gil nodded, still wandering around the trailer, looking it up and down. "I know some young guys who will probably help for cheap. And I might consider partial payment in butter tarts." He grinned.

"Deal." Will could easily come up with a reason why he needed a special order of tarts from Faye. He was humming with excitement as he and Nate climbed back into the truck. "So. I was thinking I could give Faye *that* for Christmas."

Nate quirked an eyebrow. "Seriously? Okay." He looked skeptical. "Do you think we can finish it in time? It's going to take a lot of work."

"You remember what magic we worked with the Mustang?"

"What magic Gil worked, you mean."

"You heard him. He's got some kids to help, and us, too. It'll be fine." Even if an engagement ring was starting to feel like a much simpler idea. Because Faye didn't want an engagement ring. Time to switch topics, because Will was not getting into that discussion again. "When are your parents coming?"

"You heard?" Nate asked, and when Will nodded, he said, "My mom's coming next week. Dad has to work so he'll come a day or two before Christmas."

"How are things going there?" Will still couldn't believe Nate's parents were having problems. If they were splitting up, what hope was there for the rest of them?

Nate shrugged. "I don't know. I guess there's not a lot I can do, so I should probably just butt out. Let them figure it out."

"Though you feel perfectly fine sticking your pretty-boy nose into my relationship." Will looked at him sideways.

"Well, yeah." Nate cracked a smile.

Nate was climbing out of the truck back at the farm when Will's phone rang. He gave Nate a parting wave then hesitated, like he always did, when he saw the name on the screen, psyching himself up. "Hi Mom."

"Hello, Will," she said in her version of warmth that never quite came off. "How have you been?"

All this reminiscing about Christmas past and making arrangements for Christmas present, and he'd forgotten to call his own mother and talk about her holiday plans. Since leaving

Calgary, he'd always made sure he went back every other year to spend Christmas with her. Last year he'd been here, with Faye, so he was due. But he couldn't go, not this year. Not the way things were right now.

Faye still hadn't met his mother. Now that they'd been together over two years, *that* was overdue. It was supposed to happen last year. His mom had planned to come and the proposed meet had been relatively low-stress. She'd be in Toronto only briefly, so they'd agreed on a light lunch — but his mom had bailed on them. Will had learned afterward she'd never even left Calgary, citing that, at the last-minute, she'd been called to an emergency. Was it possible his mother was just as anxious about meeting Faye as Faye was about meeting her?

"Busy," he said, finally answering her query. "Good, though."

"We need to talk about Christmas." His mom didn't waste time.

"I've been meaning to call," he lied.

"That's okay. I felt bad about last year, so I've taken a week off and I'm going to fly out. It's high time I met that girlfriend of yours."

Whoa. Will forced himself to recover. "That's a great idea, Mom. I'll talk to Faye and see—"

"The flight is booked. I'll send you the details. I'll be there on the twenty-first. I'm so excited to see you and your city."

"O — kay, Mom. Sounds great."

But was Faye going to think so?

SEVEN

Friday night, for most people, was something to be excited about — the end of a long work week with two whole days off to look forward to. Not so for Faye and those in her life, Will included. It was amazing they found the time to see each other at all. Still, she couldn't wait to get home and put her feet up — with something other than Christmas music playing on the stereo.

She was surprised to see Will's car as she came up the driveway, a warm glow filling the farmhouse windows, the light at the back door bathing the deck. Faye hadn't been expecting him — Friday night, especially this close to Christmas, he was supposed to be working. She sat in the car a moment, confronting her resentment. It wasn't that she didn't want to see him. She was just in a mood; afraid she might say something mean that had nothing at all to do with him. It wasn't fair to subject him to her current frame of mind, and would have been safer for her to spend the evening alone. Faye had been looking forward to exactly that, because Dean was out, taking his crew at the track for an end-of-season thank you dinner.

Will and Gus both greeted her at the door, looking happy to see her. *That was nice. Be grateful, Faye.* Will helped her out of her coat, then handed her a glass of wine. She had to be conscious of her facial expression to keep her eyebrows from creeping up and her thoughts defaulting to *okay, what's going on?*

"You don't have to take Gus out," he said. "He's good. I took him for a little jaunt after the horses were in."

How long had he been here? "Did you let him eat horse poop?"

"No!" he said, like that could never happen because he could totally prevent it. "He might have scarfed some feed, though, so if he asks to go out, you might want to listen."

She rolled her eyes and sipped the wine. "Thanks for the warning."

"I'm just kidding," he said. "About you listening, that is. He did get some feed, but I'll take him if he needs it."

Faye eyed him suspiciously again — she couldn't help it — but reminded herself to let it go, knowing she was completely capable of blowing just about anything out of proportion tonight. It had been a long, busy week, with the prospect of organizing Liv's Christmas on top of everything.

"Did Lemon's person pick her up today?" she asked, curling her fingers around the glass's stem and sipping, determined to be pleasant. She closed her eyes, enjoying the flavours filling her mouth and sighed her appreciation. He really was a catch, this man. She must do her level best to keep from pushing him away. Two years. Why was two years a thing in relationships? And why did she have such a problem with it being a thing? She should be grabbing him and dragging him to the altar.

"Sure did," Will said. "You hungry? I brought some soup I could heat up."

"In a bit," she said. "Right now I just want to sit." She sauntered into the living room, tucking a leg under herself as she collapsed into the couch. "I'll be so exhausted by the time Christmas actually gets here that I won't know my own name."

No matter how many times she mentioned how overworked she was, not once did he offer to step in and help at the café. There was just something hinky about that. It had gone on too long now for her to ask him outright, so she just found herself dropping endless hints, which he unfailingly did not pick up. *Great communication, Faye.* Amazing foundation for an enduring relationship.

Will slipped a hand under her calf and fished for her other leg, rotating her as he dropped onto the couch.

"What are you doing?" she asked. There was that suspicion again.

He peeled off one of her socks. "You've been on your feet all day. If you don't like it, tell me to stop." His strong fingers began kneading, releasing the tension just behind the ball of her foot. It felt so good she almost forgot her glass of wine.

"No, don't stop," she moaned, resisting the temptation to set the glass aside so she could lean back and give into whatever it was. "Don't take this the wrong way, but what are you doing here? I was surprised to see you. I thought you were working."

"Someone wanted to swap shifts. I knew Dean was out tonight and thought it might be nice to have the place to ourselves, so I said yes."

The foot rub was helping ease away her earlier irritation. She met his eyes and smiled, the warmth filling her chest from the wine and the sensation of his touch meeting somewhere at the base of her torso.

"Dean mentioned they have a Santa Claus parade in town next weekend," Will said as his hands continued to work their magic. "How did I miss that last year?"

Faye didn't open her eyes as she answered. "Because of the wedding, probably. I told them we couldn't participate. One too many things to manage."

"Participate, how? Are you, this year?"

"I said I'd have hot chocolate and coffee, and lots of cookies. We'll be busy." Busi-*er*. On a Sunday afternoon, too. *Ugh.*

"I'll help."

What was that? Faye felt like bursting into song, crooning "This Magic Moment" as she draped herself over him. Instead, she stayed where she was, thinking, *what's the catch?* "Aren't you working?"

"I'll get out of it."

She blinked. "Thank you."

He peeled off her other sock, and set to work.

"So," he said, like he was trying to sound nonchalant but failing.

The tension she'd let go crept back into her shoulders. Here it is. *I knew there had to be something going on.* She swallowed the last bit of red in her glass, waiting for it.

"My mother's coming for Christmas."

Faye almost spat up the mouthful of wine, jerking her foot away. "What?"

"That's okay, right?" His tone was casual, but he wasn't meeting her eyes.

"Did you *invite* her?" *Without talking to me first?* What was she supposed to say? It wasn't okay, but she couldn't tell him no. Because he had his own place. He could do what he wanted without consulting her.

"She basically told me what was happening," he said with

an apologetic frown. "Tickets already bought. Agenda set in stone."

"How long is she staying?"

"She arrives on the twenty-first. Flies out Boxing Day."

"So what, we're not spending Christmas together, then?" Was this payback for the first year, when she didn't go to Calgary with him?

Will's laugh was abrupt. "She wants to meet you, Faye. She feels bad about having to cancel last year. Promised it won't happen this time. What's the big deal?"

Right. Perfectly reasonable, all of it. So why did she feel like this was the straw that would break her?

Was it just because the last micron of her quiet Christmas had just been obliterated? And/or... he *wasn't* thinking ... no, he couldn't be. They'd never talked about it, only endured their friends insisting there should be a ring on her finger by now. Sure it was probably high time they got back to discussing him moving in, and she planned to do just that, didn't she? Once she stole back the portion of her brain that was completely preoccupied right now with a business consumed by holiday madness.

This was not how it was supposed to go. She'd been determined that once Liv and Nate were set for their big dinner, she'd come home to her nice, relaxing house for a nice, relaxing Christmas Day afternoon with Will and Dean. She and Will would pick up where they left off a year ago, talk about all the things they needed to talk about. Set everything right.

Except now all of it was gone. There would be no reprieve. No time to herself, not truly. She'd be fielding the barrage of questions Will's mother had stored up.

She didn't even know the woman's name. Was she still Callaghan? Dr Callaghan?

Faye swung her feet from the couch, where she'd been

perched, like she'd been cornered. "I'm really tired, Will. We'll talk about this tomorrow, okay? Sorry for overreacting. I just want to sleep."

He followed her as she returned the wine glass to the kitchen, her now-mushy feet clashing with the old hardwood floor. Will stood in the doorway, a hand resting on the jamb.

Faye turned to him. "You'll stay up and keep an eye on Gus for a bit, right?"

"Uh — yes. I said I would."

She came over to him, placing a hand on his chest and tipping her head up for a kiss. "Thanks, babe. G'night."

So, she hadn't eaten anything. She'd lost her appetite. The repetitive motion of brushing her teeth didn't settle her down like she'd thought it would, but she'd fall asleep as soon as her head hit the pillow, she was sure of it.

Except she didn't. She was still awake when Will came up but kept her eyes shut and tried to regulate her breathing; heard the pad of Gus's feet as he entered the room and flopped on the mat on her side of the bed.

The mattress sank when Will joined her, snuggling up behind her and dropping an arm over her waist.

When had she stopped turning to him when he did that, never too tired to welcome his presence, his touch; no argument enough to keep her from wanting him?

She closed her eyes tighter, and squeezed his hand, but he was already asleep. How did he do that?

THE ALARM STARTLED Faye when it went off. It was only fifteen minutes earlier than usual, but her body knew exactly what time it should wake up, and this was not it. Reaching for the phone, she resisted the temptation to hit snooze and pushed herself upright, groaning. No point trying to go back to sleep even though it had evaded her too long last night. She glanced over her shoulder, glaring — but Will wasn't there. Huh.

The shower's hot water woke her up, and she towel-dried her hair, shivering as she shrugged into her robe and shuffled to the bedroom to dress. Checking the weather app, she saw it was supposed to be snowing. It wasn't always right about current precipitation so she peeked out the window. Sure enough, fat flakes caught the light from the room, a collection piled on the window sill. She hadn't checked the weather before bed. Will must've changed her alarm to give her extra time to get to the shop. *Thoughtful.*

The old wooden stairs creaked as she stepped carefully down them. Lights were on in the kitchen and the coffee she smelled was not Dean's toxic morning brew.

"What are you up to?" she asked as she reached the door-way, discovering Will at the counter. Gus was a pile at his feet. There had to be food involved with this, Gus's loyalty unreservedly going to whoever had something tasty. She wandered over, and Will placed a mug of coffee to her palm, resting a hand on her hip as he leaned down to kiss her.

It smelled heavenly, and she saw the French Press responsible sitting next to the sink. "You're spoiling me." The first morning coffee, the kind that was just enough to keep her eyes open for the drive to Triple Shot where she could have a cappuccino, had always been Dean's burnt grocery store brand from a calcified machine.

"Have to make myself useful so I don't wear out my welcome."

It was too early for talk like that. Faye didn't want to think about the news of his mother's visit last night.

"Well, thank you." She pecked him on the cheek and

allowed herself a few minutes to sit at the kitchen table and appreciate the fine brew.

Will joined her. "The snow's slowing down. It's cold, though."

"How would you know that?"

He shrugged. "I stuck my head out when I let Gus out."

"Fair," she said, and then sighed. "This is heavenly, thank you. But I guess I'd better go." She pushed herself up, draining what was left of her coffee. "Where are my keys?" she muttered. They weren't on the hook, and she couldn't find them in her pocket or purse. "Gus, did you steal them?" It wouldn't be the first time.

"They're in your car," Will said. "I knocked the snow off of it and started it to let it warm up."

"You really are laying it on thick this morning, aren't you, honey?" She grinned at him though, leaning over to give him a lingering, coffee-breath kiss. "Thank you."

"See you in a bit," he said as she zipped up her coat and pulled on a warm hat.

"You're coming in?" She definitely did not want to revisit the discussion about his mother while she was at work.

"I have a couple of errands to run. And I hear you have the best coffee in town."

Cute. It was true. But the cup she'd just finished had been pretty special.

The wind cut into her face, but the car was toasty, all the snow brushed off, only remnants melting on the windshield. A couple of swipes of the wipers and Faye snapped in her seatbelt and backed out of her spot.

Will's sweetness, even if he was totally overcompensating, almost made up for dropping the news about his mom's visit. *This is just a test.* And not even a big one, right? But she was going to need her support group to properly process it.

She travelled past Triple Stripe, the gates lit with white lights that illuminated matching wreaths. That was Emilie's doing — Em loved the holidays. Faye wished she could borrow just a bit of that joy.

Once she had things under control at the café, she called Liv. Liv hated the phone, but Faye was on her pickup list. And sure enough, Liv answered partway through the first ring.

"Hey, everything all right?"

"In a life or death way, yes," Faye said, hesitating to draw in a fresh breath. "In the state of my life way, no."

"Why? What happened? Is everything all right with you and Will?"

"Um, yes." *And no.* "But we need to get together. Tell Em. There has to be wine. And ice cream."

"Okay, but you're the one whose life is insane right now, so, when?"

Faye drummed her fingers against the stainless steel counter. Good Question, but no sense in wasting time. "Tonight?"

"Sure," Liv said without hesitating. "My place? I think it's my turn to host. Bring Gus. Holly insists."

Emilie's Black Lab and Gus had become fast friends a minute after they first met. "But otherwise, no boys," Faye said.

Liv laughed. "That's only recently become a problem."

Faye sighed. "I suppose it's a good thing that the men in our lives are tolerable." She pressed her fingers to her forehead. It was too bad those men had to have mothers. "I've gotta go."

"I'll get everything. You just show up."

"Thank you." And she meant it with every gram of her soul. They'd figure this out. They'd conquered much worse.

CHAPTER
EIGHT

Will trudged out to the barn, Gus in tow — he didn't have time to help with stalls this morning, but he'd check in with Stacy and see if she needed anything. He was struggling with Faye's reaction last night. What was the big deal? He couldn't figure it out. His mother wouldn't understand if he turned around and said she wasn't welcome, and he couldn't find fault with that because he wasn't sure he understood himself.

Talk about it, the rational voice in his head said. Hear her out. He'd make something nice for dinner tonight, and try not to rankle her before she'd actually eaten it.

Gus trotted, nose to the ground, pausing to lift his leg on a snowbank before bounding, tail up and ears flopping, toward a horse on the other side of the fence. He stopped short of going into the paddock, giving a gruff *woof.* The horse pinned its ears and shook its head before going back to join its friends at a big round bale of hay.

"Pretty tough there, big guy." Will laughed. "Let's go."

Grinning, Gus gambolled back to Will's side. The dog was always in a good mood. *Be like the dog, Will.*

The tractor poked out the end of the main barn — which meant Stacy was halfway done. When Will entered, a flying forkful of straw and manure from one of the boxes gave away her location.

"Hey, Stacy. Anything I can do before I go? Sorry I don't have time to muck out this morning."

"Well, seeing as you're here..." She crooked a finger as she set down the fork and headed a few stalls down from the one she'd been cleaning. "This guy here is on stall rest and he tore his feed tub out of the wall last night. The eyehooks need to go back in and it would just go better if I had help. It won't take long."

Inside the stall, a horse circled, straw rustling under its feet. The horse nickered and tossed its head and Will took an involuntary step back. Stacy better be giving the thing some drugs if she wanted him to hold it. He could work a pitchfork, but had no interest in actually handling the beasts unless he had a guarantee there would be no actual skill involved.

But Stacy crouched to scoop up the power drill he'd neglected to see right outside the stall, handing it to him before she picked up a long-handled screwdriver and a lead rope.

"I'll hold him out of the way if you can put new holes in the wall. The old ones are stripped. Oh — guess you'll need these." She reached into the pocket of her vest and held a fist out to him. When he presented his hand, she dropped two screw eyes into his palm.

This he could do.

Will waited while Stacy went in and caught the horse — not that it tried to run away — then slipped in carefully.

"Hey dude. Why'd you go and do that? You like making work for everybody?"

"That's what horses do." Stacy grinned. "Make work."

That's pretty much how it seemed to Will. He glanced over his shoulder, still not entirely trusting the horse, and positioned one of the screw eyes about an inch from the first hole. "Here look good?"

Stacy nodded, tickling the horse's nose, the horse trying to grab at her gloved fingers. The power drill didn't seem to bother him the way Will thought it might — he'd been around them enough to know horses were scared of the stupidest things. The whole exercise took longer than it would have if he hadn't been looking behind himself every five seconds. Once he was satisfied the holes were big enough, he started screwing the eye hooks in.

"Here." Stacey handed him the screwdriver and he used it for leverage to tighten them.

"What would you have done if I hadn't shown up?" Will would have let the beast eat off the floor. It was covered in mats, after all.

"Tied him to the wall. It probably would have been fine. He's just getting a little stir-crazy so this is a bit safer."

Definitely safer. "What did he do?"

"Stress fractures in his hind end. Just two more weeks in solitary then he gets to be turned out again."

"I bet that'll be an exciting day."

"Oh, it will." Stacy grinned. "For all of us."

Will slipped out of the stall and grabbed the feed tub. The horse rumbled again at the rattle of it, tugging Stacy toward it as Will snapped it in place.

"How's that?"

"Perfect. Thanks Will." Stacy let the horse plunge his nose into it, and it was comical the way the big head came back up and nudged her, like he was saying, *Hello, you forgot something.*

"You've got my number, right? Next week when Dean's gone, text me if you need anything. If my car's here, I probably am, too."

"Great. I will. Not that I'm not used to being on my own. Pretty normal during the racing season when Dean's at the track. But it's probably a good thing there's someone around because you never know what could happen. The older I get, the more I think about that stuff."

Even if Faye was here, she wasn't the first person anyone would think to call if they needed a hand with the horses. If Will lived on the farm, it would be good, wouldn't it? Good to have someone nearby. For safety.

His mind kept going to it, a twinge of longing in his chest. He did love it here. It made him want to relive the most memorable parts of his childhood, those summers he'd spent at his grandfather's farm. Long days, hard work, well-earned sleep at night. What a long way he was from that now. *The older you get, the more you think about that stuff, too.*

"Catch you later, Stace," he said. "Gus! Where are you?"

The Golden's head popped out of a stall. *What's on the menu today, dude? More lost horse food with a chaser of stinky digested goodness, mmmmm.* Faye was going to be ticked at him again if it upset the dog's system. Gus should be used to it, though. Built a tolerance to whatever microbes were involved. The dog had lived on the farm almost all of his life. He'd made it through last night just fine.

"Just don't, ah, decide your system can't handle it while I'm out, okay?" Will ruffled the dog's broad blond head after they were back in the house, standing on the mat because he was going right out again. "Be good. Go watch doggy movies on Netflix or something."

The Camaro started up no problem, though the inside of its windshield had a film of frost Will hoped would melt once the blasting fan warmed it enough. *Old car problems.* By the time he climbed behind the wheel after brushing off the snow, the frost had melted into drips of moisture. He spent his time waiting for the engine to warm up googling *how to keep the inside of a windshield from frosting.* He'd been living with the issue for years, but maybe there was a fix. A cordless dehumidifier? *Cool.* He could order one online, right now. But — would Faye mind if he had it delivered here?

He tossed his phone to the passenger seat and put the Camaro into gear. He'd deal with the inside of his windshield frosting a bit longer and figure it out later. Better go pick up Nate.

He'd been surprised when Nate said he was available this afternoon, thinking he was supposed to be riding races at the track. Maybe he'd just eaten one too many butter tarts and weighed too much. Will wasn't going to probe. They stopped at Triple Shot as promised, and had to wait as Faye finished with a customer before Will could sweep in and prepare cappuccinos to go and collect a box of treats.

"Have fun!" Faye called as she sent them back out the door.

"What did you tell her we were doing?" Nate asked as they returned to the car.

"I can't remember, but I think I made it sound like Christmas shopping."

"You know that would be way easier than what you're doing, right?"

"But not nearly as much fun," Will said as he opened the driver's side door.

Nate slid him a doubtful glance from the passenger seat and sipped his coffee.

Last spring, Will had discovered the garage where they'd dropped off the trailer on a tip from a buddy of his in the city when Nate had been looking for someone to show his old Mustang some love. Gil and his guys had given it a new lease on life and Nate had gifted it to his brother, Tim. Will had thought the Camaro might be next — it was feeling its age — but they were here with a trailer instead, something the Camaro couldn't haul. And he wasn't going to be able to afford to pay insurance on two vehicles when he found something that could. He couldn't rely on borrowing Dean's truck all the time.

"Wow," Nate said when they walked in, their footsteps echoing in the space. "They've done a lot already."

Will nodded. "Some things are worth paying for."

The young guys that worked at the shop were all-in and had been working into the evenings on the trailer. Much to Will's surprise, it hadn't needed a whole new frame, just some cross pieces and a new floor. They'd sandblasted the exterior and ground down and patched the rusty spots. Nate had sourced some thick rubber matting, like the original mats that had covered the floor boards — if it was good enough for those pricey racehorses, Will was sure he could stand on it. They'd cut a large serving window into the side and fashioned a drop-down door that would double as a mini awning when open. Next would be a paint job and graphics for the outside, then insulating and setting up the inside. A shelf to serve on, a counter area for the machine, a fridge under it... it was going to be sweet when it was done.

"What are you calling it?" Nate asked as they walked around the work in progress.

"I'll have to think about that."

"Tripe Shot to Go?"

"That probably makes the most sense, eh?" Will grinned.

Continuity. Branding. "I can't believe how fast it's come together. I should have it in time for the parade."

"Parade?" Nate looked clueless.

Of course, Nate had never been here for the parade, because he'd always left for Florida before it happened. "The Santa Claus parade on the Sunday before Christmas. Faye said she'd agreed to be open and serve hot chocolate and such. This'll take the pressure off and let her focus on all the baking she has to do to fulfill the orders she's got."

"Maybe that is better than a ring," Nate quipped, but added. "For now."

"You all need to shut up about the ring," Will grumbled. "This *is* better."

The guys working on the trailer took a break, and Will doled out coffee and pastry to help make up for the guilt he felt for just watching them. He and Nate sat on overturned buckets off to the side. Will shivered, the concrete walls and floor trapping dampness, and let himself think of how cosy it would be, serving cappuccinos and treats out of the trailer in front of the café. The image softened his contrary feelings for the holidays. "It's going to be quite the Christmas this year."

"Sure is," Nate agreed. "We're going to have *all* the parents, mine and Liv's. A *lot* of people. Not something we're good at."

Will eyed him. Nate was fine with people, even if he didn't always like them, so it was Liv he meant. They'd apparently become a "we" now. That was what happened when people got married. They forged their identities. *Olivate. Nathia.* Will almost snorted into his cup. Good thing it had a lid.

"Yeah well... I talked to my mom yesterday," Will said, commiserating. "She told me she's coming, too."

"*Told* you? That sounds like your mom. How's that going to work?"

"Not sure yet. I broke the news to Faye last night."

"How'd she take it?"

"Not great."

"You're right. You should wait till after they meet to propose. Just in case." Nate grinned.

Will gave him a shove, Nate's bucket tipping, and Nate grabbed Will's arm, laughing, to keep from falling over. Then Will's phone buzzed and Will fished it from his pocket, glancing at the screen, his face falling.

A text from Faye. She was getting together with Liv and Emilie so she wouldn't be home for dinner tonight so he might as well go back to his place. He'd have to wait for another time to make her dinner and clear the air.

CHAPTER

NINE

"So what's got you all worked up?" Emilie asked, pouring the wine and handing a glass to Faye, then to Liv. Holly and Gus were already playing bitey-face, their paws overlapped, black against gold.

Faye took a fortifying swallow. "Will's mom. She's coming. For Christmas."

"But wait —" Liv started. "She came Christmas Day last year." Both her eyes and her feet shifted before returning to Faye. "I completely forgot to ask how that went. Was it bad?"

Bad? It was a non-event. Emilie knew, but Liv had been absent for their usual Boxing Day get-together because she'd been in Calgary with Nate's family.

Liv glanced from Emilie to Faye, waiting.

"It never happened," Faye said, trying to suppress the irritation the memory dredged up. "She cancelled last-minute. As it turned out, she never even came to Toronto. She had an emergency Christmas Eve and changed her plans, which I totally understand, but she didn't tell us until about half an hour before she was supposed to be here."

"Okay. So *I'm* bad at communicating, we all know that," Liv said. "But she didn't even text Will when she found out about the emergency? Or at least the next morning? Like when she knew she wasn't going to make her flight?"

Faye shook her head. "When she did tell him, it felt like an afterthought, to be honest. At least she had the decency to call. Though she wasn't overly apologetic."

But that was the way of the world now, wasn't it? Don't apologize. No more "sorry I'm late." It was "thank you for your patience." The manners Faye had been raised with were from a bygone era.

"As flakey as it sounds like Will's parents are, it's amazing he turned out as well as he did," Emilie said.

Though Faye hadn't thought of it till now, it was true. Will would never be the leader, the real go-getter his parents seemed to want him to be, but he showed up for his friends — even if he sometimes grumbled about it.

"So there's always a chance she might stand you up again," Liv said. "Right?"

"I suppose." But Faye wasn't counting on it. Because, despite the work she'd put into preparing for that visit — culinarily, and emotionally — it had been a relief when it hadn't come to pass. She could not be that lucky again. It wasn't as if she could avoid it forever — but did it have to be at the most stressful time of the year? Will didn't know how easy he had it with her. No parents to deal with, only her brother. And Dean was the most easy-going guy on the planet.

"What am I going to do?" she prodded, needing more than the acknowledgement that this was, indeed, something to be upset about.

"Drink some more?" Liv suggested, and Faye swatted her.

Faye wasn't used to drinking much anymore. It wasn't that she'd consciously cut back, it was just one of the hazards of a job that didn't leave her much social or leisure time. Not that it was a bad thing — with the new recommendations of no more than two servings a week, what was even the point? Tonight she'd make up for the last month, probably; then if she abstained until the twenty-fifth, how many drinks could she have at Christmas dinner to make the whole thing bearable? Did it work that way? Somehow Faye doubted it. Besides, she was getting too old to binge; as in, she already knew she would regret tonight, tomorrow.

"Let's sit," Emilie said, steering Faye out of the kitchen by the elbow.

"Hold up," Liv said and grabbed the bottle of wine. She topped up their glasses then Emilie passed hers to Faye to free up her hands for a beautifully prepared charcuterie board. Liv led the way to the living room.

"I'm so happy I have a sweet mother-in-law," Liv said, reaching for a cracker and slicing off a chunk of Brie.

"Me too," Emilie chimed in, and both sisters laughed.

"You two are not helping!" Faye scowled, sinking into the soft, cream-coloured couch. She'd better not spill red wine on this thing.

"This is what we're going to do," Liv began.

The wine was starting to affect Faye's brain, but she was sure she'd just heard Liv say, "This is what we're going to do." Liv. Taking charge. Of something that didn't involve a horse?

"We? What?" Faye said, shaking herself out of her shock.

Liv held up a hand, using it for emphasis. "I'm not sure how it happened, but everyone is coming this year. Nate's parents. My parents. So we'll just bundle Will's mom in with the *festivities*." She loaded the word "festivities" with repellency.

Faye had a vision of all the parents and in-laws rolled into a Yule log and giggled. Yep, her alcohol tolerance was shot. But — she could make a Yule log. That would be impressive.

"Will's mom — what's her name?" Liv continued.

Faye shrugged. "I don't know." It was embarrassing. She should probably know. "Do I have to ask Will?" She wasn't used to being the unsure one. This wasn't a good look.

Liv rolled her eyes, picking up her phone and texting someone. Faye raised an eyebrow.

"Connie," Liv said with a self-satisfied smile, resting the phone on her thigh, waiting for Nate's mother to text back. "She'll know, right? They might not be best friends, but she'll know the name of her son's best friend's mother." Her phone pinged. "Julia Ackerman. Maiden name? Remarried?" Liv suggested, because it wasn't Callaghan, like Will's.

"Wouldn't you know if she'd remarried?" Emilie asked Faye.

"Maybe? Maybe not." Faye had been too good at staying out of her short-term boyfriends' business; she still didn't like to ask questions. She figured if Will wanted her to know something he'd tell her.

"It doesn't matter," Liv said. "Though Connie might know."

"Or," Emilie said, swiping her own phone to life, "Google might. She is a doctor, after all. Here's what I've got," Emilie said, preparing to read off the screen. "Dr Julia Ackerman. Still don't know if that's her maiden name or if she's remarried. She's an ob-gyn."

Faye knew that much.

"And," Emilie continued, "she does a podcast. Should we listen to an episode? That will help give you a sense of her, right?"

"You want me to listen to my boyfriend's mother talk about women's health? Why don't you listen and get back to me?" Faye barely kept from snarling and checked herself. They *were* just trying to help.

"To return to my original point, because I did have one," Liv interrupted, a snap to her own words. "As it seems now everyone is coming, as much of a nightmare as that's bound to be — Julia, Dr Ackerman, whatever we're supposed to call her —"

"How am I supposed to know what to call her?" Faye broke in, chewing her thumbnail. She hadn't chewed her nails since high school.

Emilie laughed. *How dare she laugh?* "Didn't you sort all that out last year?"

Faye couldn't remember. Had probably banished it from her mind.

"You can ask Will that," Liv said. "Can't you? Let me finish, okay?"

Faye nodded and gulped more wine.

"Dr Julia Ackerman," Liv said, covering all the bases and nailing Faye with a *not-a-word* stare, "knows Connie and Reid, so she'll have someone to talk to."

"Will's never given me the impression they're friendly, though," Faye said. "What if they don't get along?"

"If there's some strange feud between them — which I highly doubt — my parents will be here," Liv said. "They'll be like Switzerland."

"But they have to side with Connie and Reid, because they're connected by you and Nate." *Where was the ice cream?* She needed ice cream.

"You're overthinking this, Faye," Liv insisted.

Faye stifled a laugh. Liv was the over-thinker in the room.

"They're adults," Liv continued. "She's a doctor, Connie is a sweetheart, and my mother is painfully restrained and polite. Even if they hate each other, they'll behave."

"That doesn't change that it will be stressful and awkward."

"Of course not. But it spreads it around a bit, doesn't it? We're all going to be freaking out because everyone will be here and we have to feed them like the grown-ups we have yet to become. So we need to help each other out. Many hands make light work, or whatever."

As much as it shocked Faye, Liv was right. Stronger together, and all that. Emilie seemed to sense reinforcements were required, popping up and returning from the kitchen with three small ice cream tubs.

Liv was on a mission now. "Connie and Reid can stay in Em's apartment. If they're staying in the same room. Who knows what their status is. Em and your mother-in-law —"

"Whoa!" Faye said. "She's not."

"You don't get to complain about that, *sweetie*," Liv said, her voice dripping with sarcasm as she used Faye's pet name for her. "You did that to me. Em can stay in her old room and Dr Julia Ackerman can stay in my old room. That's everyone, right? How many is that?"

Faye counted on her fingers, the conversation making her more sober than she'd like. "The six of us. Connie, Reid and Dr Mom. Wait — what about your parents? Where are they sleeping?"

Emilie started laughing. "I can't believe you forgot *Maman et Papa*."

"Is it really a surprise I'm bad at this?" Liv said. "They have to stay in our room, of course. It used to be theirs."

"So where will you and Nate sleep?"

"Right now, I'm thinking we could be in Florida by then, at the condo?"

"Oh, no way," Faye said. "You're helping me, not deserting me. It was *supposed* to be *me* helping *you*."

"We can sleep anywhere," Liv said. "The basement. A tack room. The office. Whatever."

"So far, we have eleven? Twelve, because Dean will be back." Faye counted. "What about the Cloutiers? Should we invite them? If we're feeding a horde, what are four more?" Because that would mean the Cloutier's daughter, Sylvie, and her boyfriend, Chad, too. Life got far too complicated with everyone paired off.

"Maybe Dean and Dr Mom will hit it off." Emilie grinned.

Faye shuddered. "That's just — no, Em. Please no." Then she asked, "What's Kerrie doing for Christmas?" Liv's new farm manager was almost like family now. "That would put us at seventeen." This was getting out of hand. Her heart was thudding in her chest. Was this what a panic attack felt like?

"Kerrie's spending Christmas with her parents out west," Liv said. "Emilie — did *Maman et Papa* say anything about *Grand-mère* coming?"

"I'll find out," Emilie said. "If that happens, I don't think this gathering could be any more warped." Liv's immediate family had been estranged from her father's parents until a year ago.

"I don't know how to cook for that many people," Faye said, exasperated. "I can only do dessert for those kinds of numbers."

"It's just math, Faye," Liv said.

"Says the woman who was freaking out herself not that long ago about feeding her in-laws Christmas dinner," Faye sniped. She set down her wine glass and reached for the ice cream, softened to the perfect consistency. "I was *so* looking forward to enjoying a much-deserved Christmas evening with my boyfriend and my brother."

"Your boyfriend is a chef, or close to it," Emilie said. "And Nate can cook. I say we put them to work. And our math whiz here can figure out how to scale up your recipes and do the shopping, too, for that matter."

"What am I being roped into?"

Faye's head jerked up at the familiar male voice. Nate stood on the landing adjacent to the sunken living room. "You! Out! No boys." She wasn't slurring. Was she?

Nate put his hands over his ears and continued to the kitchen. "Carry on."

"Faye," Liv said, touching her on the arm, her face lighting up. "Nate could probably help, with more than the cooking, actually."

Faye snorted. "How could Nate ever help?"

"Really?" Nate stopped in his tracks. "Or do you still hate me, after all?"

"I'm sorry," Faye said. "I don't hate you. But," she focused on Liv again. "How?"

"Well..." Liv began. "Nate knows her. He might have insight for you. Right?" She glanced over her shoulder at him, smiling sweetly.

The truth pushed aside Faye's ire. "That's a good point. You could actually be useful, Nate."

Now Nate looked suspicious. "Know who?"

"Will's mom. She's..." Faye took a grounding breath, "coming for Christmas."

His laugh wasn't encouraging. "Oh, boy."

"Miller!" Liv hissed, trying to hide her own laugh behind a hand. "Not helping."

"Will told me," he admitted. "Let me know what you need, Faye."

"Not now, we're drinking," Faye called as he disappeared from sight. She reached for another slug of red. "I guess I'm going to need to borrow your husband." She quirked an eyebrow at Liv. "Thank you for talking me down. I'm so happy you've become an adult."

Committed, now, to consuming too much wine and ice cream, Faye accepted that tomorrow she was going to feel rough. Did she care? No. Necessary evil. She was long overdue a girls' night with these two. Still, none of them were into late nights anymore. By ten o'clock, they were all fading.

Faye stared at her empty wine glass — and just as empty ice cream carton — tucked her legs underneath her, and curled up into the comfy sofa. "Can I just crash here? Just say 'no' to four AM alarms."

"You're welcome to," Liv said. "I can even give you a bed."

"I really should go home," Faye murmured.

"You're not driving," Emilie said.

"But if I stay, I'll have to get up at three instead of four." The thought was painful.

Liv, seeming far too sober, said, "I'll ask Nate to drive you home."

"No," Faye moaned. She did not want her ex taking her home in this sorry condition. "You don't sound drunk. You can drive me home."

"I'm drunk enough." Liv paused, fingers flying on her phone screen. Within a few seconds it sang back a notification that, even in her current state of inebriation, Faye recognized as Liv's chosen tone for Nate. "Done."

"Oh, come on..."

"You'll be glad in the morning, Faye."

"Fine." She propped herself up and tried to gather her wits, but Nate appeared before she'd managed to do so.

"Where are your keys, Faye?"

"What? But then you'll have to pick me up in the morning."

"If I'd known how this was going to go, I could have offered you a shuttle service here and back, but that's okay. It's a nice night for a walk."

"Are you sure?"

"Yeah. Let's go."

Faye insisted she didn't need to hang off Nate's arm to negotiate what seemed like too many steps between the couch and the car. At least for once it wasn't snowing. Nate opened up the passenger door of her Corolla and flipped the front seat forward to let Gus pile in the back, then waited for Faye to tuck herself in before swinging shut the door. He got behind the wheel and started the car, turning to Faye as he gave it a few minutes to warm up.

"Let's hear it." There was humour in his voice. "What do you want to know?"

The cold air had already cleared her head. "First of all — what should I call her?"

"Mom?"

Lucky for him, there was nothing close at hand for Faye to belt him with. "I was just applauding your wife on growing up, but it saddens me to know that you are still a jerk."

"Where's your sense of humour, Faye?"

"That's a very good question. I think I lost it the moment Will said he'd invited her."

"He didn't invite her. She *told* him she was coming."

"Details. What can you tell me about this woman?"

Nate shifted the car into gear and eased it forward. "Well — I guess to be fair, I was a teenager last time I saw her. And I didn't really ever see her much. Will was pretty independent, and she was always busy. She's one of those driven women."

"Like your wife?"

He grinned. "A little, maybe, in that she must be smart and science-y to be a doctor. She's kind of aloof."

"Still sounds a lot like Liv."

"Which means you should give her a chance, like you gave Liv a chance."

Faye admitted, begrudgingly, Nate had a point. It wasn't fair to judge this woman she'd never met.

"We'll all get through this, Faye," Nate said with admirable conviction. "We're going to be one big, happy, dysfunctional family. It'll be fun."

Faye scowled at him. "Are you bringing the psychedelics?"

Nate laughed. "There's the sense of humour."

"You think I'm joking?" She was, of course. It was the only way to deal with this, though Faye anticipated psychedelics might tempt her, should someone offer them.

"Just one more thing," Nate said.

Faye squeezed the bridge of her nose. She just wanted to be home, in her bed, asleep. "What's that?"

"Will's mom and my mom don't exactly get along. So probably best not to sit them too close to each other."

"Isn't that just great. Are we talking potential fisticuffs?"

"No." He laughed. "Though who knows, if there's wine."

Faye stared out the window, vague shapes of the towering maples that lined the laneway passing in the darkness. "How did I get myself into this? Is it too late to run away?"

Another laugh, but when Nate spoke, his tone was serious. "You're the strongest woman I know, Faye, but we're all going to help you. And who knows, maybe something good will come out of this."

"Like Will's mom and I will click and end up BFFs?"

"It's possible. But I was thinking, maybe we'll finally teach Liv how to cook. What's she going to do if anything happens to me? Live on salad?"

It was Faye's turn to laugh. "Let's hope that's something we never have to worry about."

Triple Stripe Stables was only five minutes down the road

from the Taylors' Northwest Stud. Nate pulled up next to Dean's truck, and the absence of Will's Camaro made Faye sad, even though she'd known he was returning to the city tonight. She reached for the door handle and hopped out at the same time as Nate. Gus leapt after her, stopping to pee before he ran to the back door.

Nate met Faye around the front of the car and handed her the keys. "If you think of anything else, just call or text, okay?"

Faye nodded.

"Are you okay to get from here to the door?" Nate asked, peering at her cautiously.

She smirked and gave him a shove, then pulled him into a hug. "I am. Thanks for the drive."

He grinned his charming grin, and as he turned away, breaking into a jog down the driveway, Faye was grateful that instead of thinking of him as her ex-boyfriend, the word that came to mind first was friend.

CHAPTER

TEN

The conference room at the fancy downtown hotel was decked out with antique gold garlands and pretty white lights. Table linens complemented the colour scheme and glassware sparkled, ready to be filled with the copious amounts of alcohol sure to be consumed over the course of the evening. Will checked in with the kitchen, making sure the hors d'oeuvres were ready, impressed, as always, with the menu.

Ari had recruited Will back in January to help with his thriving catering business and Will had jumped on the opportunity. He didn't make a whole lot at the casual restaurant job he'd picked up after leaving Mysticus, so the added income was welcome. Ari was busy all year so Will usually made more money with the catering jobs he did on the side than he did at the diner. He loved doing them. It was always a pleasure to be involved with great food, and he'd met all sorts of interesting people. Sure, there were difficult personalities, but, for the most part, the guests were agreeable, thanks to the celebratory atmosphere that surrounded the events.

Will didn't miss the madness that had been his job at the high-end restaurant one bit. He'd given too much of his heart and soul to that place — for nothing. It would always be what it was — a great place to eat, if you could afford it, but a terrible place to work.

As he went around the room making sure everything was just so, he had time to think. He hadn't seen Faye since the morning he and Nate had stopped by Triple Shot on the way to check in on the trailer's progress. He had catering jobs all weekend and a couple of short shifts at the diner. It made sense just to stay in the city, so it might be Monday before he caught up with her again. Dean was leaving on his ski trip Tuesday — maybe Will would plan that dinner he wanted to make for her for Tuesday night.

Faye's reaction to his mom coming still exasperated him, and it was making him paranoid. Maybe Faye was right to be upset. He'd never worried that Faye and his mom wouldn't get along — he loved Faye, so his mom would too. Except the more it bounced around his brain, the more it made him think maybe they wouldn't like each other. They both had such strong personalities, he was envisioning a clash, sparks flying once the two of them were finally in a room together.

But they didn't *have* to like each other, did they? It wasn't like his mom lived close by. If they didn't get along, it wouldn't be the end of the world.

Will strove to learn everything he could about the catering business working these parties. It was something he could see himself doing, like he might finally have found his thing. Faye had hinted there would be lots of work up in the King area, and the café was a natural place to find leads. She did a lot of dessert trays for parties around there, and Will was convinced they could steal some of that business if they could do the savoury side as well. He had the culinary skill, and he'd gathered enough experience this year; he was sure he could pull it off.

Because he needed something — something that was his, that provided a more reliable income than his bit of this, bit of that. When he'd first met Faye, they'd joked about both being underachievers, then Faye had taken the café and run with it, leaving him standing still. And Nate was right; the espresso trailer was cool, but not a full-time endeavor. Starting his own catering business would complement the café without putting him under Faye's feet, and once he built a reputation, it could be decent money.

As the wait staff began to show, dressed in their crisp white shirts and black pants, Will scanned each face. Finally he saw the one he was looking for, recognizing the bright smile and the flip of a high, blonde ponytail.

"Hey, Monique. How the hell are you?" He grinned, arms open wide.

"Will Callaghan." Monique gave him a squeeze. "I thought you'd gone and moved to the country."

Yeah, that had yet to happen. "Nope. I'm still here."

Monique stepped back and crossed her arms. "I'm surprised I haven't seen you around town."

"It's a big city."

"Yes, but it's a small world."

True, that. "I'm back and forth a lot. Are you still working at that hellhole?" He hadn't seen her since he'd left Mysticus.

"Indeed, I am, and hating every minute of it." She flashed a wry smile. "Ari said you gave him my number for this. Thank you."

"Everyone can use a bit of extra cash this time of year, right?"

"Absolutely. Have you been doing a lot of these? I could see you starting your own catering business."

"Thinking about it," he admitted.

"Don't lose my number, then. We'll catch up later, okay? Don't disappear again." She blew him a kiss and sashayed off.

Once the people arrived, Will's job was making sure both the guests and the servers were happy. He helped bring out food for the buffet, filled flutes of champagne and arranged canapés, seeing Monique only in passing. It was a good group. Respectful; no troublemakers. One of the male servers flagged him down for a break; Will took the platter of wine glasses and circulated.

A forty-something man with a bad haircut and a cheap sports coat snapped his fingers as Will was on his way by. Will gritted his teeth before pulling his lips into a smile and presented the tray to let the man exchange his empty glass for a full one — without a word of thanks, of course. There was one in every crowd.

"Do I know you from somewhere?"

Will turned at the touch on his elbow. The man did look familiar, with dark frames and distinguished grey hair, his well-cut charcoal suit refreshing after the rude fashion disaster. He juggled a napkin with smoked salmon and capers on a crostini in one hand, gripping a wine glass in the other.

"I used to work at Mysticus," Will said.

"That's it." The man nodded. "Haven't seen you there in a while. Is this what you're doing now?"

Will nodded, unsure of what else to say.

"You were good at your job. My wife and I are thinking about having a party after the holidays. You know how it gets this time of year. These things are wall to wall. We thought it would be good to break it up a bit. Give everyone something to look forward to in January." He pulled a business card from his pocket. "Give me a call. I'll tell you what we have in mind and maybe you can give us a quote. If you're interested, that is."

Will balanced the tray in one hand to accept the card, too surprised to explain that he wasn't running the show here. "Definitely. Thank you." He'd have to pass the card on to Ari, but part of him wanted to tuck it into his pocket and keep it for himself. Still, the exchange put an extra bounce in his step. It was a sign, he was sure of it. His life was coming together. The espresso event trailer; a catering business in the making. A life — a real one, not just part-time — with Faye.

It really was time she met his mom. It would be fine. And if it wasn't, Faye could hold her own. It wasn't as if his mom would be what broke them up.

The night was long, the work steady. By the time the last guests went home, everyone was worn out; ready for bed so they could do it over again tomorrow. Will was sure it would be much the same staff at the afternoon event he was working for Ari and looked forward to it. They'd all gotten along well.

Monique dropped into a chair and kicked off her shoes, rubbing one of her feet. "So what have you been up to? When you quit the restaurant, I was sure I'd be getting a wedding invitation. Or did you just marry that girl and not invite me?"

Will shook his head and took a pull on his beer.

Her eyebrows arched. "Are you still together?"

"Yep," he responded. "Two and a half years."

"So what have you been up to?"

"I work at The Downtown Diner." That really was its name. "Do this on the side."

"You made the right move quitting Mysticus," she said, switching feet. "I'm jealous."

"So why are you still there?"

She shrugged. "The devil you know, I guess."

"Well, if you ever want to get out of the city, come work for Faye. She could use someone to help out. But I can't say the pay would be as good as Mysticus." The tips Monique made at the high-end hellhole were probably what kept her there.

"I don't get it. You drive back and forth from the city, working at a place that, I've got to say, is beneath you, picking up side gigs like this. Why don't *you* help her? I thought you were partners. It's not making a lot of sense, Will."

"If we were together all the time, how would she ever miss me?" He cracked a grin.

Monique rolled her eyes. "I'm sure out in the country you'd find a way to give each other space." She nailed him with a hard stare. "Come on, Will, what's the matter with you? What are you waiting for? I thought she was the one."

She is. Isn't she?

"I'm going home. It was great catching up." Monique rose, kissing him on the cheek and strolling away, shoes dangling in one hand.

Will helped Ari finish up before heading back to his place, trying to keep *Faye* and *wedding* out of the sentences forming in his head. As the door to his loft clicked behind him, he heard the thump of Lemon landing on the hardwood before her tiny head peeked out from behind the curtain around his bed.

"There's my *chérie*. Sorry to keep you waiting."

Lemon followed him to the kitchen where he prepared her dinner, a mixture of wet and dry food. When he set it down next to her water dish, she began eating with dainty mouthfuls. He crossed his arms and leaned back against the counter, looking around his flat.

He'd grown up in suburbia, then moved to a big city two thousand miles away for school — and stayed — but he'd always felt more at home in the country. Meeting Faye had seemed like destiny. She had a city girl's heart, but was committed to her country home. Yet here he was, still living and working in the country's largest metropolis.

Turned out the city wasn't so easy to get out of.

CHAPTER
ELEVEN

"Come on. We're going to the races."

Faye looked up, rubbing her cheek with a flour-covered finger. She hadn't even heard Emilie arrive.

Lucy came over, pulled Faye from the dough her hands were in, and directed her to the sink. "Sylvie and I have got this. You go watch that horse race."

"I have to go home and change," Faye said, trying not to sound as if she was complaining when they were all doing this nice thing for her.

That was something Liv would do, a little voice in her head said. Search for reasons to get out of something fun because of her job. A job that was her life. Had Faye's job become her life? It wasn't hard to see the answer. How many times had she chastised both Liv and Emilie for that? She'd become just as guilty.

"That's why we made sure you'd have lots of time," Emilie said. "Let's go!"

Faye hardly ever went to the races in the fall as the end of the season approached. She loved Woodbine Racetrack in the summer. She loved its premier event, the Queen's Plate, when everyone dressed up. It was a chance to put on a hat and spiky high heels she'd regret wearing before the end of the day. Traditionally, she'd drink too much and always scheduled the next day off. The Plate should be a national holiday, in her opinion. It was Canada's race. An historic event, full of pageantry. A day where she and her friends played dress up and celebrated the Sport of Kings — even though they were relative paupers.

Closing day had a completely different vibe. It signaled an ending. For racetrackers like her brother, and Liv and Nate, it meant relief, but Faye found it a little sad, light years away from the excitement of summer and the Plate.

She couldn't remember the last time she'd attended the final card of racing, but their best horse, Ride The Wave, was in the featured Valedictory Stakes. Thanks to Lucy and Sylvie agreeing to fill in, Faye could be there to cheer him on. And thanks to Emilie, they arrived in time to have a drink with Liv in the Woodbine Club, where it was warm and dry, before heading to the paddock to see the horses saddled.

"Irish coffee, please," Faye said when the server came for their order.

"Oh, yes," Emilie agreed. "For me too, thanks."

Liv nodded. "I guess that's three."

"Where's Will, anyway?" Emilie asked.

"He had another catering job." Faye kept a frown from her lips.

"Are you feeling better about his mother coming?" Emilie, again.

Was she? Faye hadn't seen Will since the evening she'd

spent with Liv and Em, so she hadn't had the chance to share the plan with him. He would understand that the farmhouse was too small for Dr Mom to stay there. Liv's home was more personal than finding her a B&B — which would be next to impossible during the holidays, anyway.

"I'm sure it will be fine," she said as the server returned with their drinks. As long as the whole thing wasn't part of some hair-brained scheme that involved Will proposing. She kept those fears to herself.

Emilie scooped some whipping cream with the end of her straw. Faye felt her scrutiny, but Emilie remained silent. *If you're trying to figure it out, Em, stop,* she wanted to say. At least Liv didn't give her a hard time. She'd just been the one to target Faye with the bouquet.

When it was time to go downstairs, they traversed the escalators to the indoor saddling enclosure. It was heated, but the concrete walls and floors were far from the cosiness they'd left behind on the fourth floor. They huddled against the rail, trying to keep warm, Faye wedged between Liv and Emilie in front of the stall where Dean was saddling Ride The Wave. When Nate, who was riding the horse, joined Dean, they all gave him little waves. Faye pitied the jockeys — there were only so many layers they could get away with under those paper-thin nylon pants and tops they wore. Their boots weren't much better. Nate's hands were covered with gloves, and something under his helmet hid his ears. When he pulled what she thought was a neck gaiter up, she saw it was all one piece and would protect most of his face from December's bite. It was cold out there, and this was a long race.

After the paddock judge called for riders up and the grooms started leading the horses from the saddling enclosure, Dean joined them and they went to the grandstand's second floor.

He made them sit outside, where they huddled again. Dean pressed binoculars to his eyes, following the horses as they came onto the track with their lead ponies.

Ride The Wave wasn't the favourite, though the bettors didn't completely discount him. Faye didn't even pretend she could handicap, but she'd placed twenty dollars on the colt — more as a show of confidence than anything. The bet wouldn't change her life if he reached the finish first, but the purse money he would win would be a nice windfall for Dean and their farm, even if part of that money would go to Ride The Wave's part owner.

Faye watched the big screen in the infield instead of keeping her eyes on the starting point, far on the other side of the racetrack. Sure, she wasn't into horses or racing the way her friends and brother were, but her knee still bounced, her hands tucked under her thighs to keep them warm. When the horses broke from the gate, she leaned farther forward, just like they did, and found their farm's red and white-checked silks amid the rainbow of colours, muted in the stark artificial lighting that had come on when the sun had dropped.

Nate and The Wave ended up on the lead. Faye glanced at her brother, his binoculars still on his colt, and wondered how he felt about that. Was it okay? Was he unhappy? Dean's face didn't show emotion either way. He didn't get upset easily, her brother. She could read him at home, but watching his horse run, there was no hope of figuring out what he thought. Liv watched the race almost as carefully — she was a trainer too, after all — but her face wasn't offering an opinion, either.

The horses coasted by the grandstand for the first time — they had to go a whole 'nother circuit before the race was over — Ride The Wave leading the way, his rivals bunched behind him. The colt's ears were forward, and Nate was still — that much she knew was positive.

When they came down the stretch again, Nate and Ride The Wave were still on top. Faye couldn't help rising with the others, cheering him home. *Come on, big guy. You've got this. It's going to feed all your friends on the farm for the winter.*

She and Emilie were screaming, jumping up and down when Ride The Wave coasted under the wire, winning by three lengths with the field straggling behind him. Emilie threw her arms around Faye and Faye squeezed back before moving on to Liv, then Dean, the carefully controlled exterior he'd worn while watching the race replaced by a flush of joy. None of them were cold anymore.

Dean grinned and waved them all toward the stairs. "Let's go get our picture taken."

Faye grasped the railing as they descended the steps — the cheering had warmed her up but her knees were still stiff from sitting down in the chill. The photographer directed the groom to position Nate and Ride The Wave and they huddled in a row next to the colt — shoulders hunched, cheeks pink, but smiles on their faces. When Nate dismounted Dean folded him into a crushing embrace before letting him unsaddle.

As they walked back to the grandstand, Dean draped an arm over Faye's shoulders. "Good way to end the year."

She smiled up at him, happy for his success. In a few days he'd be on a plane to a mountain out west for his hard-earned vacation. They worked like crazy people all year, these race-track folk. There was a kinship among them, and she was grateful to be even just on the fringes of it.

Nate rejoined them after he went to the scales to be weighed — part of the rules, all the jockeys were weighed before and after to make sure no funny stuff had gone on.

Dean looked around their group. "Have we ever all been together on closing day? Can we do dinner? I'm buying."

Liv and Nate exchanged glances, and both nodded.

"Sounds great," Nate said. "Thanks, Dean."

Dean named a restaurant and said he'd go back to check on Ride The Wave to make sure everything was okay, then meet them there. Nate was finished for the day — for the year — and urged Liv to go with Faye and Emilie. He'd catch up once he'd changed into street clothes.

They ordered drinks as they waited for the men. It wasn't awkward that Will wasn't there — Tim wasn't either, away on a road trip with the hockey team — but Faye still wished he could have come. Liv updated Faye on her and Nate's plans to fly down to Florida for a few days to see how the horses down there were doing as Emilie scrolled on her phone.

"Hey, Faye? Who's this?" Emilie held the phone up to Faye and Liv.

Will was tagged in a photo. The woman in the picture had a cheesy smile, her face pressed cheek to cheek with a grimacing Will. She was pretty and looked familiar. "I've met her." *Somewhere.* "I think they used to work together at the restaurant." *Monique.* It would come to her.

Emilie pulled the phone away. "I put up some of the photos I took of the race," Emilie said. "Check them out."

Faye was sure Emilie wasn't trying to stir anything up as she and Liv dutifully pulled out their own phones to see Emilie's photos but Faye got stuck on the one of Will and the blonde just the same. It wasn't jealousy she felt, that niggling twinge in her stomach — everything about that shot said *just friends.* It was something else.

Then she figured it out. It was the same feeling she'd had towards the end of her relationship with Nate: him having a part he kept to himself, something she was never invited to share. Something she would never really be part of. Faye had never thought of Will in the same way, but maybe she'd been blind to it, and this photo was evidence. And it wasn't wrong, in theory, except it might be the thing that was bothering her about them. She shared her friends, her family, her life, with him. He was integral to it. It reminded her she wanted the same from him. She wanted all of him.

Which, of course, included his mother.

TWELVE

ean wasn't wasting any time getting out of town. Will was more jealous of the guy's trip out west to the Rockies than he was of Nate's winters in Florida.

"I haven't been skiing since I left Calgary," he said as he drove Dean to the airport. "It's tragic. You'd better invite me sometime."

"You do know Faye won't be caught dead on skis, right?" Dean asked, giving him a sideways look.

"Yeah, I figured that out. I'm picturing coming back to her in the chalet, where she's sipping a hot drink and catching up on her reading."

"Now, that does sound like something she'd enjoy."

"And then later in the hot tub —"

Dean held up a hand. "You can just stop right there."

Will grinned.

"So, are you going to share what you're doing with my old horse trailer?" Dean asked.

Will glanced over before returning his eyes to the road.

Dean had insisted they take his truck to save the old Camaro more miles, and Will was enjoying the ride. He liked the feel of the truck's steering wheel, and the height of it compared to his low-slung car. He'd need a truck to pull said trailer. Add that to his to-do list: vehicle shopping. It'd be a challenge, finding something used in his budget.

What budget? Better add that to his to-do list, too.

"I'm refurbing it as a travelling espresso bar."

Dean's eyebrows went up, this lower lip protruding thoughtfully as he nodded. "Nice idea."

"It's going to be a surprise for Faye. I know you're leaving — but don't tell her, okay?"

"Your secret's safe with me," Dean said solemnly. "So how does one make a travelling espresso bar profitable?"

Says the horse trainer. Will didn't know a lot about the horse racing business, but he'd seen enough to understand it was rarely profitable. "Multiple income streams, my friend. It's just one of many."

"You've got more balls in the air than Emilie."

That sentence hadn't ended the way he'd thought it was going to, but Will grinned anyway.

"So, Stacy has Thursday off —" Dean began outlining last-minute details. " — And Emilie's going to come and put the horses out and bring them in; make sure they're okay. She'll help with the stalls, too. You sure you're okay with doing night check?"

Will had readily volunteered to do what he could to help around the farm in Dean's absence. "Sure. I'll have Emilie on speed dial, don't worry."

"Nate and Liv would help too. When do they get back?"

They'd left too early for Will to offer his services as airport shuttle. "Not sure. They're playing it by ear."

"Well, if Emilie's unavailable and you have any concerns at all, don't hesitate to call the vet. Better safe than sorry."

"Got it," Will said, and prayed nothing went wrong.

He'd never forget the night he'd come up to see Faye, to finally tell her how he really felt about her — and to share that he'd bought Lucy's café (with a little help from his friends and his mother). A bad thunderstorm had taken out a tree, which, in turn, must've taken out a power line, because by the time he made it to Faye — on foot, because he couldn't get past the fallen tree with his car — the hydro was out. Luckily, Faye had realized it was him pounding on the door of the darkened house before she'd pummelled him with a rolling pin.

Dean had been stuck at the racetrack with a sick horse, and his live-in farm manager had called them out to the barn to help with an injured mare. A priceless moment, both him and Faye barely knowing one end of a horse from the other. Will could wield a pitchfork, but the only reason he'd agreed to hold the horse while Stacy crouched — what seemed to him, precariously close to those deadly back hooves — was because she'd given the horse enough drugs it hadn't moved. Will was more at risk of being drooled on by the dopey animal, its lower lip gaping open, than being bitten, and it looked to Will like there'd been a better chance of the horse falling on Stacy than kicking her.

That night had seemed so full of possibility. Will needed to get back to that place. He had to make the most of his time with Faye while Dean was away.

"So...can I ask you a question?" His eyes flicked to Dean and back to the road.

"About what?"

"About Faye." Maybe her brother could give him some insight; point him in the right direction.

Dean leaned back in the bucket seat, a sly smile taking over his features. "Is this where, because our father isn't around, you ask my permission to marry her?"

"What?" Will sputtered, his face turning red like a flame had flashed up from a frying pan, heat searing his cheeks. Did all of them get together and decide this was what he was supposed to do? Even Monique on the weekend, and she wasn't even part of their group. Then he recognized the humour on Dean's face. Dean would know as much as Will did that Faye would probably disown both of them if she learned either of them thought such permission could be granted by anyone but her. "I was more thinking — does she want me to move in? And would it be okay with you, if that actually happened?"

Dean's expression became neutral. "I thought you were moving in a year ago."

"Is that your blessing?"

"Consider it so."

"Has she said anything to you about any of it? Me moving in, or—?"

Dean laughed, a short rumble from his chest. "Faye? No. We don't talk about things like that."

So much for insight. "But do you think —" What, exactly? What did he want to know? He already knew Dean liked him. Dean was so easy-going; Will imagined there weren't many people he didn't get along with. He had no doubt he and Dean could live happily ever after on the farm, a couple of old bachelors looking out for each other.

"I'd say we've vetted you by now," Dean offered. "You've made it through the trial period with no red flags. You've been good for Faye. And I don't mind having you around. Have I said enough yet?"

Will laughed. "Yeah, I think so." Even if Dean couldn't tell him what was happening in Faye's head, it was still good to have confirmation her brother approved of the relationship. "So what about you?"

The way Dean straightened in the seat, his eyes widening before they dashed toward the window, almost made Will snort.

Dean said, to the window, "What about me?"

"How come you don't have someone for us to torment you about?"

A slight smile lifted Dean's lips, easing the tension in his face, and he gave Will a one-shouldered shrug. "If it happens, it happens. If it doesn't, it doesn't. I don't have the energy to put myself out there. I would like to see my sister settled, however."

"And you think that could be with me?"

"How much assurance do you need, Will?"

Will pressed his lips together and clenched the steering wheel tighter. He had it from everyone now, didn't he? Everyone, except Faye.

The little airplane icons began showing up on the big green overhead highway signs, so he made himself pay attention to be sure he went to the right terminal. He pulled up to the curb on the departures level, and both he and Dean climbed out, Will standing by with his hands in his jacket pockets as Dean unloaded his gear.

"Borrow my truck if you need it for the trailer while I'm gone," Dean said. "Maybe we can coordinate when your espresso bar is up and running. As long as I don't need it to haul the gooseneck with a horse, you can use it until you find something of your own. If you trust me with your Camaro, that is."

"Thanks, Dean. That means a lot."

"I like you." Dean clasped his shoulder. "You're a stayer."

Will opened and closed his mouth. "Stayer. Is that like a

keeper?" Sometimes the horse racing jargon still caught him off guard.

Dean patted his deltoid a couple of times like an awkward father. "Sure."

Will watched him throw his skis and duffel over his shoulder before picking up his boot bag.

"All right. That's everything," Dean said. "Thanks for driving me, Will. Take good care of my truck."

"Say hi to Banff for me," Will said, wistful.

"I will. See you next week. And Will?"

"Yeah?"

"You should know this already, but don't be afraid of my sister. And don't make assumptions. You already feel like family to me."

Dean turned away and started walking toward the terminal before Will could come up with anything resembling a response. Dean was a man of few words, unless those words were about horses or hockey. The fact he'd spoken as many as he had said volumes. Will wanted to believe Dean's support meant more than all his friends' jibes.

He climbed back into the truck and snapped in the seatbelt. The airport, as much as it didn't seem that way, was essentially halfway between the farmhouse and his place downtown.

Will made his way out of the network of concrete, paying close attention again to be sure he ended up going the right way. Signs for the highway heading north. Signs for the highway heading south. But what was the right way, really? Downtown Toronto, or the farm in the country?

Will thought of his cherished flat in the city. Of his beloved old Camaro. Both things he'd be giving up, moving to the farm. But they were symbols of his old life, and they were holding him back.

THIRTEEN

"We need something new," Faye decided out loud, flipping through the glossy *Food & Drink* magazine, looking for inspiration. That ad caught her eye again. *The only limit is your imagination.* Right now, that meant coming up with recipe ideas. She abandoned the magazine, opening her laptop, and typed *Christmas squares* into the search bar of the open browser.

Emilie and Sylvie were both helping this afternoon, Sylvie promising to lend a hand over the next few weeks and into the holidays. It was a relief for Faye. It meant she could legitimately tell Lucy she didn't need to come in this afternoon, giving the poor woman a break.

"Like what?" Emilie asked.

"Well, that's what we have to figure out. Something festive, of course."

"Mint? Gingerbread? Eggnog?" Emilie suggested the obvious flavours.

"Something layered..." Faye pondered.

"Why don't we try all three? We could have a little competition," Sylvie suggested. "Each of us take one flavour and make something, then, I don't know, have a little event? Something for your charity, Emilie."

"That's brilliant, Sylvie," Emilie said. "We can work it into the carol night. Can I have mint?"

Faye shrugged. "Sure."

"I'll take eggnog," Sylvie said.

"I guess that leaves me with gingerbread," Faye said. "I'm only the manager."

Emilie grinned. "Sorry, Faye."

"That's okay. You know I love gingerbread." She closed the magazine, running her hand over its glossy cover. *The only limit is your imagination.* She tried to imagine herself on a beach, the Christmas holidays — and Will's mother's visit — a distant memory. "Can I leave it to you to organize the details, Em?"

"For sure," Emilie said.

Perfect. Then all Faye had to do was come up with her recipe for the challenge. Gingerbread... brownies? That might be worth consideration.

The tinkle of the bell on the shop door drew her away, and she left Emilie and Sylvie exchanging possible creations. A woman Faye guessed to be in her thirties stood on the other side of the counter, eyes dropped to the display case full of baked goods. Faye smiled when the woman looked up, though the too-friendly expression and the flyers she held put Faye instantly on guard.

"Hello," the woman said. "Are you Faye?"

"I am," Faye replied, trying to keep caution out of her tone. "How may I help you?"

"I'm Mallory Steinman." The woman removed one hand from the papers she clutched and offered it to Faye. Her grip was sure and warm. "I'm head of the 'Girlfriends and Grace' group at Trinity Church here in town. We're having a little

Mistletoe Ball and were hoping you might consider a donation for our silent auction."

Of course. Everyone was always asking for something for nothing. And a church group? Hardly her thing. But before she could find a way out of the awkward request, Mallory continued.

"I know it's late notice, but we'd also like to order some dessert trays. And we'd be happy to provide you with some tickets to the event, if you might want to come."

I take that back. Faye couldn't keep the surprise from her face. Someone was actually offering to spend money. And while she wasn't sure a church dance was something she'd be caught dead at, the gesture touched her.

"I think we can accommodate you. What would you like for the trays?" Faye handed Mallory the list of items they regularly made at Triple Shot. "And I'd be happy to donate something. Which would work better: a gift certificate, or a box?"

Mallory was efficient, deciding quickly and even paying for everything on the spot. She handed Faye a business-size envelope.

"These are your tickets, if you decide to come. Bring your husband! It really is a fun event, although we don't serve alcohol." Mallory gave Faye an impish grin. "And here are a couple of flyers, if you'd consider putting them up. I'll be in touch about picking up the trays and your donation." She extended her hand again, saying as they shook, "Thank you so much. It was a pleasure to meet you."

"You as well," Faye said, then she watched Mallory depart, feeling like she'd just interacted with a friendly cyclone.

I take back everything I've ever thought about church ladies. This one was gold.

Faye caught herself humming as she rejoined Emilie and Sylvie in the kitchen. *How about that?* The little exchange with

Mallory Steinman had removed a bit of her grinchyness —
when she'd begun to understand how Lucy had ended up so
grouchy. Lucy was far more cheerful now that she only occa-
sionally came to lend a hand instead of having the entire
weight of running this place on her shoulders. As grateful as
Faye was for Emilie and Sylvie pitching in right now, it was
only a temporary solution. She really needed regular help or
she might permanently turn into a grinch. So far, the online
ads hadn't provided any solid prospects. Maybe this Mallory
woman needed a job?

*That might seem too forward, Faye. You only just met the
woman.* Her desperation was showing.

Will had texted her he'd successfully delivered Dean to the
airport, and with Nate away in Florida with Liv for a few days,
they obviously weren't getting together for their usual Tuesday
afternoon jam session. Will promised they'd make up for it
when Nate returned later in the week — clearly he'd read
Faye's mind because they were running out of practicing time
for carol night. Also, he said he was making her dinner.

It seemed like he was in a good mood. And now she was,
too, right? By the time she hung up her apron, she was looking
forward to the evening. After four days apart, she missed him.
She made herself one more cappuccino before leaving to keep
her energy up for whatever Will had planned tonight. She
owed it to him — and herself — to make the best of the next
week.

He was in the kitchen, cooking, when Faye got home. Gus
made it to her first, doing his welcome dance, then Will wiped
his hands on a dishtowel and came over, sweeping her into his
arms for a kiss. Before she knew it, he was helping her off with
her coat, ushering her into a chair, and placing a glass of wine
in front of her.

Well, hello. This might be all right. It could be worth

handling the work at the café herself if she came home to *this* every night.

"How was your evening with the girls?" Will asked, returning to the stove to stir something delicious-smelling.

Faye had purposely kept from telling him about it because she wanted to share the outcome in person. "Great." Maybe that wasn't the right word, but she and Emilie and Liv had accomplished what was needed. "We've got it all figured out."

"What?"

"Christmas."

He laughed. "Are you doing an online course? Because I think that would sell."

She gave him a wry smile and took a sip of wine before continuing. "This is how it's going to go. Liv says your mom can stay at their house. Connie and Reid are going to be there too, and her parents. It'll be perfect."

Will stopped and turned toward her, his lips pressed into a line so that Faye could see the tension in his neck. "What do you mean? She should stay here, with us. How's it going to look if you farm her out to your neighbours?"

"They're our friends, not just neighbours," she said, trying to keep her cool when her heart rate had jumped up, ready to fight for battle. "And this place — it's old and tired, Will. Don't you think she'd be more comfortable over there? Their house is more modern. I won't have to worry about something going wrong here."

"Like what? You and Dean keep this place in great shape. If I were worried about her comfort, I'd put her up in a Toronto hotel. She's not that high-maintenance. Don't stress out over this. It'll be fine."

Faye gritted her teeth. *Don't you, 'It'll be fine,' me.* She forced herself to take a deep breath, speaking with what she hoped was a note of humour. "Easy for you to say. She's your mother.

She already loves you. Her only son. Her only *child*. I'm the woman who will never be good enough for you."

Will snorted. "You've been watching too many chick flicks."

"Why did I expect you to get this? As if I don't have enough going on, now I'm supposed to welcome the woman who gave birth to you into my house?"

"Well, yeah, I thought you would!"

"You invited her without my permission!" she snarled, surging to her feet. *You had no right. This is not your home.* Faye gulped, snapping her mouth shut before the words escaped. That would be cruel. Because, didn't she want it to be?

"I'm sorry, I should have talked to you first." His face softened, his tone genuinely apologetic. "But she made it hard to say no. That's how she is. Trust me, I didn't invite her."

Faye spied the bottle of wine on the counter behind him. She needed a refill. *STAT*. He reached for her as she tried to get past him but she wrenched free. When he tried again, she relented, letting him pull her into his chest.

Great. She'd start steeling herself right now for the inevitable *when are you two getting married? I need grandkids* assault that was sure to come with the visit.

"I'll make it up to you, Faye. I promise." His words rumbled against her ear.

Sure. Whatever you say.

"I will," he insisted, like he'd felt her skepticism. "I'll help."

You? Help? She almost let the wrong response slip again. "But you have a job. And the catering gigs."

"I'll make it work. You come first. You always come first."

Faye swallowed hard, squeezing back the tears stinging her eyes before she looked up at him. "Don't you make me cry, Will Callaghan. I don't cry."

He chuckled. "I've seen you cry."

She pushed back, but he didn't let her go. "When?"

"At Nate and Liv's wedding."

"That doesn't count," she scoffed.

But the mere mention of it instantly dried her eyes, because as much as she loved Will, she couldn't picture herself as a bride.

CHAPTER
FOURTEEN

Emilie had all the horses out by the time Will got to the barn Thursday morning, which was good, because he drew the line at leading them. Or at least these. The horses he remembered from his grandfather's farm moved a lot more slowly than the ones on this place.

Will loved how Dean traded favours with Emilie, Liv and Nate. They were always there for each other, the answer always yes when one or the other needed a hand. And though Will had been known to gripe once or twice, it was nice to be part of something like that. When he'd first come to Toronto, it had taken him a while to make friends. Most of them were people he worked with, like Monique, but he'd missed the family feeling he'd had with the Millers back home. Now, since he'd hooked up with Faye, it was like he was rediscovering it, enfolded into the circle Nate had become part of after his own move. Will didn't want to lose it, now that he'd found it.

"Everything good, Em?" he asked.

"Everything's fabulous," she said, always upbeat. She

105

looped a rope lead over a hook outside of a stall. "Did you see the game last night?"

"I missed it, but I heard. Kid got a goal, eh?"

"Yes! *So* happy for him. Things are really coming together."

It was cute how invested Emilie was in Tim's hockey career. Things had really come together for Nate this year, too. Will was happy for all of them, but it was high time things came together for him, wasn't it? *Working on it.*

"I'll go get the tractor," he said

"Thanks Will." Emilie smiled her infectious smile and started dumping water buckets.

The old Massey was sheltered in a shed, out of the elements, the manure spreader still attached. Will unplugged it and started it up, giving it a few minutes to warm up. He was impressed he remembered how to work the gears, the old tractor chugging steadily out of the lean-to — and pretty proud of himself that he could back the spreader into the barn aisle.

"I really need to practice with that," Emilie said, snapping an empty bucket back in its assigned stall.

"Meh," Will said, climbing down from the worn seat. "When is there not someone else around to do it?"

"That's totally not the point, Will."

He grinned, grabbing a pitchfork. "Whatever floats your boat, Em."

He wouldn't want to do this all the time — he was too used to staying up late instead of getting up early — but Will didn't mind helping here and there, even if he still didn't understand the horse thing. He chuckled, remembering how he'd assumed Faye was a horse girl when they'd met. But while he'd learned soon enough she wasn't, these animals were still a big part of her world.

Will wasn't as fast as Emilie — or as particular — but the

stalls got done. Time flew because they talked, their conversation relaxed, but also because Emilie was a taskmaster, pushing to finish with no breaks. When he finally talked her into one, he invited her to the house for coffee. There wasn't much left to do — just refilling water pails, doling out dinner grain and tossing in flakes of hay.

"I have pastry," he said, and that sealed the deal. Emilie would never turn down pastry.

She loved up Gus while he set up the French press, because coffee maker coffee would just not do for fine pastry. Faye and Dean didn't have an espresso machine. If he moved in, he would buy one. That could be his hook — *hey, what d'you say?*

"Got your Christmas shopping done yet?" Emilie asked after he set a cup in front of her, next to the brioche he'd made yesterday.

"Not all of it," he admitted, though he didn't really have much to do. He and Nate had agreed long ago they weren't doing presents for each other and he always bought his mom the same thing, which he would undoubtedly leave till the last minute like he always did. "Faye's is going to be a surprise, so I'm not telling you."

Emilie sat up, her eyes widening. "It better be shiny."

Will rolled his eyes. It wasn't even worth commenting on. Emilie never really let up. Once the trailer had a fresh coat of paint, maybe he could throw some rhinestones on it somewhere. *How's that for shiny, Emilie?*

"We looked at rings when we went shopping last week," she said, pulling out her phone and flipping through photos. She set it flat on the table and turned it toward him. "That's the one she liked. Isn't it nice?"

He didn't want to even humour her, but he looked at the image just the same. Even with the ring behind glass, Will could see that Emilie was downplaying its beauty by using the word "nice." It wasn't lavish, though. Not too expensive, maybe. Still, he'd have to take on more catering jobs to pay for it.

The trailer had cost him the price of gas to get it to the workshop. The real expense was in what he was paying the guys for fixing it up, and everything he'd need to finish the inside. In the end, it might end up being more than the ring in the photo. But the trailer would pay for itself next year, and Faye was a practical person. She'd made a point of letting him know she didn't wear her rings anymore, having to rush back more than once to put them on whenever they'd gone out, so why would he buy her another?

But — Faye had actually picked one? That was a diamond. There was no denying what it was for. So was she actually hoping he'd propose? He thought he knew her, but right now he was having a hell of a time reading her.

"Are you thinking about it?" Emilie asked. Her voice had lost its teasing tone and when he met her eyes, they were serious.

"Maybe," he said, taking a bite of his own pastry, eyeing her. Emilie wouldn't set him up to make a fool of himself.

"What are you waiting for? Just so you know, if you decide to make a plan, I'm here to help facilitate. I've got time on my hands with Tim on the road right now."

Will doubted that — Emilie always had a packed schedule — but he was sure she'd make time for that. "Thanks Em."

"Christmas is a great time to get engaged." And with that came the cheeky twist of her lips.

Christmas was a terrible time to get engaged.

"So why were you looking at engagement rings? Are you expecting something for the holidays?" He adopted the teasing tone and gave her a cheeky grin right back.

"Me? No — I mean, I don't think so. I wouldn't say no, but — it's too soon."

Will grinned at her flustered response. It was fun to turn the tables on Em. Give her a bit of what she dished out.

"Time to get back to work?" he suggested.

She nodded, hastily gathering her plate and cup, and he followed her to the sink. "This is perfect. We'll be done in time for me to go for a hack with Curtis and get back here to bring in for you, then still be at work by five."

"I thought your horses were all on holiday right now," Will said.

Emilie said, "Hacks aren't work, Will. They're mental health."

He took Gus with them as they finished up, and the Golden snuffled around in the barn, cleaning up every minute grain he could find that a horse or broom may have missed. Faye would be mad if the dog got the runs, but hey, sometimes you had to live in the moment.

"What are you doing for the rest of the day?" Emilie asked as they put the feed cart away.

"That's part of the secret."

"Fine," she huffed, but grinned. "Don't let me down, Will."

Emilie ducked into her car and started it up, Will keeping Gus by his side, out of the way. She typed something into her phone then tossed it on the seat, gave him a little wave, and drove off.

His phone pinged. Will laughed when he looked at the text. It was from Emilie — the photo she'd shown him earlier of the ring and the name of the store and the mall it was in.

Maybe he'd check it out. Looking couldn't hurt, right?

CHAPTER
FIFTEEN

Faye took advantage of Sylvie and Lucy's presence at the café to steal away for half an hour, picking up a HELP WANTED sign at the hardware store. Emilie was just pulling in when she returned and watched as she set it in the front window.

"Going old school, are you?" Emilie asked once she was inside. She followed Faye, throwing her coat over the back of a chair — a sign that she would not be here long.

"Why not?" Faye responded. "With the number of people who come in and out of here each day, someone might know someone who needs a job. A personal reference is so much better than random people contacting you over the internet."

"True," Emilie said. She began frothing milk for the cappuccino she was making for herself. "Do you have a tree for your house yet?"

Faye shook her head, frowning. Putting up a tree was one thing Faye and Dean had always done together. One thing they'd promised they'd keep up after their parents and Shawn had died. This year, though, they hadn't been able to coordinate before Dean left on his trip. It would have to wait till he was home, even if that was leaving it late.

"I've been too busy, and Dean didn't have time before he left. You know what it's like at the end of the season. He had to find spots for some of the horses for the winter. I told him he should just send them to you, but he's got that one stingy owner. Dean just tried to intervene enough to make sure they're properly taken care of."

"I hate owners like that," Emilie said, nodding.

The bell on the door jangled, letting in a whoosh of cold air. Will stamped his feet on the mat, loosing clumps of snow, Nate on his heels, rubbing gloved hands together.

Faye's lips twisted into a smile. *"There's* who needs to get our tree."

"What was that?" Will asked as he came over and gave her a kiss on the cheek.

"We need a tree for the house. I think that can be your job."

He made a face. "Why me?"

"You said you'd help," she hissed.

"We need one, too," Nate interjected. He tapped Will on the arm. "We'll go out together. Sunday afternoon sound good?"

"That's perfect!" Emilie chimed in. "Tim will be home, so he can come along."

"How about you and Em and Tim get both trees then?" Will suggested.

"Really, Will?" Faye pressed her lips together. Was it seriously too much to ask?

"Fine," he said. He turned to Nate. "Cappuccino, buddy?"

"Thanks," Nate responded.

As Will's head was ducked at the espresso machine, Nate looked at Faye and shrugged. She mouthed *thank you*. Once Will had made the cappuccinos, the two guys sat at a table in the corner. Faye wordlessly took them a couple of plates with some of the fresh baked goods and left them alone to whatever they were plotting. Finalizing details for their part in the carol night, she hoped.

"See you, Faye!"

"Have a good rest of your day, Em," she called as her friend departed with a wave.

Every time someone came in, Faye watched them glance at the sign, but no one said anything. Well — what did she expect? She'd only just put it up. Next time the little bell on the door rang she smiled, seeing Liv unwind her scarf.

"What are those two doing here?" Liv glanced over at the two men in the corner. They both sent waves her way, then put their heads back together.

"Loitering," Faye said and pressing grounds into the filter to make Liv a cappuccino. "How are you holding up, with all your free time?"

Liv laughed. "What am I going to do with myself till we go to Florida?"

"You have a farm. There's always something to do on a farm."

"I'd drive Kerrie and the staff crazy there," she said.

"Probably true. Maybe now's the time you'll find that hobby."

"Give up on the hobby thing." Then she placed a hand on Faye's arm. "I can help you bake."

Faye snorted. They'd established Liv could make a cappuccino, but, "You? Bake?"

"Baking is just chemistry, Faye. I can follow a method. I mean — a recipe."

Faye hesitated. "Well... okay. We can try it."

"I may surprise you."

"You probably will. You're good at just about anything you put your mind to."

"Just about. Let's not get into the things I suck at though, okay?"

"And let's hope it's not this. I don't have time for screw-ups." Faye grinned and led the way to the kitchen.

They worked as a team when customers came in — Faye took the orders, and Liv silently made drinks and set out baked goods on plates. Liv didn't volunteer to be the one talking to people, Faye noticed. Was she surprised? No. And that was fine. Liv was better at peopling than she used to be — training racehorses required it — and this was supposed to be her vacation, a rare thing, so Faye would not expect her to take on such tasks here when they could be avoided easily enough. And when she set Liv to work on a simple cookie recipe to start, it went all right.

"How's this?" Liv asked, stepping back from the stand mixer.

Faye peered at the dough and scooped out a small amount with a spoon to check the consistency. "That's good. Just add a little more flour."

"But the recipe says —"

"I know, but sometimes you have to adjust for different..." Faye paused, thinking how to word her explanation for her science-brained friend. "Variables," she decided.

Liv looked skeptical for a beat. She liked following rules, to the letter. "Okay. How much is a 'little more?'"

Faye suppressed a smile and stepped in, portioning an indeterminate amount into a measuring cup and dumping it into the bowl when she was sure Liv would have preferred her to pull out a scale. "Try that."

When it did the trick, Liv shrugged and began distributing dollops onto cookie sheets, placing them equidistant from each other. Faye couldn't fault precision. It was important for baking, even if there were times modifications were necessary.

"Good job." Faye nodded as Liv pulled the result from the oven ten minutes later. "You're hired."

Liv grinned. "Told you."

Faye glanced at the clock. It was time to close. The guys didn't count — she left them to carry on in the corner as she turned off the neon OPEN sign in the front window and locked the doors. Liv wiped off tables and put away utensils while Faye scratched down the recipes she needed to replenish.

Cranberry white chocolate bars that were a copycat of the big coffee chain's, but were way better because they'd never been frozen. Dark, molasses-rich, gingerbread loaf with cream cheese icing that disappeared every time she turned around. Butter tarts, brownies, cookies. In another list, she noted ingredients to be ordered.

Then she pulled out her laptop to check the job site. There were some new applications. None that excited her, but she noticed a couple she might interview. Sometimes people were better in person than on paper. What she really wanted was for someone to walk through that door who was perfect, to save her time and energy when she had none to spare.

It wasn't too early to plan for next year — *the only limit is your imagination* — but she had to get through the Christmas rush before her brain could manage that. She'd never been the perfect planner, but still, this time of year, Faye couldn't help looking forward. She was starting to understand Liv. Never sitting still. Never being completely satisfied with her career. Always wanting to be more. More herself, which made her more to others.

So what did that mean for Faye? Achievement for Liv was more easily marked. More winners. More money earned. Faye didn't want more cafés, but she needed to grow. Personally? Professionally? What was the answer? And what part was Will going to play?

She didn't want to have to be here all the time. She wanted to be able to afford a vacation every year. And have time for another dog. And maybe a kid. Maybe she didn't want to be married, but she definitely didn't want to be married to her job. Right now, she was.

Faye returned to the job applications, selected two of the most promising, and dashed off an email to each of them asking if they'd be interested in coming for an interview. With a snap she closed the laptop and slipped it into her bag. Double-checking everything was off, she flipped the light switches in the kitchen and pushed out into the front of the shop, keys clutched in a fist. Her eyes landed on Will and Nate. Liv, having run out of things to do stood, hands on hips, watching them too.

"Get out of here," Faye said to all of them, but her tone was tender.

Both men rose, looking creaky after being there so long. Liv had long since removed their dishes and wiped the table.

"Are you coming with me?" Liv asked Nate. "Or do you two have more bonding to do?"

"Before anyone goes anywhere," Faye said as Liv wound her scarf back around her neck and slipped on her jacket. "We need to finalize a date. Now. For a Christmas dinner planning session. It shouldn't take long, but the clock is ticking."

Phones were pulled from pockets, calendar apps opened, and they settled on Saturday night at Liv and Nate's — the bonus being there was a game on. Tim was playing, so it was safe to assume Emilie would be available, as Tim's team was still on the road and Em wouldn't be working at the physiotherapy clinic.

"Satisfied?" Will said.

"Perfectly," Faye replied, grabbing her own coat then

asking him, "Are you staying over tonight?" She didn't want to assume. He had so many catering gigs right now.

"If that's okay," he said.

It was probably her fault he looked sheepish, so she looped her arm through his and smiled up at him. "Of course it is."

CHAPTER
SIXTEEN

Gus hopped into the back seat of the Corolla as soon as Will opened the passenger-side door. He closed it once Faye was settled with a container of baked goods on her lap. He'd already loaded the lasagna he'd made —in the trunk, far from Gus's nose.

Compromise, that's what tonight was. How best to get the group of them together to talk about Christmas? Do it on game night. Thank goodness the only catering job he had this weekend had been a brunch today, so he'd been finished in plenty of time to get back to King City. Good thing, because it didn't seem to take much to ruffle Faye's feathers right now.

The freaking tree cutting tomorrow. He could have lied, said he had another catering gig, but with his luck, Faye would find out and then he'd really be dead. He'd been counting on that time to work on the inside of the trailer. She likely wouldn't buy it if he said he was shopping again, though he had braved the masses to hit one store on his way up this afternoon.

Emilie and her Black Lab, Holly, greeted them at the door.

Gus merrily took off to play with his canine friend while Em took the lasagna to put in the oven as Will and Faye removed their boots and coats. Will patted the pocket of his vest — it was still there.

"Want me to carry anything, Em?" Will called, closing the door of the front foyer behind Faye.

"Yeah, thanks. Do you want to grab these two bowls? And you can leave those squares up here for now, Faye."

In the kitchen, Emilie filled their hands then led the way downstairs to the television room, the dogs bringing up the rear.

Nate was parked on one end of the couch with a guitar in his lap. Will exchanged a look with him. They needed to get in at least one more practice session before carol night. He set the bowls of snacks on the coffee table and plunked himself on the sofa next to Nate. Faye wedged herself between him and the arm, resting her notebook on it, and Liv took drink orders. The game hadn't started yet — the sportscasters were just going on with their usual drivel about what was happening around the league and their predictions for tonight.

"All right," Faye began. "Let's do this."

Emilie held up her arm. "First things first. Tomorrow. You — and you." She pointed to Will and Nate. "We're going tree hunting. Got it?"

Will sat up straighter and Nate set aside the guitar. When Emilie got in organizer mode, no one dared resist her demands, but Will complained anyway. "It's supposed to snow and be minus ten." The garage where the trailer was would be out of the elements, at least.

"Perfect tree-cutting weather!" Emilie said. "So festive. Wear layers."

"Thank you, Emilie," Faye said. "Maybe with you in charge, it will actually happen."

Will ducked the daggers she sent his way. He felt Nate elbow him, his friend's shoulders shaking as he silently chuckled, and Will had to dig his nails into his knees to keep from laughing. He shot Nate a look. *Don't get me in trouble!*

"So," Faye continued. "What do you say to a giant potluck idea for Christmas dinner? Many hands making light work, and all that."

Will peered across at her list. She had the page blocked off into sections. Appetizers, salads, veggies, main course — under which the only thing was TURKEY, written in bold — and dessert. Dessert would not be a problem — between Will and Faye, there were always sweets. At the bottom she'd scribbled Beverages — *wine, coffee, tea.*

It was kind of fun, really. The dinner would be a fusion of traditions, creating a new one. He pictured them all in another twenty years, still sharing the holiday together. The future. Faye. It was time to nail it down. He just had to concoct a plan, and pray it panned out. He had Dean on side. And Nate. Emilie, for sure. He doubted Liv would protest. The only one he was worried about was Faye.

And himself. *You can do it, Will.*

"Will?"

He snapped his head to Faye like a kid who'd been caught not paying attention in school. "Sorry?"

"We'll do the turkey," Nate piped up, nudging Will with his elbow again. "Team effort."

"Yes. Sure," Will affirmed. "The dressing, too."

"Make sure you do some that's not cooked *in* the turkey," Emilie reminded.

"For Tim." Nate nodded. "I won't forget."

"So what's Tim going to have? One of those fake things you can buy?" Faye asked, looking at Emilie.

Emilie shook her head. "He's not really into meat

analogues. I'll think of something. He'll just appreciate the effort."

Will didn't know when Tim had become a vegetarian, but they'd make sure he had plenty to eat. No one was going to starve. It was the holidays. There would be food, lots of it. Faye rapidly filled the page of her notebook with everyone's suggestions for the other areas. Food smoothed over all stress associated with the festive season.

"Silence!" Emilie commanded, cutting through the chatter. "Puck drop!"

Tim was getting lots of ice time these days. The kid was fast — flying around, making things happen. Will was proud of him, though he had nothing to do with Tim's success. He was just another guy who'd played street hockey with the kid back in Calgary. Will had never had any illusions he'd play in the NHL himself — not like Nate had, until it became obvious he'd never have the necessary height and weight — but Will still thought it was cool to say he'd grown up with a guy who'd made it.

When the first intermission began, the game in a one-one tie, Liv and Faye collected dishes, turning away offers of help, and disappeared upstairs. Will knew what that was: Faye wanted to talk to Liv, no men invited. Both dogs followed, because there might be food in it for them. Emilie stayed, because it was understood she couldn't leave the television on the off chance there would be something said about Tim.

Will's hand curled around the box in his pocket. This was his chance to get the ball rolling. "I gotta show you guys something."

Nate eyed him, and Emilie's head tilted. "Am I one of the guys in this instance?"

"Yes," Will confirmed. He pulled his hand out, and opened his fingers, leaving the box resting, unopened, in his palm.

Emilie squealed. "You did it!" She snapped the box from him to peek inside, grinning. "*So* shiny. So perfect."

Will flexed his fingers, itching to have it back in his possession, to hide it away again. "Don't get excited. I'm just trying the idea on. I can take it back."

"You will *not!*" Emilie insisted.

Will glanced at Nate. "You're being awfully quiet."

"You already know what I think."

"She doesn't even want to meet my mother." Will snatched the ring box back from Emilie and tucked it into his pocket. What was Faye afraid of? Had he made his mom out to be a monster? "How can you be so sure she'll want to marry me?"

"I'm here to watch the game and help eat the food, not give relationship advice," Nate said, reaching for the bowl of chips. "But did you ever stop to think —"

"And here we go." Will smirked. "You *not* giving me relationship advice."

Nate ignored him. "Did you ever stop to think this is actually about Faye feeling insecure?"

Will scoffed at the thought. "Faye doesn't feel insecure. She's the most confident person I know."

Nate continued. "If you hadn't dragged your ass on the whole proposing thing and Faye already had that ring on her finger — if she was your fiancée instead of just your girl-friend — she'd feel she had more cred when she meets your mom."

"Why do you have to be so hard on me?" Will groaned.

"Nate's got a point, though. When's your mom coming?" Emilie asked.

"In ten days," Will said.

"It's not too late," Emilie insisted. "You can still make it happen."

Will's hands were instantly sweaty, and his pulse raced. "If

I do this, it has to be just right. There can't be any reason for her to say anything but yes. I need help."

Emilie dropped onto the sofa arm next to Nate and draped herself over him. "Just don't take advice from this guy. He proposed in a barn. No ring. It was pathetic."

"I had to talk Liv into wearing a ring at all," Nate defended. "But the wedding was amazing, right?" Nate grinned.

"I'm pretty sure Liv gets most of the credit for that, but yeah," Emilie agreed. "Except for the part where your brother blew me off."

"Not the best first impression, I agree. It all worked out in the end, though. *Sis.*" Nate patted her on the head.

"It did." A dreamy look came over her face.

If Will didn't do this and Emilie and Tim got engaged first, he'd never hear the end of it. Which he might not care about, except the current pressure level would probably feel like nothing compared to what would come after that.

Will dragged his fingers through his hair, leaning back. "I wish we could just go away for Christmas. You and Liv did it right. You just ignored everyone and did your thing."

"You're missing something very important," Nate said. "Faye's a romantic. Liv is not."

"Don't worry, Will," Emilie said. "I have ideas."

Will was counting on it.

CHAPTER
SEVENTEEN

The music pounding through Faye's earbuds was not seasonal. Not even close. She bobbed her head in time to the beat as she started the mixer, then glanced over her shoulder. Liv's lips were moving — what was she saying? Faye didn't read lips, so she pulled out one earbud and let it fall to the front of her apron. No air pods in the kitchen; she didn't need one falling into some dough.

"Pardon?" she asked, then glanced back at the mixer to check the progress of the butter and sugar she was creaming.

"I think someone just came in. Don't make me go out there."

"Oh — thanks." She didn't miss the speculative look Liv gave her at her state of distraction. Too many things packed into her head right now, and not enough of them were about work.

Sunday mornings at the shop were always quiet, so it was a good time to get things done, before the church crowd converged on them for a light lunch or treat. Faye was happy to have Liv helping, since Emilie was on Operation Christmas

Tree with the boys today. Sylvie was coming later to lend a hand and work on her challenge creation.

Faye glided through the two-way swinging door and put on a smile for the senior couple waiting in front of the display cabinet. "Hi! Sorry for the wait. What can I get for you?" The Christmas music she'd been trying to block out played softly in the background.

The couple ordered cappuccinos and butter tarts, so Faye set the tarts on plates for them before accepting the cash the man presented. He thanked her when Faye handed him his change, and dropped it into the tip cup. At the end of every month she wrote a cheque for the total tips collected and gave it to Emilie for the New Chapter Thoroughbred Retirement charity. It wasn't much, but every little bit helped. If she ever found a real employee, she'd give it to them.

"I'll bring your cappuccinos over to you in a moment," she said.

"Merry Christmas!" they chimed in unison.

"Merry Christmas," she returned dutifully. She always let the customer decide what greeting was appropriate this time of year — because the customer was always right — right?

The high-pitched squeal of the steam foaming the milk drowned out the holiday tunes again. Faye watched the couple as she made their drinks, the two of them chatting amicably, and wondered about them. Assumed they were married, noting rings on appropriate fingers. Guessed them to be seventy-plus years. Did they have kids? Grandkids? Couples like Nate and Liv seemed to be an anomaly these days — married, and not intending to have kids — when most people their age seemed to only get married when they decided they wanted children.

Faye did, though she wasn't someone who thought she needed to be married to have them. Who knew, maybe she'd change her mind. On either the marriage thing, or the kids. It wasn't in the five-year plan, that was for sure. What was?

This. Here. If she was already overwhelmed, would she still want to be doing it five years from now? Except — what else would she do?

She realized she was still watching the couple, their drinks, a perfect combination of espresso and foamed milk, remaining before her. With a small lift of her lips, she carried the cups and saucers to the table and set them down.

"Enjoy!"

Faye hated that expression — as if it was a command to like what she was serving, the mere uttering of the word making it so — but it came out, anyway.

When Faye turned back toward the counter, Liv was leaning against the wall with arms crossed.

"Maybe time for one of those ourselves?"

"A brilliant plan," Faye agreed, and began cleaning up the machine to get it started again. If they didn't take a rest now, they might not get one. The church crowd would begin their takeover any minute.

They took their cups to a nearby table, far enough away from the couple not to feel cloying. Liv had decorated the sugar cookies she'd made first thing and Faye paused to admire one before taking a bite.

"You're good at that."

Liv's lips twisted into a wry smile. "Don't sound so surprised. I am a perfectionist, after all. Maybe this can be the hobby you keep saying I need."

Faye snorted. "Possibly not the best hobby to have when your husband has a sweet tooth and his job requires him to weigh less than he probably should."

Liv laughed. "That's the real reason we go to Florida. To get away from this place and its temptations for the winter."

"Do you think Nate's going to be one of those jocks who packs on fifty pounds after he retires?"

It was Liv's turn to snort. She shook her head. "I can't see him letting that happen. He'll probably start training for marathons or triathlons, just so he can eat more."

There was a lull in their conversation as they savoured the cookies and the break. The couple rose from their chairs, carrying their empty plates and cups to the counter.

"Oh, thank you," Faye said. "You didn't have to do that."

"You're welcome," they chimed in unison again. At least they didn't have matching outfits. That would have been too much. "Have a wonderful day."

"You too," she called after them. "Take care." She broke the last cookie in half, not sure why she'd set out an odd number. "These really are great. You're not as useless at domestic stuff as I thought." She covered her mouth as she chewed.

Liv's eyes narrowed. "What's with Mean Faye?"

"You have to ask?" Faye sighed. *She's lurking around every corner these days.* "I think I need to get it out of my system before Will's mom gets here so I don't mess up around her. Sorry, I don't mean for you to take the brunt of my irritation. Let's get back to work."

"It won't be that long till it's behind us," Liv said as they carried their own plates into the back, taking them directly to the dishwasher.

"Look at you, being all positive. Sometimes I miss dark and twisty Liv." Faye grinned.

"That is what drew us together." Liv grinned back. "I suppose it's good we've moved on from that."

They'd both had justification for being troubled when they'd met at fifteen, Faye just months after her parents' fatal accident and Liv's family fleeing her abusive grandfather in Montreal.

"It's been quite the journey, hasn't it?" Faye said with a twinge of nostalgia.

"I feel there should be wine for the way this conversation is going," Liv responded.

"You're right. After this is all over." Faye waved her hands around at the holiday work in progress. "And before you run off to Florida for the rest of the winter."

"We'll be back. Both Chique and Claire are due at the end of January."

"Good news for me, then." Though Faye guessed she might not see much of them while they were waiting for Triple Stripe's two most precious mares to have their foals.

"I wonder how they're making out with the trees?" Liv pondered.

Faye looked at the time. "I would bet they haven't gone out yet. I can't imagine Emilie not documenting the excursion in her social media stories with photos and commentary."

"True." Liv tied on an apron and washed her hands. "Are you feeling better about Dr Mom's visit now that we've got things somewhat organized?"

Faye sighed. "Some. But I can't shake the feeling that something is up with Will."

She thought she saw Liv blink before her friend turned to the fridge to grab her water bottle.

"'Tis the season," Liv said. "I get the feeling Nate's up to something too. And maybe they both are, but it's nothing to worry about."

Faye quirked an eyebrow, about to ask Liv if she knew something she wasn't sharing when the jangling bell on the door called her again, followed by the stomping of multiple feet. She glanced over her shoulder at Liv. "Here they come. You ready?"

The post-church rush was on.

A familiar face stood out amid the group of ladies who had just entered, huddled just inside.

"Hi, Mallory. Nice to see you again."

Mallory beamed, unzipping her coat. "I thought I should warn you. I told everyone about your generous donation, so be prepared for plenty of customers this afternoon."

Faye smiled. "Thank you. This is my best friend Liv. She's giving me a hand this afternoon."

Mallory exchanged smiles with Liv and introduced her own posse before the group started unleashing their order.

"Is that your new friend?" Liv whispered as they both scrambled, Liv turning out the espresso drinks and Faye gathering the food and treats, plate by plate.

Faye grinned. "She's nice and she brings me business. I might welcome a friend like that when you're flaunting the Florida sun in your Instagram posts."

Right now, she wasn't sure she wanted more business. Unless one of those ladies needed to make some extra Christmas money?

EIGHTEEN

"Hey, I didn't know you had a cat." Tim smiled as he leaned over, offering his fingers to Clementine, who sniffed them delicately.

"I don't."

Tim looked from Will to Nate. Nate just laughed.

"It's my neighbour's cat," Will finally explained. "I just look after her when Lara's away."

"She's pretty." Tim scooped the cat up and Clementine purred so loudly she threatened to drown out the music from the stereo. "What's her name?"

"Lemon," Will said at the exact moment Nate said, "Mandarin."

Tim gave them both another one of those looks as Nate and Will cracked up.

"Clementine," Will said once he recovered. "Maybe you can be the only one who calls her by her proper name."

When Will had said he had to pop down to his flat because Lara wanted to leave Clementine with him again, Nate had offered to come along — probably because he didn't trust Will to come back for the Christmas tree expedition. Because Tim had stayed at the farm last night, but Emilie was busy riding horses this morning, he'd joined them.

Will picked up a guitar, Nate already poking at the keyboard. They had a bit of time, so it made sense to squeeze in some practice. "Are you going to be around for this thing?" he asked Tim.

"When is it?"

"The twenty-second."

"Yeah, I am." Tim settled on the couch, still cuddling the cat.

"You gonna sing with us, Tim?" Nate quipped.

"Huh? I don't know. I guess I could be in the background or something, just to make sure you sound good." He grinned.

Tim was pretty shy, so Will was sure he was joking, but when they started playing, he sang along — harmony, even. They did sound better. If he actually would take part in their carol night, he'd add a welcome dimension to their sound. Maybe Tim had absorbed some of Emilie's Christmas spirit — the ingredient their previous sessions had lacked.

They stopped playing when Tim told them to wrap things up, Emilie texting him she was just getting on her last horse. She'd be done by the time they got there if they headed to the farm now.

"What about Clementine?" Tim asked as he reluctantly left her where he'd been sitting. The cat curled up on the warm cushion, unruffled by the signs of their departure.

"She's got enough food to last her till tomorrow," Will said. "I'll come back down then."

"What's Lara going to do when you move?" Nate asked, tugging on his boots.

Will frowned, a pang in his chest. He kept forgetting that part. "I guess she'd just find someone else to look after

Lemon." Last night, with Emilie egging him on, the whole proposing thing had started to make sense, but in the light of day — in this space he'd called home since he'd come east — Will's doubts came back. He'd miss his part-time cat. "It'll be hard to let this place go. And I'm convinced half the reason Faye never asked me to move into the farmhouse is because she loves it here almost as much as I do."

"She's hardly ever down here anymore," Nate pointed out. "Stop making excuses."

"Sublet it to me," Tim interrupted.

Will whipped his head around. "What's that?"

"Sublet this place to me," Tim repeated. "I should have a place in the city. You shouldn't. Then at least you can keep it in the family."

Tim thinking of him as family softened Will's resistance, just a smidge.

"That's a great idea," Nate said. "Then we could still use it."

"Hey, wait a minute — " Tim started.

"It's the perfect solution, Will," Nate continued. "Tim's away half the time during the season and then the rest of the time, you know he'll be at the farm more than here. It can still be our base camp."

"It's perfect," Will admitted.

"You took that and ran with it," Tim grumbled at Nate.

"All you have to do is ask 'where do I sign,' kid." Will grinned, patting him on the back.

And all *he* had to do was follow through with the ring.

Did it *have* to be the coldest day of the winter so far for the designated tree cutting? Would it kill the sun to come out? *Why do I have to be here again?* Will thought of Dean shushing down the slopes in Banff and wished he were there instead of here. That was what weather like this was good for.

He'd grown up with an artificial tree. Was there really anything wrong with that? No real trees had died for his childhood Christmases. But the truth was, Will had hated that tree. It stood for everything that was wrong with those so-called celebrations. They'd been as fake as the tree.

That's harsh, Will. His parents thought they were doing what was best. He'd grown up with nice things because his parents had good jobs. But money didn't buy happiness.

Holly was a sleek black bullet weaving through the woods, Gus a billowing stream of yellow fluff in her wake until he caught her, grabbing her by the scruff and pinning her in a poof of powder. That lasted for about three seconds before Holly turned the tables, growling away. Emilie laughed at the pair, Tim's hand wrapped around hers.

Will and Faye had never been that attached to each other, not even in the early days. They'd been affectionate, sure, but maybe they'd spent enough time in one or the other of their beds that PDAs hadn't seemed necessary. Either way, it irked him. He wished Emilie and Tim would just use this rare time when their crazy schedules meshed to have sex like a normal couple.

"What happened to global warming?" Will grumbled as they trudged through the knee-deep snow.

"It's —"

He cut Emilie off. "I know, I know. It's not global warming; it's *climate change.* I was trying to be funny."

"Not so funny, Will. It's probably the exhaust fumes from that beast of a car you drive. Those toxins are affecting your brain, not to mention what they're doing to the environment. Isn't it time you upgraded to something with a catalytic converter?" Emilie said.

"That's why you're here," Will responded. "To help me find a tree, because I'm too befuddled."

"You've been hanging around Dean too much, using words like that," Emilie cracked.

"Well, it's Dean's fault I'm doing this. He managed it last year. What gives?"

"Let's just get it done, all right?" Nate said. "We're under some pressure here. These trees have to be perfect, with all the parents coming."

"Like they'll be judging us?" Emilie said. "If we don't have Christmas trees that live up to their standards, we'll be failing as adults?"

"All of it has to be perfect," Nate insisted. "Think of those years they did it for us. Did we really appreciate the effort? The torch has been passed, so we're doing this, and we're doing it well. We're going to wow them."

"All right, Miller," Will said dryly. "What have you been smoking, cedar boughs?"

They kept trudging, passing several conifers Will was sure would have done the trick. The little wooded area on Liv and Nate's farm was thick with evergreens; it could probably stand to lose more than a couple of them. Nate ducked under a snow-laden branch and before Will had a chance to react, it thwacked him in the face. He grumbled to himself as he brushed cold flakes from his coat and skin.

Emilie stopped, spreading her arms wide, staring up through the trees. "It's so beautiful in here. Can we just take a moment to appreciate that?"

Will was about to snap — he just wanted to be done with this. A crack had developed in his right boot and he could feel his sock getting wet from the snow packed into the crevice. But something about Emilie's expression chipped away at his resentment. She was right. If she could set aside the season's challenges and enjoy this, couldn't he?

Tim swept up behind her, wrapping his arms around her. She squawked as he picked her up and swung her around until she twisted free — then launched herself at him. Tim caught her, and it soon turned into kissing.

Will growled, "Why are they even here?"

Nate shrugged. "It's Emilie. It's Christmas. That's just how it is."

"Let's find a damn tree," Will said.

"Two damn trees," Nate corrected, pressing on, leaving Tim and Emilie to catch up. "I just got a small one last year — Em had it picked out already, so all I had to do was cut it. That's not going to be good enough this year."

"No half-assed trees." Will grinned.

"Nope."

Snow began falling like some kind of holiday TV special, drifting down through the boughs. It *was* beautiful. He tried to do as Emilie advised.

"So what's up?" Nate said.

Will glanced over, catching his friend's expression. It shouldn't surprise him Nate had picked up on his mood. Will hadn't really been trying to hide it.

"I'd been counting on using this time to work on the trailer. Clock's ticking, man."

"You're giving her the ring. It's not all that important to get the trailer done now, is it?"

"Of course it is. I'm giving her the trailer for Christmas. The ring isn't a present."

That shut Nate up. Because it wasn't, was it? Nate should know. It was something bigger. Much bigger.

"I can help."

Will looked at Nate sideways. "Huh?"

"I know you're busy. It's not as if you can give up any more catering gigs. You've got a ring to pay for." Nate nudged him. "I've got time. I'll go work on it. I could use something to do while Liv's helping Faye that doesn't include sampling their product."

Nate's offer made Will feel just a little mushy with gratitude. "Thanks. That means a lot."

Before it got awkward, Emilie scooted up next to him and looped her arm through his, Holly bounding at her side. Tim was just behind her, playing tug of war with Gus, a branch between them.

"About those ideas to sweep Faye off her feet. I was up late waiting for Tim last night, and I made you a spreadsheet."

Will's eyebrows crept up. Was she serious? This was Emilie. She probably was.

CHAPTER
NINETEEN

"Maybe you and Will can come down to Florida for a few days this winter," Liv said as she shouldered on her jacket.

On the other side of the café's large front window it was getting dark, something Faye was sure would be easier to take if it were eighty degrees out. They'd accomplished a lot and she was looking forward to putting her feet up. "If I ever find some help, maybe we will."

"For the number of times you've lectured me about being all work, I'm going to have to turn the talk on you," Liv said. "You know you could just close for a few days. Small businesses do things like that. People understand."

Liv was right. The locals could get their coffee somewhere else for a few days in February. "I'll think about it."

"Condo on the beach, Faye. For that matter, if you could pull that off in January while we're up here waiting for Chique and Claire to foal, you and Will could have the place to yourselves."

That sounded heavenly. Faye slipped on her own coat and straightened her desk. A brown manila envelope caught her eye. The tickets from Mallory for the dance.

"Hey, you want these?" Faye lifted the envelope and waved it at Liv, who gave her a questioning look. "Mallory, the woman you met today, gave me a couple of tickets to the dance. The thing I'm donating is for a silent auction they're having at it."

Liv choked back a laugh. "Thank you for the offer, but, come on, Faye. You know better than asking me that."

"I just thought because you're adulting so well these days..." Faye grinned. "And Nate would love it. But okay." She tucked the envelope under her arm and followed Liv to the door, turning out the lights and locking up along the way.

Liv pulled out of the parking lot first, and Faye followed her until Liv turned up the lane to Triple Stripe, the farm gates lit up and adorned with wreaths. She knew she'd find nothing that festive at Northwest. But as she pulled into the driveway, she couldn't miss the bright red and green bulbs outlining the front door they never used. It was like the old Victorian home was dressed up for a party.

No one greeted her as she entered through the back door and dropped the envelope with the dance tickets on the kitchen table. She heard Will in the living room and Gus belatedly ambled over to welcome her. Faye raised an eyebrow at the Golden as she hung up her coat.

"Hey," she called.

Even before Will appeared she could smell the tree and wood smoke from the fire, a smile curling her lips. He met her, kissed her, then Faye glanced down at Gus. "You must've tired him out."

"He and Holly had a blast. So did Emilie and Tim, I think."

"And you?"

"It's done," Will said, his tone not quite flat but close to it. "I fed Gus. He talked me into it."

"He's very persuasive."

"I haven't made anything for us for dinner though, sorry."

"You've been busy. The lights outside look great."

"You sure? I tried to remember how Dean did them last year." He leaned over to the table, picking up the envelope. "What's this?"

"Tickets for that church dance I'm doing the dessert trays for. Don't worry, we don't have to go."

He nodded, tossing it back on the table. "I'm starving. What do you feel like?"

"I can figure something out."

"Nope," he said. "You sit down. I'll throw something together."

First Will brought her a glass of wine — yes, she could definitely get used to this — then he opened the fridge and began pulling things out. Before long, bread was being buttered, a frypan on a burner, and the already wonderful smells in the house were joined by onion and melted cheese. Faye closed her eyes and breathed it all in. A few days at Liv and Nate's beachfront condo would be fabulous, but this would do just fine for now.

"Let's eat in the living room," Will suggested. He found a tray, put the grilled cheese sandwiches on plates, and led the way to the couch.

The tree filled the front window, lights already wound around it. Twigs crackled in the hearth, dancing flames creating flickering shadows in the room.

"It's a beautiful tree," Faye said, taking a moment to admire it.

Will handed her a plate. "Where are the decorations? I found the lights, but that's it."

"In the basement. Didn't you put them away last year?"

"Nope. Must've been Dean."

When she bit into the sandwich, Faye hummed with pleasure. "This might be the best grilled cheese I've ever tasted." It wasn't just any cheese — it was Brie, with caramelized onions and raspberry preserves. "You're outdoing yourself today, Will Callaghan."

He looked at her sideways, a wry tilt to his mouth. Probably overcompensating for his mother coming, but she'd take it. He inhaled his sandwich while Faye, as hungry as she was, savoured every bite.

"Pretty amazing that something as simple as grilled cheese can be so good, isn't it?" he said, setting his plate back on the tray.

"This is no ordinary grilled cheese." And the red wine paired perfectly with it.

Will shrugged, rising and rubbing his hands on his jeans.

"Where are you going?" she asked.

"Why don't I get the decorations?"

"That would be brilliant." She might have to forgive him this whole thing with his mother for not making her go down there. The basement in this old house was little more than a crawlspace, with a dirt floor and an old furnace. It had always terrified her as a kid with its steep, narrow stair and a door that locked at the top. Her parents had kept it locked so none of the kids did anything stupid like trap themselves down there by mistake. Just the thought made her shudder.

"It's locked," she called after him. Because of course she still had that nightmare. "The key's in the everything drawer. It has a big fob on it, you can't miss it."

It was a relief when he reappeared with a hefty cardboard

box — Faye had dreaded the idea of needing to go down there to help him — and Will set it on the floor near the tree. Faye finished the last bite of her grilled cheese, stacked her plate on top of Will's and wandered over with her wine glass.

"Let me get you a refill," Will said, taking it from her and sliding past.

"What are you doing? Get back here!"

He raised an eyebrow. "You want me to help?"

"Of course I want you to help. Why wouldn't I?"

Will retreated to the kitchen, coming back with the wine. "Because decorating the tree was always my mom's domain. I thought because your tree last year was so perfect, you were probably the same."

Faye accepted the glass, sipping. "Are you saying I'm like your mother? Because that would be important to know."

"I don't know what I'm saying."

The reality dawned on her. "Were you not allowed to help?"

"Mom's tree always looked like something straight out of *Canadian Living* magazine. Look, don't touch, you know?"

"That's really sad, Will. Decorating the tree should be a family thing." Last year Will had been too busy with work to help, or else she would have invited him for sure.

He shrugged. "I didn't care. It wasn't even a real tree."

"Well, this is. Thanks to you." She slid closer to him, looping her arms around his neck.

"That is true."

"Tell me it was just a little bit fun?"

He smirked. "Which part? The part where my feet got all wet because I have a hole in my boots, or the part where I had to put up with Tim piggybacking Emilie through the woods?"

Faye snorted. "Did he really?"

"No word of a lie."

"That is so cute."

"Nauseatingly."

"So you wouldn't piggyback me? I'm hurt."

Faye squeaked as he dipped and scooped an arm behind her knees, lifting her up to him, their faces close. Her heart thumped, the heat that enveloped her from more than the warmth of the fire.

"Put me down," she murmured, clutching his back, eyes drawn to the upward curve of his lips. "We have a tree to decorate."

She was disappointed when Will slowly let her feet drop to the floor and she didn't want to let go.

"You might have to show me how it's done," he said, like he was just finding his voice.

Faye reluctantly stepped away from him. "Did you not decorate a tree at school or anything?"

"We made paper ornaments and strung popcorn. Does that count?"

"Kind of, I guess." She'd bet there were no handmade ornaments or strings of popcorn on Dr Mom's tree. Faye cracked open the box, the musty basement smell embedded in the cardboard quickly dousing the flames she'd felt as Will held her. She dragged out a golden garland and handed it to him. "Start with this. Pretend it's popcorn."

He grinned and snapped it from her grasp.

This was how it should be between them. How she'd imagined it would be, last Christmas when she'd joked that leaving the fancy restaurant meant he'd be here all the time. It was as if when they'd taken down the tree, they'd packed the moving-in idea away with it, because they'd never spoken about their plans — either seriously or in jest — again.

It was her fault. She'd done that. Because she hadn't asked

him to move in, had she? What was she afraid of? *The only limit is your imagination.*

And she'd imagined all of it, which was exactly what she feared — because she knew better than anyone how quickly it could be taken away.

CHAPTER
TWENTY

It was Monday morning, and, unlike the commuters around him, Will was not headed to work. The roads were covered in slush leaving all the cars a uniform dull brown. He already ached for the pristine white fields of the farm and the cosy old Victorian house, calculating how soon he could be driving the other way.

He was running out of time. Dean would return from his ski trip soon. His mother's arrival was just over a week away. Forget the spreadsheet; he should have just done it last night — dropped to one knee, held out the box, said a silent, desperate prayer. For the first time in a long time, everything between them had felt right, and that moment when he'd scooped her up, looking into her eyes, he was sure she would have said yes. It had been a magic moment, and he'd let it slide by. Now, he was racing away from her, to the city. Why? Because of a cat.

Clementine was waiting for him at the flat, the tone of her meow and the flick of her tail all judgment. Will felt guilty for leaving her overnight, but what was he supposed to do? Lara's timing had been terrible, calling on him last minute — as she did often enough he'd resolved to give her a key so she could drop Lemon off whether he was there or not — but he couldn't say no. And he couldn't say no to Faye, either. He'd had to get the tree for her. He'd told her she came first — not following through wouldn't fly. Besides, the cat could survive perfectly well in his absence for less than twenty-four hours. Still, he felt as if he was juggling two relationships.

It didn't help that this was the worst time for Lara to be away, when he had a few days without work where he could have stayed in the country, repurposing the trailer while Faye was at the café, and spending the evenings — and nights — with her. He needed to talk to Lara. It was getting out of hand.

As Lemon delicately nibbled her food, Will stared at the spreadsheet of ideas Emilie had made for him. The tricky part was he had to get Faye to go out with him. Ha! Funny he'd never asked her out when they'd first met, unless you counted the coffee they stopped for when he'd driven her drunk ass home after that party at the racetrack. Their courtship had come in car rides when he was rescuing her from more awkward situations with her ex. He probably should have recused himself from that responsibility, her ex being his best friend and all, because she'd caught his eye the minute Nate had introduced her, and ex's best friends were in "hands off" territory, weren't they? A bit of a grey area of the bro code, maybe.

His phone pinged with a text, and it was Monique. Huh. *When are you in town next, country boy?*

Will cracked a smile and responded, *Right now, actually. You off today?*

Yeah.

The phone pinged again, but it was Nate this time. *DON'T*

PANIC. Everything's under control. Just pick up these things we need on your way back up.

Will blew out a breath, consciously trying to relax his shoulders as he scanned the list in the text, then the video Nate had attached showing the progress on the trailer, inside and out. The exterior was finished but for the graphics. All they had to do was work on the interior. It might even be done ahead of time.

Thanks, dude, he responded, then to Monique typed, *Wanna grab a coffee?*

No response. He changed Lemon's water and replenished her dish of kibble, then his phone pinged again.

Monique. *Sure.*

She was waiting outside the coffee shop when he got there, dressed in black leggings and a long coat, blonde hair piled messily on top of her head.

"How's the country boy?" She grinned.

"Still living in the city," he answered.

"I can't tell if you're happy about that or sad."

"Neither." Conflicted was a better description. He brushed it aside. No, he was doing it. Moving forward. Making the change.

They ordered drinks and found a table in the corner and Monique draped her coat over the back of her chair.

"So, you haven't gotten married since I saw you last?" she asked.

"Does anyone even get married anymore?" he said, when it felt a bit like a skewer being jammed in his side, considering the ring box he'd been carrying around since he'd purchased it.

"Didn't your friend get married last year?"

"Nate? Yeah. That's just him, though. He's an old-fashioned guy. Getting married is an old-fashioned thing."

"Marriage is a timeless thing," Monique insisted, leaning forward, hands wrapped around her cup.

"You want to get married?"

She laughed. "Not to you."

Will laughed. "You know that's not what I meant."

"Someday," she said.

"Why, though?"

"Do you have a single romantic bone in your body, Will?"

"I guess I didn't have the most romantic parents. I'm pretty sure they hated each other. I think my mom is happier alone, and my dad seems to still be chasing it."

"Didn't he get married again? Are they still together?"

"Yeah."

"Are they happy?"

"How should I know?"

"I don't know, ask? Aren't you old enough to talk to your father like an adult now?"

"What, people get to that point?"

Monique leaned back in her chair and sighed with a subtle shake of her head. "Are you going to be one of those guys who never grows up?"

"Actually..." Will took a deep breath. "I'm trying to come up with just the right time to propose to Faye."

"Seriously? And you going on, all, 'who gets married anymore.' I'm so happy for you!"

"Don't be, yet. She has to say yes first."

"She will."

"How would you know?"

"Call it intuition." Monique rested her elbows on the table, lacing her fingers together and propping her chin on them, her eyes bright. "How are you going to do it?"

"Well, because you're not wrong about me not having a

romantic bone in my body, my friend Emilie is determined to help me out. She made this spreadsheet for me."

Monique grinned. "She did not! Let me see!"

Will opened it up on his phone. As Monique reached for it, the sleeves of her shirt crept up her arms and he caught sight of the discoloured skin on one of her forearms. The bruise was still dark, yellowing around the edges.

"Hey — what's that?" He gestured toward it, and she snapped her arm back and tugged the sleeve over the mark.

"Nothing."

"Monique. What the hell? Who did that?"

"Don't worry about it, Will. Please?"

Red flags, that had merely been fluttering, whipped wildly now. "Tell me," he growled.

A flash of fear passed over her eyes until she blinked it away, her gaze falling to her lap. Monique's shoulders slumped, a sigh escaping through her lips. "Gerry."

He bristled at the name of the chef at the restaurant he'd left last year. Will had stuck it out there for longer than he should have — because he'd thought his presence mattered — until finally he couldn't take it anymore.

"You're back with him." His voice was flat.

"It's on again, off again. You know how Gerry is."

He did, and he hated the guy because of that more than his prickly personality. The man was a first-rate misogynist — and worse, apparently. Will would never get how women were attracted to that. *Charisma*, Monique had told him once. *He has charisma.* But it was selective charisma, reserved for the pretty servers and the guests.

"My roommate moved out, and I couldn't carry the apartment on my own. He offered to let me stay with him." She wouldn't meet Will's eyes, a hand unconsciously running over the bruised forearm. "It was just one time. He got carried away."

"I don't really care."

"It's not your problem, Will."

"You can't stay there, Monique. You've got to get out, and away from that damn restaurant, too. Nothing's ever going to change if you don't. I wish I could convince you you're worth more than that."

She blinked, still refusing to look at him. "I can't afford to leave."

"Oh, come on. You're good at what you do, and there are a million nice restaurants in this city. And people are always looking for roommates. You'll find something." He pinned her with his eyes. "The truth is, you can't afford to stay."

"I'm fine, Will. He won't do it again. That's very sweet of you to worry about me, though. Now drop it, okay?"

"No, I won't. Listen." He pulled out his keys, separating the ones for his car from the spare for his apartment. "Stay at my place. I've got to be up in King most of the week, anyway. Feed the cat. You'd be doing me a favour. Please? I'm serious. I need to do this with Faye, and I love that damn cat, but she's cramping my style." He grinned.

Monique stared at the key, extending a finger cautiously, as if she thought it would give her a shock to touch it. "You're a good guy, Will. That girl would be lucky to have you. I bet she knows it. So turn on the romance a bit. Surprise her. She might surprise you."

Take the key.

Monique picked up his phone instead, the screen still lit up with Emilie's list. "She's good. There are some great ideas here. Can I add one to it?"

Will nodded, and she opened up his browser and navigated to a site, sliding the phone back to him.

He studied it, glancing up at Monique. "You think so?" It wasn't on the spreadsheet.

"I do. You can get tickets for tonight. It's bound to be quiet on a Monday. You can order them right off the site."

"I'll order the tickets if you take the key."

She pressed her lips together, catching his gaze. Then she snapped it up.

CHAPTER
TWENTY-ONE

'm taking you out tonight. We'll leave from your place at six.

What? Faye laughed. She couldn't help it. Will knew she couldn't go anywhere that required her being ready to leave at six. Was he drunk? He'd gone into the city this morning to check on the cat; maybe he'd met up with a friend for lunch and there had been too much alcohol involved.

How should she word her response? Maybe she should call him. She didn't want to be misconstrued, because it was a nice thought. Her thumbs hovered over the keypad but another text came in before she'd decided what to do. Emilie.

See you at two-thirty. Got you covered.

Faye's lips crimped on one end. So, Emilie was in on the conspiracy. Why did that not surprise her? Well, fine, then, a night out in the middle of her holiday mayhem would be wonderful. Will was definitely overcompensating for the Dr Mom thing. She had to tell him it was okay, that she'd accepted the visit was going to happen — probably *needed* to happen — and she was fine with it.

Emilie blew into the kitchen at two-thirty on the dot with

her usual whirlwind of energy. Faye didn't know whether Em's enthusiasm tired her out or inspired her. *Pick inspired, Faye.*

She crossed her arms and watched Emilie bounce over. "What's this all about?"

Emilie grinned. "If I told you, it would ruin the surprise."

"So you do know, then. I might have to withhold butter tarts until you spill."

"Oh, well." Emilie sighed dramatically. "I should really cut down on sugar. They say it's not good for you, can you imagine?"

"That's commitment," Faye said before the door's jangle distracted her, sending her to the front. She couldn't help laughing again, seeing Liv.

"I brought reinforcements," Liv said as someone came in behind her.

"Connie! You're here!" Faye exclaimed, rushing over to give Liv's mother-in-law a hug. "The best kind of reinforcements." This woman was enough to make Faye believe in angels.

"Put me to work!" Connie said, clapping her hands together.

"Let me at least make you a cappuccino first," Faye insisted.

"I'll do that," Liv said and marched directly to the espresso machine.

"Give me the tour," Connie suggested. "Then, I hear you have a date, so you need to leave."

"Right this way," Faye said with a sweep of her arm.

Liv brought them both cappuccinos as Faye showed Connie around. Not that there was much to see, but Connie was excited by the workspace, *oohing* and *ahhing* her appreciation and commenting on all the shiny stainless steel.

"Mine's going to look so drab after this," Connie said.

"It's all yours for a few hours," Faye said. "Seeing as I have this mystery date that no one will tell me about."

"Surprises are so fun," Connie said. Clearly she wasn't sharing any clues if she knew what was happening — which Faye would bet she did. "How is Will doing these days? I always felt so bad for him when he was a boy. His mother was hardly ever around. You'd think someone who spent so much time bringing babies into the world would be a wonderful parent, but it was as if she only had him as a science experiment."

"Connie!" Faye snorted into the back of her hand. Liv had turned away and Faye could tell by the way her shoulders were shaking that she was stifling a laugh of her own. "See Liv, we really do have this backward. Dr Mom should be *your* mother-in-law. Is it too late to swap, Connie?"

"No way," Connie said, and threw her arms around Liv, squeezing her so Liv looked like Max the dog in *How The Grinch Stole Christmas* — except, of course, there was nothing grinchy about Connie. She was more like a slimmed down Mrs Claus.

Faye stopped herself from joking if Connie had another son hidden somewhere. She'd never been jealous of Liv's status in life, but she wanted Connie as her mother-in-law, not that woman who had produced Will. How had that happened? Will was too sweet a guy to have Dr Mom for a mother. But, in a way, Connie had raised him so that was probably why he was so sweet.

She watched as Connie began chatting with Emilie and tilted her head toward Liv, whose face finally seemed to be recovering from the flush that had coloured it as Connie squeezed her. "If I'd met Connie while I was still seeing Nate, I never would have broken things off with him. Have I said that before?"

"Possibly. Still so, so wrong, Faye. Hands off."

Liv's tone surprised Faye, but when she slid her friend a glance, Liv was grinning.

"It seems I'm right to be worried about meeting Will's mom, though."

"You should probably take what she says with a grain of salt," Liv said. "Nate said they don't get along."

"He told me that. But who doesn't get along with Connie? That alone speaks volumes."

"You'll get to form your own opinion when you meet her. Can you just let it go until then?"

No, she could not. But she had to.

The next person to come through the door was Nate. Who were they missing? It was becoming like a party around here.

Nate hugged his mother and gave her a kiss on the cheek. "You causing trouble?"

"You have no idea," Faye said, laughing. "You need to come out to play more often, Connie."

"I'm here as much as you need me to be for the next two weeks. Just give me an apron and tell me what needs doing."

Connie looked ready to dive in. Faye couldn't wait to see her and Lucy side by side. Would they work well together, or was that a recipe for friction? She found a clean apron and handed it to Connie, giving the older woman a squeeze.

"Thank you so much. Am I too old to ask if you'd adopt me?"

Connie patted her on the back. "Consider yourself adopted. Anytime you need an ear or a shoulder, I'm here. Just don't expect any financial gain. I'm counting on my sons to support me in my old age."

"Fair enough." Faye chuckled.

When the next person who came through the door was Sylvie, Faye couldn't remember the last time she'd seen a customer. Besides Lucy — and Will — that's who'd been missing. *I have the best friends.*

Sylvie tapped an imaginary watch on her wrist. "You need to leave."

Nate pointed from one helper to the next, doing a headcount. "It only takes four people to take your place, Faye. I think you're good to go."

"At least tell me what I should wear, Em," Faye said as she slipped on her coat.

"Something warm. Now go."

Something warm... it just better not be anything sporty, like skating. She would not be caught dead on skates. Faye was giddy as she climbed into her car. She was leaving the café in capable hands, and she'd even have time to walk Gus in daylight. Dates with two of her favourite guys tonight. Too bad it wasn't dancing; she felt like dancing.

Gus was as pumped as she was. Okay, so he was always thrilled to go for his romp. A quick change of clothes and Faye was back out the door, the happy Golden romping ahead of her.

She was too excited to take him on their usual route, wanting to be sure she was ready when Will arrived. Gus didn't seem to mind, especially when she gave him a kibble snack to assuage her guilt. He finished the handful before she bounded from the kitchen, the rattle of his aluminum bowl on the floor chasing her as she skipped up the stairs.

After a shower, her hair in a towel piled on her head, her robe wrapped around her, Faye rifled through her closet. What to wear? She was counting on Will not daring to make her do anything athletic. It needed to be cute, but practical. Thermal tights and her favourite pair of black skinny jeans. A slouchy boyfriend shirt to go under her warm white Irish wool sweater. She put the outfit on and sized herself up in the mirror with a nod. Next, makeup and hair. She kept the makeup simple, just a bit for her eyes and some colour for her lips. The cold would take care of her cheeks.

When was the last time she'd worn her hair down, outside of lounging on the couch? In the café, it was always up in a neat bun. Faye dried it, hesitating a beat at the pair of silvery hairs she uncovered in its dark length — she'd deal with the grey some other time — then styled it in loose waves. What was the point in having great hair if you didn't flaunt it once in a while? That alone made this night worth it.

Now, her feet. Faye gave her heels a sorrowful look. *Sorry, heels. Not tonight.* Boots. Sensible. Ankle-height, or tall? Snatching the suede shorties, she skipped back downstairs. This was the perfect chance to wear her wool coat — warm white like her sweater — and the knit hat Emilie had given her last Christmas, with its faux fur pom-pom, matched perfectly. She even had a matching scarf. Matchy, matchy, matchy.

Checking that the coat was actually clean, Faye draped it over the back of a kitchen chair. It was a relief she could still put herself together. Lack of practice hadn't dulled her ability.

But wait — it had. She needed a necklace. And her rings, even if they'd be under the fleece-lined mittens that went with the hat.

Upstairs in her room, she opened her mother's jewellery box, choosing a necklace and setting it on the top of the dresser as she found her rings. Before closing it, one other caught her eye. Her mother's engagement ring. Like Faye, her mom had often removed her ring as she prepared food, preferring to keep them in the safety of the box instead of on a window sill where it could end up down a drain. Practical and organized, her mother had been. Her father must've had a nice racehorse in training to pay for it when he'd decided to propose, because it was a sizable diamond.

Faye felt the familiar twinge of grief at the sight of it. The day of the accident, her mother had forgotten to put the ring on, wearing only her wedding band, so it always felt as if she'd left that tiny piece of herself behind.

Reaching in, Faye picked it up, then slipped it onto her ring finger, something she hadn't done since she was a little girl — tilting her hand from side to side to let the stone catch the light — and tried to let herself feel what that little girl had felt, full of hopes and dreams for the future.

Now, she was just scared. Scared of not being able to sustain the café. Scared of meeting Will's mom. Scared of ending up alone.

She didn't believe in ghosts, didn't believe her mother could talk to her from beyond, but it was as if someone whispered in her ear with perfect clarity:

Imagine being fearless.

CHAPTER
TWENTY-TWO

Monique's idea had grown on Will. It would be a bit public, but Faye wasn't shy. When he picked her up and she was dressed in an Instagram-ready Outfit Of The Day, she looked ready to walk into a photo shoot in a winter wonderland. She'd love being that girl, the star of a picture-perfect proposal. Monique had even made sure there would be someone secretly shooting video evidence once Will had secured the tickets.

The event was set out in the country, so the glow was visible in the distance against the dark winter sky as they drove toward it. Faye was antsy, he could tell. Dying to know what was up.

"I wonder what that is?" she said, pointing at the glow.

"That's where we're going."

She looked at him sideways with a wry half-smile. "I was wondering why we were driving away from civilization instead of toward it. What is it?"

"Just wait."

The sign was lit up, but Will wouldn't blame anyone for

missing it because what was behind it drew his attention away, the glow becoming a vibrant village of light.

Faye didn't miss it, though, announcing theatrically, "Twinkle and Freeze Festival." She cracked a grin, looking relieved when he pulled into the parking lot. "I wasn't a hundred percent sure you weren't going to try to get me to skate or toboggan or something."

Huh. Tobogganing would have been fun. Will wouldn't tell her there was a skating rink at this place. Skating wasn't part of tonight's plan.

She was good at accepting chivalry, waiting as he came around to open her door for her, offering his hand and lifting her out of the low-slung car.

"Shall we?" he asked, proffering his arm.

For once, Faye seemed at a loss for words, hooking his elbow. He maneuvered her around the patches of ice dotting the frozen ground on the way to the entrance, then held out his phone to the attendant for the tickets to be scanned — and hoped Faye didn't think the whole thing was lame as they joined the modest group strolling in front of them.

They were met with a sparkling maze of snow and ice illuminated by lights and travelling projections. Faye's eyes lit up like a little girl's, and that alone made it worth it — even if Will was still having doubts. *I don't know about this, Monique.*

"This is what old people do for dates," he muttered.

Faye tipped her head to the side, looking up at him. "What did you say?"

He decided it was best not to repeat it. Time to conjure up some holiday spirit. "It's cool, eh?"

"It really is. I wonder how long it took them to make this?" She gazed around, the different coloured lights dappling her white hat and coat. It made her look magical, which helped him better appreciate the spectacle.

"Let's get hot chocolate," he said, steering her to a booth along the trail. As he passed money to the teenager working the cash, he wondered if he could do events like this with the espresso trailer.

Faye grinned as they walked away from the booth, mitted hands wrapped around her cup. "Now, if this was mulled wine instead of hot chocolate, they'd really have something."

Will pulled her to the side so they were out of the way, then looked around furtively before extracting a stainless steel flask from the inside pocket of his jacket like a salesman in a back alley.

Faye snorted. "Will Callaghan, you rebel. You are *so* bad."

He grinned and handed her his cup, cracking open the plastic lids one at a time and dosing them. "It's not wine, but rum tastes fantastic in hot chocolate. Have you ever tried it?"

"I have not," she admitted as he tucked the flask back out of sight. "Were you the guy who smuggled candy into the movies, too?"

"Didn't everyone?"

"Probably." She handed him back his cup and tapped hers to it. "Cheers."

They wound along the path, taking in the ice sculptures, and trees and structures adorned with strings of light. Will felt himself coming around. It was beautiful, and Faye was beautiful. Really, they could have been standing in a snowy field staring up at the stars, for all he cared. It just felt good to share something with her. If they made a life together, it wouldn't be about spectacular moments; it would be about making the ordinary, extraordinary.

When they stopped to throw out their empty cups, Will felt a hand drop on his arm.

"Hey, would you take a picture of me and my girlfriend? Then I'll take one for you two."

"Sure," Will said, eyes landing on a young guy with a beard and buffalo-check jacket next to a girl with purple hair. They posed for a few different shots and Will handed the guy back his phone, then held out his.

The bearded guy snapped a few, then paused. "That's great! How 'bout a kiss?"

Faye didn't wait for Will to initiate, pulling him down and pressing her lips to his. He made the guy wait a little longer than necessary, just to be sure the shot was a good one, though this was just the warmup.

"Thanks, man," he said as the guy passed his phone back.

"No problem." Then he winked and rejoined his girlfriend.

Will stifled a laugh. Monique's friends.

He draped an arm around Faye's shoulders as they started walking again, and she curled against him. A glance behind told him the other couple was discretely trailing them. As stodgy as it had seemed at first, now Will could almost feel the small velvet box in his pocket calling to him.

This is it, dude! This is your moment. Seize the day!

Then with a fizzle and a pop, all the lights went out, followed by a series of gasps from the crowd.

"Are you kidding me?" he growled.

Faye laughed, unperturbed. "Guess the show's over!"

Whispers and chatter bounced around them as others stopped in confusion. Default human behaviour: the cell phones came out. People texting, probably posting statuses, some of them turning on the phones' flashlights. At least no one was panicking. Everyone was being civilized, stuck in a holding pattern, waiting for an explanation and orders how to proceed.

Forget that. Will wasn't waiting for orders, now that the night was trashed. He grabbed Faye's mittened hand and started weaving through the bodies. Instead of the light show, cell phones dotted the path like at a concert during a ballad.

"It's just a different kind of pretty now," Faye said.

And as much as he loved her for trying to find a silver lining, Will wasn't about to get down on one knee by cell phone light. With his luck, someone would trip over him.

The power was still out when they made it through to the end. Faye remained snuggled up to him as they trudged to the car.

"It was a neat idea," she said as he opened the passenger door for her.

He needed to keep his foul mood to himself. "I wonder if it's successful. We could do one at the farm." He glanced over, attempting a smile as he shifted the Camaro into gear. At least he'd beat the exodus of cars leaving.

"Right, because we have time for that." But she was smiling. Maybe tonight wasn't a complete loss. He hadn't seen her this relaxed in a while.

"It could be Dean's off-season project. Speaking of Dean..." Will frowned, then trained his face into a neutral expression. It wasn't the end of the world that her brother would soon be back. Dean was good at keeping out of the way. "Want me to pick him up from the airport tomorrow night?"

"Can you? It's a late flight so I could, but..."

"Consider it done. I have to go down to feed the cat, anyway." He didn't, now that Monique was there; he had to work on the interior of the trailer — but Faye didn't need to know that.

A week from now, it would be his mom he'd be picking up. Plan A had flopped. What was Plan B?

TWENTY-THREE

aye's temporary team at the café was a godsend. They'd gotten so much done today. If Connie's marriage really was falling apart, Faye wondered if she could talk the woman into moving to Ontario. She'd love to be closer to her boys, wouldn't she?

No, she did not want Connie's marriage to fail.

While she didn't get away as early as yesterday, Sylvie offered to stay till close which meant Faye almost got home in time to walk Gus before the sky went inky-black. When Dean was back, she wouldn't worry about it as much — which was good, because for the next week and a half, her work at the café would snowball until Christmas Eve.

She knew Will was disappointed about last night, but the evening had felt like a mini-vacation to Faye, and she loved the photos. When she posted them on her personal account, she realized how long it had been since they'd done something, just the two of them. The business got all the attention, daily shares of filtered product shots. Faye put a few of the pictures of her and Will in the cafés stories; it was high time she reminded her followers there were real people behind the baked goodness.

Gus led the way past the barns, in between the back paddocks. The outdoor horses were on alert: heads up, stock-still. Faye could see them like shadows in the encroaching dark. One of the old mares gave a snort that reverberated through the air. Then Faye figured out why.

Gus had spotted the coyote too, and she didn't trust him not to try to make friends, so she called him back, worry interfering with her volume, relieved when he responded immediately. Protective and smart, Gus was not. He'd rush up unsuspectingly and quickly find himself outmatched. Faye grabbed his collar when he was close enough just to be sure, and couldn't help watching the observer — because that's exactly what the coyote was doing. Standing there, casually sizing things up. Literally, she expected.

"Good boy," she praised Gus lavishly and loudly, rubbing her hands over his thick coat.

She hoped all of them — she, Gus, and the horses — looked too big to be an easy meal. The coyote was large, almost wolf-like. Healthy, which equalled well fed. There were enough rabbits around that he likely didn't need to attempt larger targets. That didn't mean Faye didn't have a healthy respect for the potential threat. She wished she could enjoy his beauty instead of fearing it, but dug into her deep pocket to retrieve her phone, opened the music app and looked for the most obnoxious tunes she had, turning the volume up full. Then she belted out, *Go away! Get out of here!* over top of the actual lyrics.

The coyote remained still for a moment, then nonchalantly strolled away. He probably still lurked in the grove of trees. Keeping Gus close — much to his chagrin — Faye headed back toward the house at a steady, slightly hurried, pace.

Sure enough, as they neared the barns, when she glanced

back, the coyote had resurfaced. Will's Camaro was parked next to her Corolla, and she walked faster. Thank goodness he was home. *Don't run,* she reminded herself. But, even though she was not a runner, it was hard not to. It wasn't till she was in the house, Gus running over to his water bowl to lap messily, that she felt safe again, her heart rate slowly returning to normal.

"You okay?" Will asked.

"Is handling a gun among your Calgary-bred skills?" Faye hated that she even had to think about it

His eyebrows went up, and he stepped further into the room. "Uh — yes? Kind of. No one's going to call on me for sniper duties or anything. Who pissed you off?"

"Hilarious," she said, frowning and heading for the cupboard for a wine glass.

"Sorry. Why?"

"We met a coyote out there who was a little friendlier than I liked. Dean keeps a rifle just in case, though I don't think he's ever used it."

"So you want me to, what? Shoot him if I see him?"

"Maybe it's time I learned how to use it. I don't want to shoot him, not really, but if I could just scare him away?"

He strode toward her. "Don't take your coat off."

"What?"

"Let's go." Will tugged on his boots and reached for his coat.

"He might still be out there."

He walked back into the kitchen and she didn't even scold him for not taking off his boots. Will started rooting through the cupboards, pulling out a couple of her mother's sturdy old pots. He handed her one and opened the door, nudging her out in front of him.

"What are we doing?" she asked as they stepped down from the deck.

"You'll see." He grabbed her hand and marched, heading for the first barn, its windows bright, meaning Stacy was in there. She was watering off and looked at them both strangely as they walked in.

"Hey, Stace," Will said. "I saw a couple old rasps in the tack room. Can we borrow them?"

"Sure."

"Are you moving any more horses around?"

She shook her head as she came out of a stall with a bucket. "Nope."

"Don't be alarmed if you hear a bunch of noise, okay?"

Stacy looked as confused and suspicious as Faye felt. Faye shrugged and turned her palms up as she followed Will from the barn, carrying the pots while he grasped the rasps.

"Should I gather kindling? Are we building a fire?" she joked. "I'm not sure we have time for a campsite if you want to get down to feed Lemon and make it to the airport in time to pick up Dean."

He smirked and kept walking. She wasn't comfortable being out here after her earlier encounter. It was like they were inviting the coyotes to come out and play. Maybe that was the point. And sure enough, as if summoned, three coyotes roamed on the other side of the pond.

"Are you, in fact, crazy?" she whispered. "Are we going to wait till they start singing and accompany them with instruments?"

"I'll get you some cymbals," he said. "In the meantime, the pots will have to do. Here. Trade." He held out a rasp and reached for a pot.

"Are you going to give me ear plugs, too? This might be a workplace safety violation."

"I don't work here. Do you?"

Faye stifled a laugh despite the way the tiny hairs stood up on the back of her neck.

The three coyotes stood watching them now. Who could blame them? She and Will must look ridiculous.

"Get out of here!"

Faye jumped when Will yelled and began beating on the pot with the rasp.

"Help me out," he shouted to her. "Pound that thing."

So she started. The metal on metal sent vibrations through her forearms to her elbows, making her funny bone hurt. The coyotes stared, and then took a few steps before stopping.

"Now, let's hear you yell. You know you want to." Will grinned.

Faye joined in, mimicking him. Before long she was jumping — up and down, side to side — as she screamed. The coyotes almost seemed to look at each other, agreeing these humans were dangerous because they were *crazy*, and trotted off to the fenceline, ducking under a broken board, into the sparse copse of trees beyond it.

Her screaming turned to laughter, and she collapsed to her knees in the snow.

"Felt good, didn't it?" Will said, still grinning at her. "Relieves stress, and scares coyotes away. Without guns."

"You learn how to do that in Calgary, too?"

"How can you have lived in the country your whole life and not know about coyote hazing?"

"I sort of knew. I yell and play raunchy music at them. It hasn't been working. The coyote dance was new to me."

"The dancing was all you, Faye."

She caught his look — one that made her think in about three seconds he'd be down here in the snow with her. But he held out a hand and she let him pull her to her feet.

"I haven't been dancing in forever," she said as they headed back to the house. The coyote hazing left her with a warm glow, and she was sorry Will had to go down to the city.

"Let's go to that church thing."

She stuttered a step, almost tripping. "You're not serious."

"Why not? You've got free tickets. What's the harm? If it really sucks, we'll just leave. And before you use work as an excuse, I sprung you from work yesterday. I can do it again." He gave her a crooked grin.

"Well — all right." Mallory would be pleased.

Faye had no intention of going outside again tonight. She'd let Gus out on a long line when he had to go before bed. Will kissed her, then left, and she wished she were going with him. After the scare with the coyotes, the house would seem extra-lonely. At least he'd be back with Dean later.

She'd always imagined herself eventually living in the city. She loved Will's loft. Every now and then, that girl would resurface, the one who, as a teen, had resented living on a farm. Not A Horse Girl Faye. Not A Farm Girl Faye. But she was still here.

And, let's face it; she would never be the girl with the income to have both lifestyles. And Will was not the man who was going to give it to her. She'd really screwed up somewhere along the road. It was just as easy to fall in love with a rich man as a poor one, wasn't it?

But instead, she'd fallen for Will.

TWENTY-FOUR

The trailer, at least, was coming together. At this point, it was the only thing that seemed to be going right in Will's life. Nate was already at the garage, working on the inside. Distinctly not-Christmas music was playing on his phone, and Nate was singing along.

"I need you," Will yelled.

"What now?" Nate reached for his phone to turn the volume down, looking at Will suspiciously.

"Faye has tickets to the dance at the church."

Nate choked on a laugh. "One of the last things I've ever pictured is you and Faye in a church. At a dance."

Will waved him off. "I don't know how to dance like that. You've gotta help me."

"You want *me* to teach you how to dance?"'

"How else am I going to learn?"

"I don't know. YouTube? Lessons? There are places that teach that stuff, you know."

"Of course I know that. But what good is a best friend who knows how to ballroom dance if he can't teach you so you can do something nice for your girlfriend? Especially if that girl-friend is also your buddy's ex. You probably owe both of us."

"That's ancient history."

"If it works for coercion, I'm using it. Plus, you're kind of the right height. You did such a great job playing the woman's part at the Plate Ball." Will still couldn't believe Nate and Tim had teamed up to do a demonstration, of sorts, at the biggest social event of the Ontario horse racing season. It had been both hilarious and brilliant at the same time.

"That's not the way to talk me into it," Nate said, but he was laughing.

"Please? I know you don't owe me anything, so just name your price."

"If you're willing to pay, it's better if you go somewhere and take lessons."

"No, it's not. I don't want to make a fool of myself in front of a stranger. You've seen me make a fool of myself countless times, so I'm used to it. Besides, I don't have time for that."

"When is it?" Nate asked.

"Saturday night."

"Saturday. *This* Saturday? You expect to learn how to dance in four days?"

"You're going to have to go slow with me. And I'll need lots of repetition. 'Ballroom for Dummies,' something like that. Hey — *is* there a book?"

"Will —"

"I don't need to be an expert or anything. I just want Faye to know I made an effort. You gotta teach me that dip."

"I've got a better plan. My mom's in town. She can teach you to dance. Or, you know, help you enough that you can muddle through."

"You think she would?"

"Of course she would. She loves you." Nate walked down

the ramp of the trailer. "I should warn you, though. Be prepared for the old ladies. You've never been to one of these church things. I grew up getting dragged to them. Those widows are fierce!"

"That'll be Faye in fifty years," Will grinned. "Picking up young guys after I'm dead and gone."

"I can see it," Nate agreed. "Okay. You don't have time to waste. There's lots of room here, so let's get started. I'll set you up with my mom tomorrow."

"If those guys that work here show up, I'm never going to live this down."

"You're never going to live down going to a church dance." Nate grinned. "Because I won't let you."

Will picked up the bag he'd left on the trailer's fender and offered Nate the pastry he'd saved.

"You were holding out on me," Nate said, reaching in. "But thanks."

"I thought you'd give me a harder time."

"Is Saturday night the night, then? Seeing as last night didn't pan out?"

Will pressed his lips together, not appreciating the reminder. At least they'd gotten a couple of nice photos out of it. Monique's friend was good with an iPhone.

"Here's hoping," he said.

"You know Will asked me too, right?" Nate sat on the edge of the sofa arm in the TV room of his and Liv's home, arms crossed, looking skeptical.

Faye grinned. "I know. It's hilarious. I would have asked Tim to save you, but the timing of his road trip sucks. And Emilie says she's not good enough to teach me. Please?"

Nate scratched the back of his neck and looked at the ceiling. "You're sure about this?"

She laughed. "Not completely, but he's really trying to do things that make me happy right now, so I can endure a little hardship."

"I'm so glad you think of dancing with me as a hardship."

"I didn't mean it like that. It's just this ballroom stuff has always scared me, you know? I'm not the most athletic being on the planet."

"I know you can dance, Faye," he said, meeting her eyes.

She smiled at the positive memories. They had some.

"Besides, this isn't about athleticism, it's about coordination," Nate said. "You have rhythm. And poise — and you've got plenty of both."

"Was that a compliment?"

"You say that like I've never given you one."

"I'm sorry. Apparently old habits die hard."

"I'll say one thing, both of you are gung-ho. But it would be so much easier if you learned at the same time. You know, together?" Nate cranked an eyebrow.

"He can't know you're doing this for me though, okay? It has to be our secret."

Nate grinned, popping to his feet and sauntering over in what looked to be his best dancer walk. "You know you're a closet romantic, don't you, Faye?"

Her lips twisted. "I never really thought I kept that in the closet."

Nate just laughed and held out his hand, and started singing, because that was Nate — something about God giving her style and grace and putting a smile on her face. Which did make her smile; she couldn't help it.

How did people do this? Faye was over him, there was no question, but this was more awkward than she'd anticipated

— the way he held her, even though there was considerable space between them — especially with Liv right there. *Deal with it, Faye.* Liv was not the jealous type. She was propped on the couch, immersed in a book.

"Is this too weird?" she asked.

"It's fine, Faye," Nate said. "Focus."

If things had been different — as in, if Liv hadn't existed — it's quite possible she and Nate would have ended up together. And knowing it was him who considered marriage important, not Liv, it would have come up, eventually, if he'd been with Faye. He would have asked. And Faye knew she would have said yes, as much as now that seemed ludicrous. So why not Will? He was learning how to dance properly for her — to make her happy — and it did.

Of course, the fact remained, Will hadn't asked, though neither had she given him reason to.

"You can reel my mom in, too," Nate said when he decided they'd done enough, Faye stepping back to reclaim her own space. "She can practice with you when you take breaks at the café. Make Liv practice with you, too."

Liv raised her book to her face, hiding behind it — to no avail, as Faye watched Nate drag her to her feet. Getting Liv to dance was no small feat. Faye had never been able to talk her into it. The structure of ballroom probably appealed to Liv, though.

"You'd better watch it. You're starting to look as if you know what you're doing," Faye quipped. "Now I know what you've been doing with all your free time."

"I'm practicing for your wedding," Liv said dryly.

Faye nearly choked on the mouthful of water she'd just taken. *"Et tu?"*

"It's worth it just to see your face." Liv smiled sweetly.

"I think it's time for me to get out of your hair. Some of us still have to be up before dawn."

Liv and Nate probably were up then anyway — you didn't get up at four AM for years and just turn around and sleep till noon just because you had a few weeks off — but right now they didn't *have* to. That was an important distinction.

Looking relieved for the chance to break away from the whole dancing thing, Liv saw Faye out and they parted with a hug. It was a crisp night, the sky clear, the stars sparkly diamond chips against the darkness overhead.

Tonight, Faye didn't mind if Will was up to some grand thing. Why fight it? Seeing Liv and Nate together... It was a solid endorsement of matrimony. Liv never would have gotten married, if Nate had never asked. And Faye had been over the moon when she'd heard. *Face it, girl. If Will asks, you're not saying no.*

CHAPTER
TWENTY-FIVE

"Aren't we fancy," Faye said, curling her hand around Will's elbow as they walked to the hall.

This wasn't anything like the snazzy Plate Ball Emilie helped put on to raise money for the Thoroughbred retirement group — everything looked as if it had come straight from the dollar store. It was cute, though. It had a homey feeling, reminding her of a school dance, right down to the decorations. Faye wondered if she'd met Will in high school, if her life would have played out differently.

She had to give him credit. He'd sprung her early from the café again, made her dress up, and gotten her out for another evening. Five years ago, that would have been an easy thing to do. Is that how life went? You got close to thirty, became your parents — until your kids grew up, and then you started doing things like this. That's what it looked like. They were the only ones under forty-five, Faye was sure of it. But she was already having fun. Good, clean fun. She wasn't sure she'd known before now what that was.

This was the stuff of sweet romance fiction and squeaky

clean, holiday made-for-TV movies. She could pretend she was in a scene from one of those shows, though she'd probably over-prepared with the whole getting Nate to teach her how to dance thing. Not that she was any good. She might just be able to keep from stepping on Will's toes, if Will was agile enough to keep his out from under hers.

"Let's get punch," she said. *Meet my new friends.* That almost made her laugh out loud. Faye Taylor, chummy with the church ladies. At least they hadn't invited her to bible study. She might have to draw the line there.

She dropped her hand from Will's elbow, finding his fingers and lacing hers through them. When she glanced up at him, he gave her the cutest look, which just made her want to ravish him right there. She didn't want to shock the ladies, though. *Decorum, Faye. Ravish later.*

"Hello, Mallory!" She waved as she caught the sight of the organizer, envisioning herself as a fifties girl with saddle shoes and a poodle skirt. What a fun theme that would be — tried and true, not cliché, right?

The woman looked up from straightening napkins, and smiled. "Oh, hello, Faye! I'm going to be honest. I didn't really think you'd come. I'm so happy you did."

So, Mallory was possibly a little sharper than Faye had given her credit for. "This is my boyfriend, Will."

Will removed his free hand from his pocket and smiled his most charming smile. "Nice to meet you, Mallory."

Mallory blushed. Really, who could blame her when Will looked so edible tonight?

"Would you have some punch?" Mallory asked, dipping her eyes, looking flustered. She served Faye first, then Will.

"Thanks so much, Mallory."

Will's lips brushed Faye's ear as he dropped words into it. "You're laying it on a little thick, aren't you?"

Faye grinned from behind her cup as she sipped. Not a drop of alcohol in it. She should have thought to suggest Will bring his flask. *No. Bad, Faye. You can have fun without alcohol. No hangover!* That alone was exciting.

"Don't you feel as if we've been tossed back in time?" she asked, bumping Will's arm with her shoulder.

"Sure."

"This was your idea, remember. You're required to have fun. Hurry up and finish your punch. We need to dance!" Faye was looking forward to seeing what he'd picked up from his lessons. She wasn't expecting him to have the prowess of Nate or Tim, but it didn't matter. He'd done this for her.

"All right," Will said, taking her glass from her and placing it on one of the round tables set at one end of the hall. "If we don't, some blue-hair might steal me away." He raised his eyebrows at her with a wolfish look.

"I don't think they do blue hair to older women anymore," Faye said, looking around. "I should look so good at their age. Look at them. They're fabulous. I'm a little worried you might find one with money and leave me for her."

"Better be on your toes, then." He grinned, grabbing her hand. "Shall we?"

We can try. But instead of speaking, she stepped with him to the floor where couples were moving in time to the music with varying degrees of expertise.

Uncontrollable laughter threatened to bubble up as the two of them stood off to the side like a couple of awkward teenagers trying to remember where to put their hands. *Okay. My left hand on his shoulder, my right hand in his.* Will placed his right hand lower than he should, but they weren't being graded here. This wasn't a competition. Nate wasn't standing on the sidelines ready to bark instructions at them. He really had been a sport, agreeing to teach them what he could in such a limited timeframe.

"Ready?" Will asked.

She nodded, and waited, listening to the music. It was a waltz, she knew that much — which was good, because it was the only one Nate had taught her.

Will began counting before he moved. "*One* two-three, *one* two-three..."

Faye did her best to follow, staring down to make sure her feet were doing the appropriate thing even though she could hear Nate's voice telling her to keep her head up. Once they found their groove, she'd raise her chin, find Will's eyes, looking just like those beautiful ladies sweeping around the floor in the competitions. *One two three, one two three.* Will led the steps in a little box just like Nate had done. Well... not *just* like Nate. It was more of an approximation.

"We're killing it," Will said.

"Don't make me laugh, I'll lose my spot."

"Your spot, like you're reading a book?"

"I might be safe with a book. " Faye clutched his shoulder tightly and redirected him before they bumped into a sweet elderly couple. "Sorry! Didn't mean to take over."

"When are the Tai Chi classes? That might be more our speed." Will asked.

Faye snorted and tripped. "Stop it!"

"No — bingo! I'll come for that," he said.

"I hear those bingo players can get pretty rowdy," Faye countered.

Will focused again, looking down, so Faye kept watch in case they were on another collision course. *One two three, one two three.* Faye's shoulder brushed a woman nearby and she glanced over in horror. "I'm so sorry!"

The woman just smiled pleasantly as her partner maneuvered her away.

"If we were in a club she would have chewed my head off," Faye whisper-shouted over the music. "This is so civilized. I think we should invite them all to the Plate Ball next year." Then she stepped the wrong way and caught Will's toe.

"Ouch! Would you pay attention?" he hissed.

"Shit, I'm sorry!" She dropped her arms, a hand flying to her mouth as she looked around. "Damn! Do you think anyone heard that?" Could she say damn? Probably not.

Will grinned at her and repositioned her hands, then tried to get her to spin. Faye ducked under his arm and grabbed his shoulder again, feeling dizzy, and not in the right way.

"Maybe that's enough dancing." She laughed, her forehead dropping to his chest. "At least I'm not wearing heels."

"I agree," he said. "You could have maimed me there. Let's see if there's any punch left."

"You don't have your flask stashed and filled with vodka, do you?" She glanced up at him as they tried to get off the dance floor without causing any more problems.

"Sorry. That would just be wrong. Punch should have rum, not vodka." Will grinned.

He didn't have rum, either, but the punch soothed her parched throat. They were both sweating — or did dancers glow? As if either of them were dancers. "The punch is nice. Not too sweet. Should I ask for the recipe?" she whispered. Will chuckled as he slung an arm around her shoulders.

"What are you thinking about?" she asked, seeing a look she couldn't put a finger on in his eyes.

"I'm imagining the two of us chaperoning our kids. Do they still have chaperones at high school dances?"

A warm sensation spread from the middle of her chest. She

grinned up at him. "I don't know why they bother. It's not as if it stops anything."

"How *ever* would you know that, Faye Taylor?"

"That's just what I heard. I didn't go to school dances."

"Why do I have a hard time believing that?"

"It's true. Ask Liv." Will's eyebrows crept up, and Faye admitted, "Okay — maybe I went to a few. But they really weren't my thing."

They wandered to the dessert table and picked up a couple of treats to nibble on, Faye studying the different squares for the most enticing ones. She taste-tested them to see if they were as good as they looked and wondered about recipes again. Maybe the church had a cookbook, but she could deconstruct them if need be. That wasn't stealing, was it? She even bid on a couple of things in the silent auction, but she didn't expect to win. Faye had no intention of battling it out with the old ladies who made the rounds at the table every so often to check the numbers. She'd bet it was war in those final moments as the bidding came to a close.

"We really should go. I kind of hate to leave though, you know?" she said.

"I won't tell anyone you had fun tonight." Will squeezed her. "But yeah. No sleeping in for you on Santa Claus Parade Day."

"Don't rub it in."

"I'll get up with you," he said, and Faye believed him as they set their glasses on a tray near the kitchen, wandering toward the coat rack.

Mallory intercepted them. "You're not leaving already, are you?"

Faye almost said. "No rest for the wicked," but caught herself in time to reconsider. "It's been lovely, but —"

Mallory leaned in conspiratorially. "The older folks will be leaving soon. Then we age the music down. Something tells me that's more your scene, Faye."

Faye looked sideways at Will. Was this woman serious? Age down how far? Then the ballroom-friendly music died away, the quiet hush of voices and shuffling feet filling the room.

"Just another half hour?" Mallory said.

Faye looked at Will again, hoping he'd bail her out, but he just shrugged, no help.

When the music started, Faye got her answer. Eighties music. She could do eighties music. She'd been with Nate long enough to be exposed to Connie's playlist, even if she'd never met his mom when they were dating. She laughed, and Mallory grabbed her hand and pulled her to the middle of the floor with a growing group of middle-aged ladies, some of whom Faye thought she recognized as visitors to the café. Faye glanced over her shoulder at Will and he grinned and waved.

It was fine dancing with the bunch, all of whom no longer looked old to Faye as they bounced to "She Bop" and "Footloose," but when they played Bowie, she skipped over to Will and dragged him in, because "Modern Love" was timeless.

"One more," she gasped, breathless, sure it had been over half an hour. "Then we *have* to go, because now I'm going to be sore *and* tired tomorrow."

She prayed it was a good one, and maybe someone was listening — this was a church, after all — because they played Peter Gabriel's "In Your Eyes."

Faye smiled up at Will as she snaked her arms around his shoulders and he rested his hands on her waist. She said, just loud enough for him to hear, "Slow dancing feels so much better than that ballroom stuff."

He ducked his head to whisper in her ear, "Do you think there are chaperones here?"

Faye caught the glint in his eyes. "What do you have in mind?"

But he just closed his arms around her, and she rested her head against his chest. She could hear his heart beating, a steady thing, like he was a steady thing. *They* were a steady thing — and there was nothing scary about that.

FAYE WAS BUBBLING AS WILL CLIMBED behind the wheel of the Camaro in the church parking lot. "Who knew that would be so much fun?"

He smiled as he started the car then tried to inconspicuously pull his phone from his pocket.

"Who are you texting?" she asked.

"Nate," he lied. It turned out to be good that Dean was home, because he'd agreed to start a fire then disappear to bed when he heard them drive in. Will found himself humming, "Tonight's The Night." That eighties music had messed with his head.

The temperature had risen above freezing today but dropped with the sun, and as they left the streetlights of town behind, snow started to fall. Houses along the way were lit up with colour, making the usually dark drive to the farm festive. He took it slow as the snowfall became heavier. They probably should have taken Faye's Corolla instead of the Camaro, but he'd been driving this car in Canadian winters since he was sixteen; he was used to the way it handled in this weather.

The sideroad was clearer, allowing him to increase his speed a smidge. It wasn't far now to the farm. His palms were sweaty and his throat dry. This time would really be it. The cosy living room, the beautiful tree they'd decorated, the champagne Dean promised to hide, chilling. The perfect end to a brilliant evening.

Something big and dark flashed in front of the car and Will instinctively hit the brakes hard, bracing with hands clutched tight on the wheel. The back end fishtailed and he corrected before it spun out...only to hit a patch of ice and spiral in slow motion the other way. The car hit the bank with a thud and came to a stop, lodged in the frozen pile.

Will's heart hammered hard in his ears, hands still white-knuckled on the wheel. The deer had leapt away safely.

Finally he heard Faye's voice. "Are you okay? That was close." Her voice quavered.

"Yeah. You?"

She nodded.

He unsnapped his seatbelt and hefted the door open — it was clear, at least. Will opened his phone flashlight to assess the situation. The hind end was wedged into the snow bank, and, given the bank hid the ditch, he had a feeling they weren't driving out of this predicament.

"Shit, shit, shit." Will stared up at the sky, the softly falling snow not seeming so majestic anymore. *Why tonight?*

Faye climbed out her side. "Well — it's not far, at least. We can walk home. Worry about getting it out in the morning?"

"I guess. And hope no one bashes into it." Will wondered if he should call a tow truck now just to get it out of the way for exactly that reason. Or — "I guess I could bring the tractor down."

"In the morning, Will. If you're worried about it getting bashed, that means there's a chance you could get bashed, too. Wait till the snow stops. Please?"

He didn't want to agree with her common sense. She worried too much.

"Please?" she repeated.

The fear in her eyes brought it back. Most of her family had been killed in a car crash. Maybe this wasn't the same scenario — a country sideroad wasn't a highway — but the weather, and her memory... Will couldn't blame her for making the comparison.

"All right. I wonder if insurance would give me anything if it got totaled?"

"It'll be fine, and tomorrow morning, everyone driving by it will wonder what yahoo was driving an old Chevy Camaro on these roads." Her lips crimped up at one end and she theatrically rolled her eyes. "Some city driver."

He wrapped his arm around her neck, and she laughed as he crushed her against him. She was being a good sport.

"Guess we'd better get walking," he said.

Strike two, Will. Strike two.

CHAPTER

TWENTY-SIX

An unfamiliar humming woke Faye before her alarm. Not fully alert, she sat up, trying to figure out what was wrong as the fog of sleep wore off. She'd been having the strangest dream about shopping at the bulk store with Will's mom. Shaking her head with the weirdness of it, Faye pushed back the covers. As usual, Will remained dead to the world.

Her calves screamed as she climbed out of bed, the night of dancing coming back to her — and reminding her Will had promised to get up with her because it was the parade today. She'd let him sleep a while longer because he'd been so incredibly sweet lately.

Nothing happened when she flipped the light switch in the bathroom, and it dawned on her what that humming was. The power was out, but Dean was up and already had the generator going because priority number one was water for the horses — which meant, at least, she could flush the toilet. She rummaged for her clothes, going by feel, then dressed in the dark and made her way downstairs.

184

Squinting in the kitchen's brightness, the first thing she did was check her socks matched. The fridge hummed — also part of the circuit fed by the emergency source — and the little red indicator on Dean's coffee maker was lit, of course. As she helped herself to a cup, Dean came in the back door, preceded by Gus. Only one of them stopped to knock off snow, Gus bounding over to lap at his water bowl.

"Hey," Faye said, cradling her mug. "Everything okay out there?"

Dean hung up his coat, nodding. Stacy would have both water and illumination so the horses could be cared for.

"How long has it been out, do you know?" she asked.

"It was out when I got up. I haven't checked to see how widespread it is."

Faye brought up the hydro company's app to see if there were updates and frowned. "Looks as if it's in town, too. I'm not going to be able to open the shop."

Dean grinned. "You deserve a day off, Faye."

"But today's the parade."

Dean's expression transformed to sympathy. "They'll restore it by then. The parade doesn't start till two, isn't that right?"

At least she didn't need to be in a rush, but she still needed to go in and put a sign on the door because there would inevitably be people who either were coming from a different area and didn't know about the hydro outage, or hadn't figured out that places of business were affected too. It wasn't as if they got preferential treatment and few of them had a backup power source.

"What's going on?" Will blinked at them in a rumpled sweatshirt and jeans, his hair askew.

Faye laughed quietly. "What are you doing up?"

"There are no lights upstairs."

He clearly wasn't awake yet. This was not Will's usual time for functioning. Faye poured him a cup of coffee and pressed the mug into his hands. "Hydro's out." She turned back to Dean. "I guess I'll just go in and wait it out."

"Won't it be cold?" Dean said.

"Probably, but either it'll come back on and I'll be fine, or if the expected time for it to be restored is too long, I'll come back here. Not much else I can do."

"Want me to come with you?" Will asked, seeming a little more with it.

"That's okay," she said. "I might be home in an hour. I'll keep you posted." She rinsed out her cup, then sauntered over and kissed him. "Go back to bed."

It wasn't until she saw Will's car, lodged in the snowbank on the edge of their sideroad that she remembered it was there — an unfortunate end to what had been a wonderful night. She'd text him when she got to the café to remind him about it because it might be awhile before he remembered himself. Dean would help him extract it.

At least the roads were clear. Everything in town was dark without the streetlights and it was chilly enough in the café Faye figured the power had been out for a few hours. There was still no update from the hydro company. She'd signed up for text notifications, and only one message stared back at her: *we are aware of an outage in your area and we are assessing the problem.*

Hurry up, she wanted to text back, but that wasn't one of the options the bot offered. After rifling through paper on her desk for a blank sheet, she grabbed a black Sharpie marker and wrote in block letters: POWER OUT. CLOSED TEMPORARILY. SORRY FOR THE INCONVENIENCE!

Like it was anything she could control. She found a roll of blue painter's tape and broke off four pieces so she was ready to put the sign in the door at her usual opening time if needed, then began appraising the fridge. With the low temperature in here, she might get away without having to throw away any perishable stuff — milk and cream being the most vulnerable — as long as the hydro didn't stay off too long. She could take the items most at risk of spoilage home with her.

Her phone pinged with an update from Hydro. *Crews have been dispatched and will work as quickly and safely as possible to restore power. The current est. time of restoration is 2:30PM...*

Had something blown up? That was her whole day gone! And all those kids looking forward to the parade would be so disappointed. Well — maybe the parade would go on, so it was the parents needing their afternoon caffeine fix who would be dismayed. Where were those crews? If she took them cappuccinos and butter tarts, would they get the job done faster? But she couldn't run the espresso machine without hydro. Sugar alone, then. Faye would never underestimate the power of butter tarts.

She was making a list of the things she'd take home with her when she heard a vehicle pull up in the parking lot. Was it time to open already? Faye grabbed the sign, rushing to the door to make her apologies. A truck with a two-horse bumper-pull trailer backed in. What did they think they were doing? It wasn't unusual for a truck and trailer to make a quick stop, but they usually pulled up onto the shoulder in front of the strip mall instead of taking over the lot. Its lights went off, the exhaust from the truck's tailpipe dissipating into the air, and a man came around the hood. Even though he was bundled up against the cold, Faye would recognize Will anywhere.

"What is that?" she said, staring out at the trailer as she let him in, the sign still in her hand.

"We were going to put the final touches on it today, but other than that and the graphics, it's done, so this seems like a good time for it to make its debut. Merry Christmas?" he said tentatively.

"That doesn't really answer my question."

Will gently removed the sign from her hands, glancing at it. "Put on your coat and come out."

When she came closer to the rig, she recognized the truck as Dean's — every pickup looked the same to her, especially this time of year. Will opened the small door on the side of the trailer and waved her in first.

Faye glanced at him, hesitating before she grabbed the edge to pull herself in. "This is the first time I think I've actually been in one of these things. You'd better not be planning anything fishy."

He climbed in behind her, laughing. When she stopped abruptly, he ran into her, grabbing her hips to steady himself.

"Wow," was all she could say at first.

The inside of what looked on the outside like a nondescript old-model horse trailer was finished better than any room in her house. Faye could smell the new rubber mats underfoot, almost overpowering the more pleasant scent of the wood that formed counter space and shelving. On the left was what would open up into a serving window, on the right, a shiny espresso machine, and at the far end, a small fridge and some cupboards.

Finally she stepped further into it, running her hand over the counter, eyes travelling over all of it. "This is amazing. Incredible. Fantastic. Brilliant. Have I missed any words yet?"

She turned back to him, met by his pleased smile, Will rocking on his heels with hands jammed in the pockets of his jacket, making her close the distance between them.

"Here you are, saving the day," she murmured.

He met her lips and pulled her against him, a kiss that started soft and slow becoming something deeper, and it was much too soon when she admitted this wasn't the time or place to take it where she wanted it to go.

"I guess I'd better let you open," she said, catching her breath, when it was the last thing she wanted to do. She wanted to hide in here — preferably until the New Year. "Fire this baby up."

Faye ran back to the café — realizing she'd left the front door unlocked — and grabbed the A-frame sign proclaiming COFFEE to set close to the road like she did each day. Will flipped up the serving window which gave a nice overhang that would keep people out of the elements as they waited, should such elements be a factor. The generator was noisy, but it probably sounded worse because everything was so quiet — everywhere — with the hydro out. Ducking back into the shop, she put together an assortment of baked goods and ran them back to Will. She could travel from shop to trailer all day to replenish supplies as needed. What else was she going to do?

She passed the container to Will through the window. "Do I get to be your first customer?"

"Absolutely." He grinned.

"Cappuccino, please, sir!"

The squeal of steaming milk warmed her soul — maybe not as much as that kiss had, though. Will handed her a paper to-go cup from his perch.

"What do you think we should charge?" he asked.

"On a day like today, this is priceless. We'll be the only game in town. We can charge whatever we want — but we should keep it the same as if the shop were open. When you take the show on the road, you'll be able to jack it up a couple of bucks. People will throw money at you for this."

And they did. It wasn't long before cars started pulling in, immediately attracted to the open trailer once they saw the café was closed.

"Are you serving coffee?" seemed to be the common statement of the obvious, followed by gushing gratitude when the answer was "yes."

"Lifesaver" was used often.

"Tell me coffee's not addictive," Will said, laughing.

"I will not debate that." Faye grinned.

She finally remembered to snap some photos with her phone, posting them on the Triple Shot Instagram page, filling her stories with them. *Power out? Never fear! We've got coffee!* People kept coming, even after Faye realized the hydro was back on, earlier than expected. The crowd thinned out around the noon hour, but it would pick up again for the parade. They were going to have to chase everyone away when they wanted to close.

Her entourage began to arrive — she'd been fielding texts all morning, keeping them up to date as she dashed back and forth, restocking Will's supply of treats. It was possible he'd sold more from the trailer than they would have on a normal Sunday morning at the café. Food trucks were big right now; the as-yet unnamed espresso trailer was a novelty — and, more importantly, a hit.

CHAPTER
TWENTY-SEVEN

Faye was inside organizing her crew, and Will sized up the shifting crowd, more people gathered on the sides of the road than lining up for coffee. After an overcast start that morning, it was a perfect day for the parade. The sky was clear, the air crisp, and last night's dusting of snow freshened the greying banks.

Emilie marched over from the café loaded down with a large box in her arms, bags dangling from the fingers of each hand. She'd dressed appropriately with a red jacket over black leggings and a Santa hat on her head, the white ball at its tip bouncing in time with her step.

"Whatcha got there?" he asked.

"Decorations. Faye suggested dressing up the outside — then no one will care that you don't have graphics yet."

"Great idea," Will said. Not that the trailer's plain exterior had kept anyone away that morning, once they figured out there was coffee.

Emilie pulled out sparkly garlands, draping them on every edge she could find, then she popped inside with him. "This is so cute! Such a brilliant idea. And just in time for the parade. We'll need to have a proper celebration one day. An official grand opening."

"I'd suggest doing that in January," Will said wryly. "There's enough going on right now."

"Agreed," Emilie said. "It'll be a nice way to add a little something to an otherwise quiet month. We'll keep it simple, nothing over-the-top. That said, we'll require live music."

Will laughed. Emilie would have it exactly over-the-top before any of them knew it.

"Does Faye love it?" she asked.

"I believe she does." He nodded, a smile coming to his lips, thinking of the way she'd kissed him, and set up the espresso machine so it was ready to brew. Folks were congregating in the parking lot and would be lining up to grab drinks before the parade began.

"So how was the dance?" The arch to Emilie's eyebrows suggested she wanted more of a report than he expected he was prepared to give.

"It was fine," he said anyway.

"I can't imagine Faye would hold out on me if someone had given her something *shiny* last night. What happened, Will?"

"Did you not hear that I spun my car into a snowbank on the way home? It kind of killed the mood." His, anyway.

Emilie gaped at him. "Are you both okay? Is the car?"

"We're all fine. All that died was my intentions." He cleared out the steam wand with a noisy blast. "I'm beginning to think the universe is trying to tell me something."

"You can't give up because of a couple of little bumps, Will."

They were feeling like roadblocks to him right now.

"Tonight, then," Emilie said. "After the skating party."

He frowned, giving her a look. "Skating party?"

"Yes. We're going skating on the Taylor's pond after this."

Because this day wasn't packed enough?

"That's great, except Faye doesn't skate," Will reminded her, wondering who had come up with that idea. It wasn't on the spreadsheet.

"That's why it's so perfect," she said. "You do. That's all that matters." Emilie elbowed him with a grin.

Will's brow furrowed, but a customer was approaching. He'd figure out the skating thing later. It would probably be a case of making it up on the fly.

"I'm here to help." Emilie popped up beside him. "Put me to work."

"You take orders, I'll make the drinks. Hey, there you are," Will called over the heads lining up. "Where've you been?"

Nate stood off to the side. "Looks like a success to me."

"I've got you to thank for making this possible."

"Glad I could help," Nate said. "Want me to take over for a bit? Sounds like you've been stuck in there for a while."

It would be good to get out of the cramped space while things weren't too busy. He could try his little experiment. "You got this, Em?"

"Yes, sir."

Will took the bottle of liquid from the fridge, still impressed he'd remembered to bring it along, and Nate traded places with him.

There were tons of little kids, too excited to feel the cold yet. They were bombing around, parents trying to corral them to keep them from running into the road, even though it was closed for the event. No one noticed Will as he unscrewed the top of the bottle and tucked the lid away. He'd stashed the straw in the inner pocket of his jacket and probably looked like a drug addict as he put his mouth to one end, dipping it in the solution and drawing a small amount into the straw. He positioned the end in a crevice on top of the snow bank and gently blew out.

The bubble popped. *Shoot.*

He tried again with the same result. This was going to take some practice. Finally, he got a perfect transparent globe and watched with fascination as frost crept over the surface, the crystals building into a delicate network. It was so beautiful — but after a few moments, he had to pop it to see it crack. Then he made another one and took out his phone to take a picture, catching sunlight sparkling on the fragile sphere.

"Wow, what's that? That's so cool!"

Will grinned, looking sideways at the boy, maybe ten, who had snuck up beside him, and noticed a collection of mesmerized kids with him. "It is, isn't it?"

"Is that just a regular bubble solution?" one of the parents asked.

"Just google it," Will said. "You'll find the recipe. It's simple."

"Can I try?" the first boy begged.

Will looked at the parent. "Is that okay?"

"What's in it, exactly?" the woman asked.

"Water, corn syrup, sugar and dish soap," Will answered.

She shrugged. "Okay. Don't swallow any though, right Logan?"

The kid gave his mom a *"duh"* face and Will had to keep from laughing.

He realized he only had one straw and it wasn't exactly hygienic to let the kid use it— then he saw Faye coming out of the café.

"Faye!" he called. "Can you grab some straws?"

One of her eyebrows shot up — predictably — but she went back inside, returning with a fistful of paper straws. Of course, Emilie, environmentalist that she was, would insist on those useless ones —but they should still work.

Will handed one to the kid. "Just draw up a little, okay? Else you're going to get a mouthful and trust me, it won't taste so good."

Logan's grin was brash and Will was worried he was going to ignore the warning.

"Careful, Logan," his mother reiterated. The kid rolled his eyes at Will.

"Don't get me in trouble, kid," Will hissed. He hadn't thought this through — it might be an insurance liability.

It was a relief when Logan didn't suck any into his lungs, placing the tip of the straw on a different part of the snow bank and breathing out a bubble of his own — first try. After that, all the kids wanted a turn, Will doling out straws and coaching each one.

"Parade's starting!" one of the parents called.

The kids stampeded away. Will stooped to pick up a straw that had been lost in the fray.

"Where did you ever learn how to do that?"

Will straightened, catching Faye's smile. He hadn't noticed she'd stayed. "The internet. There's no end to the possibilities."

A strange expression crept over her features. "Imagine that," she said. "You were pretty good with them."

"Not bad for an amateur." He grinned. "It was a lot of fun."

"Can I try?"

"Sure." He handed her an unused straw. "Remember not to swallow."

Faye swatted him and reached for the bottle of solution.

It was no less engrossing now than it had been the first time — or maybe it was more so, because this sphere came from her lips. They both crouched to catch the glittering it, watching the crystals racing over the surface, encasing the membrane in a brittle shell.

Will was afraid to breathe. "Yours is the most perfect of them all."

Faye tilted her head toward him, the same light that illuminated the frozen bubble catching the rich brown of her eyes, and he thought for a moment she was going to kiss him.

Instead, she straightened. "I feel like we should be pouring maple syrup on the snow, next."

"Crossed my mind," he said. "But this was enough of a question mark for the parents. Doing something they were actually supposed to ingest would be a bad idea."

The crowd in front of the trailer was down to two or three people, everyone wandering away to find a spot to watch for the floats. Emilie gave Will a thumbs-up over her own cup and went back to chatting with Nate.

"I'd better get inside," Faye said.

"Not waiting to see Santa?" Will quipped. "C'mon. Stay with me. You still have Lucy and Sylvie and Liv and Connie in there. I think they're all right."

"Will Callaghan," she said, her lips crimping on one side. "It's almost like you've caught some Christmas spirit. What's going on?"

What's going on is, I'm picturing you and me here in ten years with our kids — and it's kind of nice.

He grabbed her hand and pulled her to the edge of the group that had gathered by the street, then wrapped his arms around her from behind. As parades went, it was definitely small-town. A few different businesses had floats, there were some old cars, and this was horse county, so there were horses. Santa was on a hay wagon pulled by a tractor, sitting on some bales of straw, no reindeer to be seen.

"Where did you get it, anyway?" Faye asked, leaning back against him. "The trailer."

"It was sitting at your farm."

She laughed. "I didn't even miss it. Someone could have stolen it and I wouldn't have noticed it was gone."

Will chuckled. "According to Dean, the thief would have been doing him a favour."

"So it makes both me *and* Dean happy? That's a win." She turned away from the parade, slipping her arms around him. "Thank you. It's genius."

He wondered if his first instincts were right, if the trailer was all it took to make her happy and he should just take back the ring. Time was nearly up — his mother arrived tomorrow. How was he supposed to turn a skating party into an opportunity? But maybe doing it when all their friends were around to witness it was right.

CHAPTER
TWENTY-EIGHT

A warm front swept into the area late afternoon, turning the frosty temperatures of earlier in the day upside down as night fell. Fog billowed, setting a scene more appropriate for Halloween than Christmas, mist rising off the snow, sublimating.

Dean had set two spotlights up, the beams criss-crossing over the ice lighting up the surface and creating long shadows. Faye watched from her post on the bench under the tree, bundled warmly because even though it was above freezing, it wasn't exactly July. Skating party had turned into shinny hockey, giving her the perfect excuse to remain on the sidelines — no one in their right mind would want her on their team even if it left them uneven.

It was three against two — Emilie, Liv and Nate versus Dean and Will — and Faye did not feel the least bit guilty about sitting out. Will and Dean were better off without her, despite their disadvantage. Dean was better than Will, but Nate was small and fast, and Liv and Em held their own, more agile than the two taller men.

"Come on, Faye," Dean prodded. "At least stand in goal for us. It would even things up a little."

Faye laughed. "Absolutely not." She was not about to be their target. When this gang got together to do anything athletic, they forgot about being careful — all of them were too competitive for that. Instead, both sides played with empty nets.

They looked like a bunch of kids reliving their childhoods. It made Faye smile. There was no fighting, only skating and shooting and group hugs when they scored — which was a lot. She liked this kind of hockey — not watching elite athletes with seven-figure salaries. This seemed more like real life, the essence of Canadian winter.

In a surprising display of footwork, Will deked around Nate when Nate hit a bump in the ice and wiped out.

"Go Will!" Faye yelled, sitting on the edge of her seat.

He shot the puck at the space between two buckets acting as the net, but Emilie dove, blocking it, spinning into the bank.

"Augh!" Will groaned, stopping sharply with a spray of shaved ice. He skated over and helped Emilie to her feet. "Nice save."

Faye started when a dark shape moved in her peripheral vision, her hand flying to her thumping heart until she recognized what — or who — it was. "Tim!"

He dropped to the bench beside her and let her give him a squeeze.

"Good to be home?" she asked.

Tim paused for a moment, his eyebrows slightly raised, his trademark mild smile on his lips. "It is. It was a good road trip, though."

"Maybe you'll be the one to break Toronto's Stanley Cup curse."

He just laughed and trained his eyes to the figures on the ice. "How's it going?"

Faye said, "You need to get out there and show them how it's done."

"Nah. I'd just make them look bad." He grinned.

"Dean and Will could use the help. They're getting their asses kicked."

Tim chuckled. She noticed he had skates with him, but he made no effort to put them on.

"Tim!" Will called, spotting him. "Get down here!"

"It's my day off," he called.

Emilie raced over the ice — Faye had no idea how she could do that on skates — and jumped onto the bank, scaling the short incline. Tim stood up to catch her when she threw herself at him.

She couldn't really hate Emilie's all-in enthusiasm for Tim, so it wasn't resentment Faye felt for such an overt display of emotional freedom. A touch of envy, maybe, because she hadn't experienced that kind of sweet, uncomplicated, first love herself. Somehow Emilie had kept herself from truly falling until she met "the one." She hadn't protected herself the same way Faye and her sister had. It was nice that at least one of the three of them hadn't needed to.

Emilie finally released Tim with a shove. "Put your skates on."

"It's my day off," Tim repeated.

"Skating is like walking to you. You don't want to seize up from inactivity, do you? I'm a physiotherapist. I know these things."

"You're not *my* physiotherapist."

"Quit whining and come skate with me." She hopped nimbly back down to the ice.

Tim rolled his eyes, but he sat next to Faye again and laced up.

"Poor Tim." Faye laughed.

Tim slid his eyes her way. "Where are your skates?"

"I outgrew them long ago."

"Now I know what I'm getting you for Christmas." He eyeballed her feet, his lips twisting just a little, and he elbowed her before getting up, jogging down to the pond's smooth surface with the sure-footedness of a mountain goat.

Will skated over, still holding his hockey stick, and climbed up to park himself beside her. "Aren't you getting cold sitting here?"

"I'm perfectly fine, thanks."

Emilie and Tim were showing off their fancy footwork, almost like they were doing a figure skating routine. Nate and Liv just talked, because no doubt Liv would not go for the cute stuff, though she'd probably take to ice dancing better than the ballroom Nate was trying to teach her.

"Hey, Faye!" Emilie called. "Watch!"

Emilie and Tim locked wrists, and Tim spun her, around and around. Faye was impressed Emilie didn't fall over because just seeing it made her dizzy.

"What do you think, *Battle of the Blades?*" Emilie asked once she was upright and skating easily again, her face flushed and chest heaving from exertion.

Faye laughed. She'd watched the show where professional hockey players were paired with world-class figure skaters. Tim would be a natural, with his ballroom background, but Faye had to wonder if Emilie might be a little jealous of him ice dancing with another woman.

Will elbowed her. "C'mon Faye."

She elbowed him back. "I don't have skates."

"That doesn't matter."

"Forget it. I'd need a pillow for my butt."

"I won't let you fall. Or if you do, I'll make sure you fall on me." He grinned.

Faye smiled wryly. "Who said chivalry was dead?"

"Please?" He pulled a flask from his pocket, raising his eyebrows and waving it in front of her. "I'll share this."

"You'd better share that with me anyway." Faye laughed and grabbed it from him. She popped it open and took a slug, nearly choking on the whiskey that burned her throat. "Why?" she sputtered.

"Warms you up, doesn't it?" Will tucked the flask away and pulled her toward him, planting an alcohol-infused kiss on her lips. "Now, let's go."

When he scooped her up, holding her against him as he descended to the ice, it felt an awful lot like déjà vu.

She yelped. "What are you doing?"

One of her first encounters with him Will had shamelessly tossed her into the pond after helping with hay. It had felt as if they were in middle school — like that was his way of showing her he liked her. Apparently, in two and a half years, he hadn't grown up.

"Relax. I won't drop you," he promised.

"Not on purpose, anyway."

"Give me some credit."

"For what, exactly? Being aggravating?"

Will set her down carefully on the frozen pond, holding her elbows. "That better?"

"Mildly."

"You're out here now, so might as well humour me." He slid his hands from her elbows to grasp her fingers, and began skating, slowly, backward.

Faye's teeth and her butt muscles clenched as she slid

along, trying to keep her balance. "Have I told you lately what a jerk you are?"

"I don't think so. I've kind of missed it."

At least he was good enough on skates that she started to feel safe. As long as he didn't do anything fancy, or keep her out here too long, she might survive. He eased to a halt and drew one arm up, holding her hand.

"Give me a twirl?"

"You have got to be joking," she said, feeling even sillier.

"It's gotta be easier on ice than it was when we were dancing. Try it."

Faye sighed. Her hand was going numb from being held up in the air as blood drained from it but Will wouldn't let go, so she ducked under his arm, shuffling her feet in a three-sixty.

One second, Will was looking down at her with a goofy smile, then his eyes popped at something to his right and he grabbed for her abruptly. Faye glanced the same way in time to see Nate wipe out — and the next thing she knew, she was tumbling to the ice with a gasp, pulling Will down on top of her as Nate's momentum took out her legs. They landed together with a grunt, Faye sucking in a breath.

"Are you okay?" Will's face was contorted, trying not to laugh as he propped himself up on his elbows.

Faye was stunned, still lying flat on her back. This is why she should have stayed off the ice.

"Wind knocked out of you? Need mouth-to-mouth?" Will grinned, lowering his mouth to hers.

Faye grimaced as she shifted. "Ouch."

"What's the matter?" he frowned, his expression finally turning to concern.

"I think I hurt my foot."

Nate appeared beside Will on his hands and knees looking

horrified. "Shit, Faye, I'm so sorry. Are you okay? Do you need help?"

"Can we get off the ice now?" she pleaded.

Will rolled onto his side and climbed to his feet. "Can you sit up?"

He helped her upright, and Faye absently rubbed the back of her head, though thankfully her wool hat had cushioned the impact. It was her stupid ankle, pain beginning to radiate from the joint.

"Give me a hand, Nate," Will said, and they each took one of her arms and hoisted her up, supporting her as she balanced on one foot.

"Get her inside," Emilie ordered. "If she broke it, she might have mild shock."

No, no, no. It can't be broken. Faye glowered at Will, but he looked so guilty, she eased off.

"I could piggyback you," he offered.

"That's all right," she grumbled. *You've done quite enough.*

TWENTY-NINE

My life is officially a disaster. Not only had Will *not* created the perfect moment to pop the question, he'd broken Faye. Literally.

The waiting room of the emergency department wasn't busy, but they were in no hurry to see her. It sucked that it was a Sunday night and the walk-in clinic was closed. All Faye needed was an x-ray requisition.

"I told you we should have called an ambulance," Nate quipped with a crooked grin. "That gets you seen a lot quicker."

Liv and Nate were experts on hospitals and injuries — it came with riding racehorses. Will didn't know what they were doing here. Nate said he felt guilty, but it hadn't been intentional. He wasn't the one who'd dragged Faye out onto the ice. It was a good thing she *hadn't* been on skates.

"Let's just go home," Faye said, glancing at Will after staring at the clock on the wall. "It's not that bad. Emilie said she'd tape it for me."

"You're here now. Might as well get the x-rays to be sure

there's no fracture," Liv, former vet student, was the closest thing their group had to a medical expert. "You know Em would back me up on that."

True enough. And as a physiotherapist, Emilie was probably just as qualified as Liv to offer advice.

"It's embarrassing," Faye grumbled. "This is like a broken fingernail to you two." She glanced from Liv to Nate, then sighed, resting her head on Will's shoulder.

After her initial grumpiness following the injury, Faye's ire toward him had died. It did nothing to remove his guilt, though.

"Would it be wrong to play music?" Nate asked, looking bored, playing with his phone. "We're the only ones here."

"I think you two boys should sing," Faye said. "Give us a preview of carol night."

Was Faye seriously suggesting Christmas music? As he exchanged a look with Nate, Will had to stop himself from asking if she'd hit her head harder than she'd thought.

"All they can do is tell you to stop," Liv said. "Maybe they'll like it."

"Maybe it'll get you seen faster." Nate grinned.

"Because they want to get rid of us?" Will quirked an eyebrow.

"Only if they're as grinchy as all of us." Faye finally smiled.

Will sat up straighter, rubbing his hands on his thighs. Broken girl got what broken girl wanted. "Requests?"

Faye tapped her phone against her leg. Her ankles were crossed; the hurt one on top, and Will wished he could find something to elevate it. All the tables, with their requisite waiting room magazines, were between the chairs, making it awkward.

"What do you think, Liv?" Faye asked.

Please don't ask for "Little Drummer Boy/Peace On Earth," Will begged silently.

Liv pressed her lips together, a slight furrow to her brow for a beat before she said, "'A Huron Christmas Carol?'"

Nate snorted. "Trust you to pick the only one we probably haven't practiced."

"'Feliz Navidad?'" Liv tried again.

"Make that two," Will said. "We should have asked *you* for ideas."

"They both would've been good ones," Faye agreed.

"We could probably do that one on the fly," Nate said. "The other one, not so much."

Will said, "Just don't judge us on the Spanish parts."

"I'm not judging anyone tonight," Faye said.

Will quirked an eyebrow at her, and she reached over and patted his leg. She looked beyond tired, and he wished he could speed things up and get her home.

"You okay with the melody?" Nate asked.

Will wasn't in the mood for this, but there was a good chance that wouldn't change before the real carol night, so this was a good drill. Time to dig up his musical self and put on a little show. Will nodded at Nate and began tapping the beat on his thighs. When he started to sing, he mumbled through the Spanish bits after the three *Feliz Navidads,* and when he broke into the English part, Nate joined in, singing harmony.

Will forgot everything temporarily, not caring about impressing anyone or performing for a crowd, instead closing his eyes and imagining they were around a crackling bonfire on a cold winter's night — which would have been a nicer way to end the evening.

As they trailed off at the end of the song, fading out the English part, the clapping Will heard came from more than

Faye and Liv's polite applause. A small group of nurses stood by the triage, smiles on their faces.

"Come this way, Faye," one of them said.

"See?" Nate whispered.

Faye grinned as Will helped her up. She tried a step, and then hopped the rest of the way.

"Go home, you two," she called over her shoulder.

There was more killing time in the curtained-off examination room until Faye was seen by the doctor on call, and more yet before she went to radiology. When Will went back to the waiting room, Liv and Nate were still there. It didn't surprise him, really. They'd probably stay until the doctor had seen the x-rays. Liv would probably demand to see them.

He sat next to Nate, blowing out a long breath. "This is not how tonight was supposed to go."

"That's three though, right?" Nate said. "The light show going poof, the car crash, now this. You should be free and clear."

"I hope you're right."

"But you should just ask her tonight, anyway."

Will looked at Nate like he was crazy, then at Liv — but Liv was nose-down, reading something on her phone. "Liv. I need a woman's opinion."

She looked up abruptly, her eyes shifting from side to side. "I don't think it really matters where you ask her, to be honest. Just that you do."

"It would be a great story, don't you think?" Nate prodded. "Popping the question in the emergency room?"

"Says the guy who proposed in a barn. Em told me not to take advice from you."

"The barn was perfect," Liv interjected quietly.

Maybe they were right. None of his romantic ideas had worked out. Maybe this was his and Faye's story, like Nate and

Liv in the barn had been their story. It was real. It was messy. It was life. But when he shoved his hand in his pocket, his whole body turned to ice.

It can't be.

"What's wrong?" Nate said. "You look like you're about to pass out."

"The ring. It must've fallen out of my pocket." *I think I'm going to throw up.*

"When? At the pond?" Nate asked.

"Must have. When we fell." If that wasn't the ultimate case of kicking a guy when he was down, Will didn't know what was.

"You'd think someone would have seen it," Liv said.

Except everyone had been concerned for Faye. "I'll call Dean. Maybe he'll go look." Will couldn't very well leave Faye now. How would he explain that? Then he remembered. "Or not. Dean will be asleep by now."

"We could go," Liv offered.

"But how's that going to look if we get back and you guys are there?" Will almost pinched a fold of skin because this had to be a nightmare. "I'll go after I've got Faye settled. I'm going to check to see if she's back from radiology."

The man who had pushed Faye, in a wheelchair, away for her x-rays was rolling her back as Will found the spot where he'd left her.

"Not broken!" Faye shot her arms in the air like she'd just scored a goal as she hopped up and sat on the edge of the bed. "It's just a strain. I can't even injure myself thoroughly."

"What a relief," Will muttered, hugging her. "Can we go now?"

"Thank you!" Faye waved at the departing man before returning her attention to Will. "I guess I have to wait for the doctor to make it official. The radiologist said he wasn't supposed to tell me, but I talked him into it."

Of course she did. Probably bribed him with butter tarts.

He could have done it right now, if he had the ring. The good-news diagnosis had flipped her mood. Everything was right in Faye's world at that moment.

She seemed to notice his twitchiness. "What's wrong with you?"

"Nothing. I'm sure you're ready to get out of here, that's all."

She scolded Liv and Nate for still being in the waiting room, and Liv promised to drop off the crutches she still had from a far worse injury a few years ago. Emilie had already offered to meet them at the farmhouse to apply her magical kinesiology tape, but Faye wouldn't let her, promising to ice it and take some anti-inflammatories to get her through until tomorrow. Once they were in the car she faded, which was fine with Will, because he was too preoccupied with losing the freaking ring to make conversation.

"I'm exhausted," Faye said, letting him support her as she hobbled up the steps to the deck. A pair of crutches somehow already rested by the back door.

"How's the pain? Can I get you something for it? Another shot of whiskey?" He hoped she was tired enough not to care that his words were clipped. He needed to get out to the pond.

"Those liquid ibuprofen capsules Liv gave me are already helping, thanks. Just take me to bed."

Any other time he would have taken advantage of that offer, but tonight he only made sure she was comfortable and was grateful that her eyes were already closing as her head hit the pillow. Gus settled on the floor near her night table.

"G'night," he whispered and turned out the lights. "Gus! C'mon."

The Golden seemed a little unsure, but scrambled to his feet and followed as Will rushed back downstairs. He grabbed a flashlight, threw on his coat and boots, and headed out, Gus romping ahead of him. When they reached the pond, he plugged in the spots, their powerful beams flooding the ice, and began his search. How hard could it be to find a blue velvet box against the white landscape?

He tried to recreate the fall, but he couldn't even recall where it had happened — which meant scouring the entire surface of the rink and the bank. When his first pass came up empty, he picked up a broom that sat with the shovels used to clear snow and started gently prodding, thinking it must be buried somewhere. *Nothing.* He could be here all night, and still not find it until spring.

Gus did his best to help, poking his nose into the snow, intermittently finding sticks and bringing them over. Will dutifully took each one and threw it. Bringing the dog had been a stupid idea. He'd just wanted the company, but the Golden was a pain in the butt.

Give up, Will. Just give up. Obviously this was not meant to be.

He looked around for Gus, done. The Golden trotted toward him, amazingly surefooted on the slippery surface.

"What've you got this time, buddy?" Hopefully it wasn't decomposing.

Gus sat, his tail sweeping the ice, and tipped his face up. Will's jaw went slack as he fell to his knees and reverently removed the box from the dog's jaws. He opened it up to be sure the ring was still there, tucked it carefully in his pocket, and threw his arms around the Golden's generous ruff, blubbering, "I love you, Gus. Will you marry me?"

CHAPTER
THIRTY

Today was the day.

Was it too late to run away? She could hop in her car, drive to the airport and get on a plane somewhere warm. Pick up a bartender looking for a ticket to Canada and let him think it could happen. That girl was still in her. Somewhere.

Last year Will's mom had canceled at the last minute. Stood them up, really. It could happen again. Faye clung to that hope. Because she was not hopping on a plane. She wasn't picking up any bartenders. She wasn't leaving Will. And Will had a mother.

I hope she has a sweet tooth.

Will had been grouchy that morning and he'd looked terrible. She was the one who should be grumpy. What was worse than meeting Dr Mom in the middle of her busiest season? Meeting Dr Mom in the middle of her busiest season, on crutches.

Her ankle felt much better than expected today — that tape of Emilie's really was magic — but Em had made her promise to stay off it for a couple of days. Once they were at the café, Liv gave Faye a lesson with the crutches, and she could hobble around reasonably well. All her helpers made sure she didn't overdo it — probably under strict orders from Emilie.

Will had never answered when Faye asked if she and his mom were similar. Weren't men supposed to fall for women like their mothers? Liv wasn't anything like Connie, but it wasn't practical to use Liv as a point of comparison. Or had Will — consciously or unconsciously — gone for the opposite of his mother? Because really, Faye was not the driven career woman. She'd be all for staying home with her kids, like Connie had, if they could afford it. If she and Dr Mom did get along, it would be a shame that she lived so far away. She'd want to spoil her grandkids. That was a biological imperative, wasn't it?

Time flew when Faye wished it would drag and delay the inevitable. It was already afternoon. Sylvie would be here in two hours to relieve her so she could get home and get the house ready. Dean had promised to help her because she wasn't one hundred percent, and it was comforting that he'd be there. She'd have an ally, someone unreservedly on her side. Though he'd be in bed by the time Will arrived with his mother.

The phone interrupted her rampaging thoughts. Emilie.

"Your package is here. Want me to drop it off on my way to work?" Emilie said.

"Could you, please? That would be amazing."

With everything that had been going on, Faye had forgotten she'd had the gift she ordered for Will sent to Emilie to hide it from him. It would be easy to stash in the back of the café.

"You got here quick," she said when Emilie showed up what felt like minutes later, slipping through to the kitchen carrying an oblong box. Faye finished serving customers then joined her. Connie and Liv had gone out to stretch their legs, so only Lucy worked away on one of the stainless steel surfaces.

"Quick?" Emilie's eyebrows arched. "I called forty-five minutes ago."

Faye glanced at the time. *Seriously? How did that happen?* Time was racing by — like her pulse all of a sudden. She forced herself to breathe.

"Check that it's right," Emilie said, helping herself to a butter tart.

"Good idea." If she didn't do it now, she'd forget about it and only find out Christmas Eve if something was wrong — leaving her really scrambling for a gift for Will. She pulled an X-Acto knife from a drawer and slit the tape to open the outer box, removing the inner one.

"Are those boots?" Emilie asked, frowning. "Muck boots?"

Faye laughed as she cracked open the box. "Isn't that hilarious? But functional, too."

"Faye! You can't give Will those for Christmas."

"Why not?"

"He got you a —" Emilie waved one of her hands around, then finally sputtered, "Mobile espresso bar."

"What if," Faye said slowly. "It came with an implication?"

"Such as?"

"What if the boots were just a prop, and the story behind them is, he's going to need them if I ask him to move in?"

Emilie tipped her head from side to side. "Better." But she still looked disappointed. Emilie was holding her enthusiasm for a bigger step than that.

"I'll stuff some socks in them, how's that?" Faye added.

Emilie rolled her eyes. "That would make it infinitely better. I've got to go. Stay off that ankle, and good luck with Dr Mom!"

Faye hid the boot box away; she thought it was a perfect gift. Will would see the humour in it. Now, she just had to survive long enough to see him wear them. When Sylvie came, her heart started thumping so hard Liv began coaching her through deep breathing exercises and had the common sense *not* to ask her if she was ready when it was time to leave.

Liv carried the box of cookies and squares Faye had readied as they made their way to the car. Faye had chosen simple classics: gingerbread, sugar cookies, and Nanaimo bars for a touch of something fancy. She'd bought half a dozen types of loose-leaf tea and an infuser from an online tea shop, and sparkling water, so her bases were covered for light refreshments. Thank goodness the woman was arriving after dinner.

"Somehow this feels familiar," Liv said as she helped Faye in the passenger side and slipped the crutches behind the seat.

It was an admirable attempt on Liv's part to make Faye smile. It felt like an age ago, that Liv had been the one on crutches, and all the memory did was remind Faye what a wuss she was, to end up in a hospital emergency room with an insignificant strain when Liv could have died in the racetrack accident that had fractured her femur.

She gave herself a pep talk. *You are a successful small business owner. You have a degree, even if you're not a doctor. You've been taking care of yourself since you were fifteen.* This woman would not intimidate her. They both loved Will; that was common ground. She would keep that in the front of her mind.

"Are you sure you don't need help here?" Liv asked once she'd seen Faye safely inside.

"I'm sure. Dean's here, and Will did a lot before he left. Go back and make sure Connie and Lucy don't get on each other's nerves."

The old farmhouse seemed so drab compared to the image Faye had in her mind's eye of where Dr Julia

Ackerman must live. She knew Will's mother had moved from the house he'd grown up in and bought a condo in downtown Calgary. Faye envisioned white walls and white painted trim and grey hardwood floors and granite counter-tops. Expansive pieces of abstract art done on gallery wrap canvas.

And certainly not a large Golden Retriever who drooled in your lap trying to get you to play fetch with his favourite ragged toy, hair wafting in his wake as he wagged the plume of his tail no matter how often Faye brushed him.

She sighed. "I love you, Gus. But what are we going to do with you while she's here?"

It was a rhetorical question. Will insisted she didn't have to do anything which was good — because it wasn't as if Faye would put Gus in a kennel for the duration of the visit. If the woman didn't like dogs, too bad for her.

Now. Would it be wrong to pour herself a glass of wine to boost her morale?

Yes. Yes, it would. Best not to meet Will's mom with alcohol on her breath.

The guest room was ready with her best linens on the bed and extra pillows, a set of towels on the chair. All Faye had to do was open up the door to let the room warm up. Dean vacu-umed while she hobbled around, wiping things. She tugged down the blinds to help keep the cold out. Dean started a fire so the house would be cosy. When they were done, the clock above the kitchen let her know she had an hour left. Dean apologized and went up to bed, taking a reluctant Gus with him.

Faye sighed, longing for wine again. Maybe some music. She decided on smooth jazz, picked up a book, then set it back down in favour of her phone and found her last group conver-sation with Emilie and Liv, her foot propped on the coffee table. She fired off a text. *T-45 minutes. House is ready. Distract me.*

Emilie responded first. *At work, wishing I was at the game. Watch it for me and fawn over Tim on my behalf.*

Liv: *Sounds like a worthy distraction.*

Not a bad idea. Faye reached for the remote and switched the TV on. It was already tuned to the sports channel. After a few minutes of following the action and listening to the commentator, she located Tim, decked out in the blue and white. *I do like a man in uniform,* she texted.

Emilie: *Sigh. [Heart-eyes emoji] Okay, gotta go. Patient. Thanks Faye. I'll text you later.*

Liv: *You okay, Faye?*

Faye: *Best I can be without a glass of wine in my hand.*

Liv: *You're watching the game for Em; I can have a glass for you.*

Faye: *You'd do that for me?*

Liv: *I would.*

Faye: *Such a trooper. Why are you still up, anyway?*

Liv: *We're watching the game.*

Faye: *Never thought I'd hear you watching a Leafs game.*

Liv: *I know. Sacrifice for family, I guess.*

Faye: *That's going to be the theme this Christmas, isn't it?*

Liv: *Sucks to grow up.*

Faye: *It does.*

How silly to feel comforted knowing her friends were with her via an electronic device, but Faye appreciated their solidarity. She tried to follow the game, but her anxiety had worn her out.

The rumble of Will's old car caught her just before she dozed off. That would have been a disaster, Will and his mother coming in to find her passed out on the couch.

Faye scrambled to her feet, trying to figure out what, exactly, she should be doing when they came through the door.

Heading for it, probably. She took a step and flinched as she felt a twinge in her ankle, and resigned herself to the crutches. Then she tried to predict when they would appear. Getting out of the car... Will grabbing his mom's luggage... walking up the path to the steps, across the deck...

The screen door clicked, and Faye swung her way awkwardly toward it. Will pushed open the inner door.

His grin eased her tension for a split-second and he mouthed, "Hi, honey, I'm home." Faye controlled her smile because it wanted to twist and distort, and in her current state, her face would come off looking maniacal. As Will set down the bags, Faye did a quick study of the woman with him before she realized Faye was watching her.

She was tall, probably five-nine, and had that long, leggy look of someone who could have once been a model. Her hair was a warm grey in a short, stylish cut, and when she finally found Faye's gaze, her lips parted in an expensive smile of straight white teeth. When Faye was close enough to see, she noticed the woman's eyes were almost the same colour as Will's, honeyed champagne, but somehow sharper. Maybe it was just the fine lines around them.

"So nice to finally meet you, Dr Ackerman," Faye said. *Do I shake hands? Hug her?* She opted for the former, slouching on the crutches. How did one look together on crutches? This really wasn't the image she'd wanted to present.

The woman reached out politely, her hands soft in contrast to Faye's own, which spent too much time being washed throughout the day to not be drier than Faye would like. She missed the life that had allowed her regular manicures.

"Please, call me Julia."

Faye tried not to exhale too obviously. One question answered. "How was the flight?"

Julia smiled the smile of a tired traveller. "It was fine, thank you. Will told me about your accident. How are you?"

Faye felt her face flush. What, exactly, did Will tell her? "Oh, I'm fine," she said, dismissing the concern. "I'll be back to normal in no time."

"It's good you had it looked at. If it's still troubling you in a couple of days, be sure to go back. Minor fractures don't always show up right away."

Yes, Dr Mom. That would be, what, Christmas Eve? Faye would not be repeating her emergency room experience on Christmas Eve.

Will helped Julia shrug out of her coat. "I'll take your things to your room."

Faye fought the urge to stop him as he gathered the bags. *Don't leave me alone with her!* Then she chided herself. *Grow up, Faye. You talk to strangers all day. This woman is just another stranger.*

"Can I get you anything? A glass of water? Coffee or tea? Are you hungry?"

"Some wine would be lovely. Thank you, Faye."

Faye swallowed her reaction. *All right then. Gotta love a woman who knows what she wants.* But Julia was teeth-clenchingly polite. Why was it rubbing her the wrong way? It didn't sound or feel fake. What was it, then?

Clinical. That's what it was.

Well, she's just doing what you're doing, Faye. Because you're a stranger to her, too.

Will reappeared shortly, and Faye beamed in relief. "Can you pour some wine for us?" *Sweetheart? Honey Bunches?* "Why don't we sit in the living room, D — Julia?"

Once Will's mom was seated, Faye positioned herself on the opposite end of the couch, which looked its age under Julia's tailored suit. Dr Ackerman was old school, apparently, still believing travelling by air required professional attire. Faye removed her cardigan because the cosy fire now made her much too hot.

Will brought a plate of cookies and squares — letting the wine breathe — then handed his mother a glass before presenting one to Faye. Faye kept herself from grabbing it and guzzling it down.

Julia brightened. "Are these some of your creations?"

"They are," Faye said. The tension eased again; it ebbed and flowed. She watched as Julia paused with her hand hovering before selecting a Nanaimo bar.

"Good choice." Faye realized she was grinning.

Julia nodded. "I think I deserve chocolate after a day of travel."

"You certainly do. Chocolate goes nicely with red wine." She looked at Will, who had retreated to the doorway between the kitchen and living room, looking perplexed. Finally Faye asked, "Aren't you going to have a glass?"

"Leave us to get to know each other," Julia interrupted. "Don't you have errands to do, Will?"

At ten PM? What was she thinking?

"Um — ah," Will stammered. "I'll go see if I can catch the end of the game in Dean's office."

Faye sat up straighter, keeping herself from calling after him. *What do you think you're doing? Get back here!*

"So what do you do in your free time, Faye?"

Faye snapped her head back to Julia and tried to recall what Julia had just said. She let herself take a breath before answering. "Free time is a rarity these days, but I like to take my dog for walks and drink with my friends." Might as well be candid.

Julia's laugh was rich. "I think we could be friends, Faye. I'll have to consider getting a dog. So much more reliable than a man."

Faye almost snorted. Why had she been afraid of this woman? Julia was delightful.

"Your boy is lovely — Will's shown me photos," Julia continued. "Where is he? I'd love to meet him."

"I didn't want to assume." Faye assessed their wine glasses. Will should have brought the bottle. "He's a lot of dog sometimes. It can be overwhelming."

"And so much hair. I'd like something with less hair. What do you recommend? One of those Doodles, maybe?"

"Please, no," Faye said, choking on her last mouthful. "No overpriced mutts. Please."

"Well, I like to run. What can I get that could run with me?"

Of course she liked to run. The universe had this backwards. This woman should be Liv's mother-in-law. Faye was better suited to soft, sweet, Connie. Except she was warming to Julia, quickly. Or maybe that was just the wine. She excused herself to grab the bottle, swinging out to the kitchen but leaving the crutches behind when she returned. If she took it slowly, her ankle didn't hurt too badly.

"You sure you don't want a boy toy instead?" Faye said. "If you do it right, they really are less work."

Julia's lips curved into a coy smile. "Is that the voice of experience I hear? Give me some tips."

How had they ended up here? This was going swimmingly. "More wine?"

"Please," Julia said, proffering her glass. "You're smart not to get married. And kids! Just don't. Of course I love Will, but kids make it messy when things don't work out."

Well. This was not how Faye thought it would go. "You don't want grandchildren?"

"Oh, I'd love grandchildren. But I'll live without them. You won't hear me putting pressure on another woman to have kids. I know how much they tie a woman down."

Fay's mouth opened and closed, at a total loss for a response. This woman, the mother of the love of her life, was counselling her not to get married. Not to have kids. A woman who brought babies into the world *all the time.* Though that probably meant she prevented them as well.

Was Julia really saying something more? What Faye had feared, that she didn't think Faye was good enough for her son? Didn't want Faye as the mother of her grandchildren?

Wasn't that just dandy?

Maybe Julia realized Faye's discomfort because she diplomatically redirected to safer subjects, asking about Dean and the farm. Alcohol mixed with fatigue, and the conversation tapered until Faye suggested showing Julia to her room. Julia waved her off, asking Faye to point her in the right direction because of her ankle. Faye didn't argue, though the wine had done a good job of killing her pain. She'd pay for that in the morning, when that pain was in her head instead.

By the time she crawled into bed, Will was asleep. In no time, Faye would be too. She collapsed into the mattress less than gracefully.

"Sorry!" she whispered.

Will's eyes cracked open. "You two have fun?" he said, his voice gravelly with sleep.

"Yes? No? I really don't know. She's not what I expected."

He threw an arm around her waist, pulling her in, nuzzling her neck. "See? I told you everything would be all right. 'Night," he rumbled against her ear.

The thing was, Faye wasn't sure it *was* all right.

CHAPTER

THIRTY-ONE

Faye was gone when Will woke up. As usual, he hadn't noticed her leave, but he'd thought she might wake him up. Dean wasn't around, either. Gus, looking lonely, curled up by the back door. The Golden scrambled to his feet with a grin when he saw Will.

"How's my favourite dog in the whole wide world?" he asked, crouching to give Gus a proper welcome. Will had given Dean the ring for safekeeping. All plans were on hold — probably until his mother left.

He felt as if his life was playing out by the lyrics of "Paradise By The Dashboard Lights," except he was the one ready to scream that he needed to know right now if Faye would love him forever. Instead of cornering her and finding out, he'd be playing dutiful son until Boxing Day.

Will poured himself a glass of juice and sat at the table while he waited for the French press to brew, one hand on Gus's broad head, the Golden's chin resting firmly on his knee. No sign of his mother. She was on Calgary time, two hours

223

behind, but it had been pretty obvious when Faye came to bed that those two had tied one on.

Faye and his mother getting drunk together. Will shook his head. He didn't know how to take that.

Gus scrambled to his feet, and Will followed his trajectory. There was Julia, a red robe wrapped over top of black silk PJs, her hair looking almost as perfect as it had when he'd picked her up. Otherwise, she looked rough. He kept that thought — and the grin it inspired — to himself.

The dog made it to her first and Julia fussed over the dog briefly. Will called the Golden before he got too carried away.

"That's enough, Gus. Go lie down." Will leaned down and kissed his mother on the cheek. "Coffee?"

"Please."

Will placed a steaming mug in front of her and joined her at the table. Gus thumped his tail from his spot by the door, dropping his head to his paws when he wasn't invited over.

"Thank you," she said, spinning the handle and staring into the cup's black depths.

"You're welcome," he said. "Can I get you anything else? Ibuprofen? Acetaminophen? ASA?"

Her lips curled into a wry smile. "Not right now, thank you. This will do just fine." She tentatively brought the mug to her lips, risking burning the roof of her mouth. "Where's Faye?"

"The café, I guess. She was gone when I got up." Will kept eyeing Julia with a brow cranked.

"Everything okay?" she asked.

"Sure. She's usually gone before I'm up."

"I enjoyed getting to know her. She's refreshingly blunt."

Uh oh.

Julia noticed his expression. "Oh, don't worry, Will. I adore her. I'm sure she's a lot of fun."

Fun? Is that what it looked like they were — just casual, having a good time? *Who could blame her though, right buddy?*

"So what are your plans today?" she asked, sipping more bravely.

"Tonight we've got a carol sing at the café. We did it last year, and it was a hit, so we thought we'd do it again. Nate missed that one, so it's great he'll be part of it this time. Will you come?"

"I'd love to. It's always wonderful to hear you boys sing together."

He would say this much for his mother: sure, she'd wanted him to be more — a doctor like her, a lawyer, an engineer, *something* — but when he'd gotten the music scholarship in Toronto, she'd done nothing to dissuade him, and even contributed to his expenses. He had her to thank for his education, so hearing that she got some enjoyment from it was meaningful — even if it hadn't led to anything that would make him rich.

"Do I get to see the famous café before then?" she asked. "I expect it will be crowded this evening."

"Sure, if you want." She was an investor, after all; though she'd insisted the money she'd given him for the startup had been a gift.

"Of course I do. I must have one of those butter tarts I keep hearing about."

"I'll make sure Faye saves you one. They sell out pretty quick. When you're ready for another coffee, we'll go." He grinned.

They headed out at eleven — nine, Calgary time — and got to Triple Shot before the lunch rush. Faye must've been parked on cash register duty, because she was seated sideways on a stool behind the counter so she could monitor both the kitchen and the front door.

"Good morning, Julia," she said, rising, her face betraying nothing, though she avoided Will's eyes. "Let me make you a cappuccino."

Will couldn't wait to get her alone. He needed feedback. But when was that going to be?

"You want one, Will?" she asked.

He tried to read her face — he was usually pretty good at that — but no luck. "I can —"

"I've got it," Faye said. "Sit down with your mom."

"Can you sit with us, Faye?"

Faye hesitated, then glanced behind herself as Liv appeared.

"Go ahead, Faye," Liv said. "I'll make them."

He had no problem reading that look. Liv suppressed a smile as Faye glared at her on the way past.

"I'll grab the butter tarts," Will said, so he didn't feel completely helpless, and prayed the sugar and caffeine would boost everyone's moods.

Was it awkward? Of course it was awkward. How was this supposed to go? Will felt like he should set the record straight, with Faye here. Tell his mom they *were* serious. But it turned out Nate was right. Because Will had failed to get that ring on Faye's finger, and in the process determine how she felt about their future, he didn't really have the authority to comment, did he?

Liv brought two cappuccinos over, moving with caution. Wordlessly, she placed one in front of Julia, sliding the other toward Faye.

"This is my best friend, Liv," Faye said, grabbing Liv's arm with a ferocity that made Liv's eyes bug out. Will glanced at Liv sympathetically.

"Nate's wife, right?" Julia said.

Liv seemed to flinch, like she still wasn't comfortable with that word, and then offered her hand.

"Nice to meet you, Dr Ackerman," she said. "I'll just get Will's cup." She dropped a look on Faye and twisted her arm free.

Will was scared something was going to blow up after Liv brought his cappuccino before disappearing, but they fell into small talk. His mom tried to find nice things to say about the very plain café, Faye asked her what there was to do in Calgary, and Will noted a longing in her eyes as Julia talked about the city. It made Will think he should have planned outings in Toronto rather than the quaint country events he'd taken her to. Faye lived in this small town; he should have realized she might want to get out of it when she managed time off.

"I should get back to work," Faye said when their plates and cups were empty.

Julia rested a hand on one of Will's. "Let me take you to lunch. Is there a nice restaurant nearby?"

They could have lunch at the café, but that wasn't what his mother meant. Will glanced at Faye, worried she would be offended by the fact she'd clearly been excluded.

But Faye said, "Have a lovely time," in a cheery tone, rising carefully and gathering dishes.

There was only one real option. Will took his mother to Hooligan's, in what served as downtown. It wasn't Mysticus, but the food was excellent and the service top notch.

"Do you come here often?" Julia asked once they were seated.

Will lifted the cloth napkin from the place setting and draped it over his lap. His grandmother — his mom's mom — had schooled him on that, growing up. He knew what all the forks were for, too. "We don't go out much."

"Why not?"

Will shrugged. "The café keeps Faye pretty busy, and I'm still in the city a lot." It sounded lame, but his mother didn't challenge him.

They ordered, and Julia stuck to drinking water so Will followed suit. There was more small talk. He asked about her work and told her about the espresso trailer.

"That's fun, Will. But what are your plans? Let's be honest. You're coasting. You're almost thirty. It's time."

Time? Time for what?

"You get that from your father," she continued. "Look at him. He still hasn't grown up."

Great.

His mom was right, though — his father still acted like he was twenty-five. Any day now, Will expected his dad to say he was divorcing his young wife of two years. Ashley was probably getting too old for him. Fatherhood had never been Ron Callaghan's forte.

"I really like Faye, but it's not as if you're going to marry her. You've been going out what, two and a bit years? If you're staying in Toronto for her, well... I'm just not sure I understand, that's all. She's obviously putting her business first."

It's. Our. Business. Isn't it? "That's great, coming from you Mom."

She'd always cared more about her career than her family. Will had a feeling Julia had only married because it was what she was supposed to do, and in her field she'd felt it was important to have a child by thirty because the risks increased, as a woman got older. She'd ticked that box off on her life plan, and then gone back to work.

"That's why I'm nearly sixty and single, isn't it?"

Yikes. How could she be almost sixty? Maybe that's what this was about. Maybe it had nothing to do with him and Faye at all.

"William."

Oh. No. His mother was the only one who called him William.

"Come back to Calgary. A friend of mine has just bought a restaurant. I was telling him about you. If you want to get serious about the restaurant business, this could be your chance."

Will was speechless. *What the actual...* but, it's what he should want, wasn't it? All that time at Mysticus, he'd dreamed of running his own fine dining establishment. Then he'd met Faye, and the café had happened — except that hadn't turned out the way he'd anticipated.

"Faye's very self-sufficient. She doesn't need you."

Which was too true. He'd figured that one out on his own, hadn't he?

"You're my only child. I'll be turning sixty the year you turn thirty. We'll be sharing milestones. Your life should be soaring as mine winds down. This is a tremendous opportunity."

"You look like you're forty, Mom. You look amazing."

Julia smiled sadly. "You've always been a sweet boy. I miss you, Will."

She'd succeeded in making him feel guilty. She wanted him closer — an unexpected sentiment from his independent mother. Julia hadn't said it outright, but the implication was there — she was getting older. She would need him one day.

Faye didn't need him. But he didn't need her to need him. They had a good thing. Here.

Or did they?

THIRTY-TWO

By afternoon, Faye's hangover had morphed into exhaustion. She felt as if she was running at a caffeine deficit; it had started when she'd missed her quick cup of toxic sludge before leaving the house and she had yet to catch up. Away even before Dean because Liv had driven her to the shop again, Faye hadn't wanted to wake Will's mom. Liv was an early riser, even when she didn't need to be.

Come on, Faye. The truth. You couldn't get out of the house soon enough this morning. Because if she'd woken Will, it would have gone one of two ways: either she'd have had to endure his wisecracks about getting drunk with his mom, or an inquisition covering what they'd discussed. First thing in the morning, Faye didn't want to talk to anyone. It suited her just fine that she was at the café an hour early, even if she could have used the sleep. She could count on Liv to leave her alone, and by the time Lucy showed up and Nate dropped off Connie — whom Liv didn't feel could be expected to come at dark o'clock — Faye had felt almost civilized. Good thing, because when the text from Will had come in that he was bringing his mother by, it wasn't as big a jump for her to be gracious.

She still couldn't believe Julia's words last night. Fine, the woman was welcome to her opinions about marriage and kids, but in the light of day, all of it felt like a thinly veiled insult. Faye had been too stunned — and too drunk — to respond properly.

The little sit-down she'd endured with Julia and Will — no thanks to Liv *(some best friend)* — had gone fine. And Faye did not feel slighted that Julia hadn't invited her for lunch. It was fair that the woman wanted to catch up with her son, and it wasn't as if Faye could disappear for the afternoon and leave her friends to carry the load yet again. They'd already been too generous with their time.

You totally feel slighted. Julia should *have at least asked, even if you would've had to decline.* It was carol night; Faye's to-do list was a mile long.

By the time Sylvie walked in, Faye had worked herself into a silent fury.

"What happened to you?" Sylvie asked, hanging up her coat and exchanging her slush-covered boots for dry running shoes.

Faye cast her a sour glance. "Will's mother kept me up late chatting."

Sylvie's eyes widened. "How did that go?"

"Let's just say it was interesting. I quite like her, actually. But I'm not sure drinking with your boyfriend's mother is a good thing to do."

"Why?" Sylvie laughed. "Did she tell you things you don't want to know? It wasn't just embarrassing baby photos and childhood stories?"

"No. She seemed to want to talk more about herself, actually."

"Oh. That's no fun."

It should have been. Faye was all for Julia's point of view. Or had been, once. What had happened to her?

Will had been raised by this woman — which explained a lot. It explained why they'd never seriously talked about all those things. Because if Faye wasn't bringing them up, neither was he. That was going to change.

"I'm sure you'll get to meet her and form your own opinion," Faye said. "She's coming tonight."

If Julia was trying to discourage Faye about those things — marriage, kids, *Will* — it was backfiring.

WHEN WILL SHOWED up with Nate, there wasn't really time to talk. He paused from their setup to kiss her, and Faye buried everything, writing off his distracted mood. He needed to prepare. To get in the zone, or whatever was necessary to sing and play guitar in front of a group of people. Faye had no time to worry about it. It could wait until later.

"Can I bring either of you anything?" she asked.

Will shook his head.

"Thanks, Faye," Nate said, and Faye thought he shot Will a look.

C'mon, guys. Just get along for the next few hours, all right? She was *so* looking forward to this night being over. Then there would only be two more days to get through. Or three, really, because Christmas Day would be no holiday.

The kitchen felt like controlled chaos. Faye enjoyed the unexpected company of all her friends, who made the madness bearable, but it would soon come to an end. Connie would go back to Calgary. Liv would go to Florida. Sylvie was finishing up her Masters and trying to decide if she was going to do a

PhD or find a job. Emilie would continue to be Emilie, popping in and out as her schedule allowed. Faye just wanted someone who was hers, all the time.

Will's voice reached her as he warmed up and she wanted to believe it was a sign.

Emilie had organized their bake-off. Sample-sized pieces of the three creations were plated and set on each table with voting slips, and they'd prompt the guests to rank the squares in order of preference. Whichever recipe won would be added to the menu for January. They were all good, so each could be used as a feature flavour in the following months.

Emilie had swapped flavours with Sylvie because she wanted to make a vegan Eggnog mousse square. Her boyfriend, Tim, was vegetarian, not vegan, but Em liked the idea of a challenge. The squares had a dark chocolate crust topped with the mousse, and more dark chocolate drizzled on top.

Sylvie's creation was like a reverse mint Nanaimo bar, with a golden crumb crust followed by a thin dark chocolate layer, glazed with mint white chocolate and a dusting of crushed candy canes.

Faye felt she'd cheated a bit with hers, adapting her ginger-bread loaf into a bar, the rich, dark base topped with molasses cream cheese icing, chunks of candied ginger sprinkled on top.

The event was sold out. They'd had to turn people away, or they'd have violated the fire code. Faye gave Emilie the okay to open the doors, and people steadily poured in, recorded music through the speakers welcoming them. Dean arrived with Julia, and Faye wondered what they'd talked about. As much as Dean lived and breathed horses, he was educated and could pull off normal conversation when needed. Just so long as Julia wasn't clocking him as a boy toy.

Once everyone was settled with drinks and Emilie and

Sylvie had gone from table to table explaining about the baking competition, Nate said some opening words, introducing himself and Will — and, Faye still couldn't believe, Tim. Then they started singing. The crowd readily joined in, warming the room so much Faye had to keep sticking her head out the back door to cool off.

"Another success," Faye said into Emilie's ear. "Great job."

"I'm just one member of the team," Emilie answered, smiling.

The guys did a balance of carols and secular songs, some easier to sing along to than others. A few less familiar tunes showcased how good the three of them were. Faye had never realized Tim could sing, though she only recognized it by the way the three of them harmonized.

Will's voice would always stand out to her, though, and she isolated it, letting it become the only one she heard. Other than the brief exchange when they'd initially met, his first words to her had been in song. Or that's what she'd let herself think, that night of the Queen's Plate party — that he was watching her as she watched him, singing to her as she danced for him — letting herself believe, for the briefest of moments, they were meant to be.

And Faye finally believed they were. The fury Julia had roused turned to determination.

This was her town. Always had been, though she'd never quite fit in anywhere in the horse-centric world until Will had helped her find her place with this café — not horsey, but serving her horsey friends and neighbors — giving her a kind of acceptance she'd never quite felt before then.

It wasn't flashy. It was steady, like Will was steady. And what could it be, if they were both fully committed to it? What could *they* be?

The only limit is your imagination.

They finished up with "Rockin' Around The Christmas Tree," which brought people to their feet, dancing — including Sylvie and Emilie and Connie — so Faye shrugged and joined in, as best she could with her gimpy leg. Even Julia tapped her fingers on the table, lips upturned, her head dipping in time to the beat.

The crowd was in no hurry to leave. Emilie and Sylvie went around and picked up the ballots for the baking challenge as people milled. There was a hum of holiday cheer. It was almost infectious, but Faye just wanted everyone to go home, so she could go home and have Will to herself.

She caught it out of the corner of her eye — Julia, slipping into her coat and pushing out the door with her phone pressed to her ear — and felt guilty for hoping it was the hospital in Calgary, calling the doctor back early.

"Where'd my mom go? Were we that bad?" Will quipped as he appeared at Faye's elbow.

"She went outside. She was on the phone." Faye flashed a smile, turning toward him and lacing her fingers behind his neck, pulling him down for a kiss. "You were fabulous."

But he raised an eyebrow, looking over her shoulder, then released her as Julia reappeared, placing a hand on Will's arm and drawing him aside.

Faye watched him as he stooped to listen; watched his expression change, his face falling before he hugged his mother. There were no tears from either of them, though they both looked solemn. It was the first time Faye had seen Will maintain any prolonged physical contact with his mother, an arm around her shoulders as he ushered her back over.

"My grandmother," Will said, meeting Faye's eyes. "Mom's mom. Mom just learned she's passed away."

"I'm so sorry, Julia," Faye said automatically, remembering how often those words had been directed at her after the car accident that had changed her life. She didn't feel comfortable enough with the woman for a physical display but stepped in to give Will a half-hug, all she could manage with the crowd around their little bubble.

"I'm going to wrap things up then take her to the house," Will said. "Talk when you get there?"

Faye nodded. "See you then."

She stood rooted as she watched him go over to Nate, Nate patting him on the arm and clearly telling Will he'd take care of it. Will met Faye's eyes once more before he held the door open, letting his mother through.

"What's going on?"

Faye jumped. She'd been too intent on their departure to hear Liv sneak up. "Julia just had a call." She glanced at Liv. "Her mother's passed away. Will's taking her back to the house. That's all I know for now."

"You go ahead, Faye," Liv said. "There are enough of us here to take care of things."

Faye shook her head. "I'll give them some time."

Maybe when she got home, Will would have answers to the questions pummelling her mind like a jackhammer. Would Julia go back to Calgary for the funeral? Would Will go with her?

If he went, would he be back for Christmas?

She was the last to leave, the one to put the key in the lock and secure it. Liv and Nate waited in their car until Faye climbed into Dean's truck. They followed Liv and Nate, Dean flashing his high beams goodbye as they turned up the Triple Stripe lane.

Will and Julia were in the kitchen. Will had made tea, her mother cradling a cup at the table as he sat opposite her. Even Gus was subdued.

Julia pushed herself up. "I'm going to get to bed. Thank you both for tonight. It was lovely." She smiled at Faye and Dean and Will kissed the cheek she proffered before she left the kitchen.

"I'm going to head up to bed too," Dean said, excusing himself.

Will sank back into a kitchen chair, gesturing at the pot. "Tea?"

Now that she knew his mother could hold her own with alcohol, Faye wondered why he'd opted for tea. Alcohol seemed an appropriate choice after news of a loved one's death. But if he was staying sober, so was she.

"Yes. Thanks."

She found a cup and sat adjacent to him. Will poured from the old teapot and regressed into silence.

"I'm sorry about your grandmother," she said, because she realized she'd only offered Julia condolences. Even if they felt like empty words, they needed to be spoken.

"Thanks. It's not like we were close."

"So tell me what's going on," she said, reaching for his hand. "This wasn't a sudden thing, I take it."

"No. She'd been failing for a while. Obviously my mother didn't think it was imminent or she wouldn't have planned to come. The timing's inconvenient... but I'm going to go back to Calgary with her. She doesn't have anyone else. Even if it wasn't entirely unexpected, I wouldn't want her to be alone."

"Of course not. I would go too, if I could. But like you said, inconvenient timing."

His eyes snagged hers, flickering with appreciation. "We'll leave tomorrow. Funeral's the twenty-third. Fly back the twenty-fourth." He propped his elbows on the table, head in his hands. "Yep, the timing sucks."

She tried to hide her relief that he'd said he'd be back for Christmas, and it surprised her how much that mattered.

"How was lunch?" she asked.

"It was weird. She wants me to move back there. Has it all planned out." He rolled his eyes. "A friend of hers just bought a restaurant. She thinks I should interview for the manager's job."

And he didn't seem to be dismissing the prospect. This was a hard left-hand turn. "You're actually thinking about it," she said.

Will didn't speak, just slid her a miserable look.

"Is that what you want?" Faye asked, intent on sounding civil when she was seething at Julia — and at Will. *Your mother brings out the worst in you.* "If it is, go for an interview. Spend some time with your mom. Maybe it's high time you figured out what you want from life."

"I guess that tells me everything I need to know."

"What's that supposed to mean?"

"Nothing," he muttered.

He looked frustrated, like he wanted to leave, go back to his place in the city, but it wasn't as if he could do that with his mother staying here. *Go, and take her with you,* Faye felt like saying. But they were stuck in this. No childish stomping away.

"I don't want you to move back to Calgary, Will. Is that clearer? I want you here. I want us to figure out what we're going to be. But if that's not what you want, I won't hold you back."

How had she been so totally wrong about him? Maybe Will *was* her rebound guy after all, and she'd end up true to type. Go back to having meaningless flings, because clearly she was not good at relationships.

Say something, damn it. But Will remained silently sullen.

"I love you, Will, but I'm not moving to Calgary. I've

worked too hard to finally find myself. To find my purpose. I don't want to start over."

Will's gaze remained fixed on his teacup. "This is not how I thought tonight would end."

"Yeah. Me neither."

Was this really happening again? Losing the guy she loved to another woman? With Nate, it had been Liv. But Will's mother? That was worse.

THIRTY-THREE

Will couldn't believe how far off track things had gone; never would have imagined his mother's visit would send everything off course. *It'll be fine,* he'd told Faye. But it was not fine. Nothing was fine. At least Faye and his mother seemed to get along. If sharing a bottle of wine wasn't bonding, Will didn't know what was.

When they reached the airport, he parked the car, trying not to think how much that was going to cost. There wasn't much to retrieve from the hatch, just carry-ons for each of them and a garment bag. Dean had loaned Will a suit, so he didn't have to go downtown to get his. Will had tried it on at the farmhouse, and it fit well enough to get by.

"I need a coffee," he said once they were in the terminal. "Would you like one?"

Julia shook her head. As he stood in line, his phone pinged with a text from Nate. *You are coming back, right?*

Will frowned, thumbing in the response. *What makes you think I wouldn't?*

Just making sure.

He'd told Nate about lunch with his mom. It unnerved him that both his best friend and his girlfriend were worried his mother might convince him he wanted to run that restaurant. But two days ago, he'd been planning to propose to Faye, and today he felt as if life had turned the tables on him. Did he even know what he wanted?

Once they were in the air, Will pulled out the box of samples Faye had packed for him because he hadn't had the chance to try the new recipes last night. She was so amicable. No resentment. Letting him decide what was important to him when she'd made it clear what was important to her.

Faye was good at breakups. She'd had more practice than him. But this wasn't a breakup. He was just honouring his mother and grandmother. The restaurant prospect Julia had dangled in front of him was just an annoying taunt. She'd been so supportive of what Will was sure she deemed poor life decisions. He had to go for the funeral; what would it hurt, talking to her friend who owned the restaurant? Except he knew it had hurt Faye. He hadn't done a good enough job of assuring her that wasn't what he wanted. No, it was worse than that. He hadn't even made an attempt.

Well. Thanks to technology, he'd just have to send her repeated reminders that he was devoted to her.

He held the box out to his mother, but Julia shook her head.

"I tried them last night. They're all exceptional. Be sure to vote. My favourite is the gingerbread." She went back to her book.

Will raised an eyebrow. Mint had always been Julia's favourite flavour. The gingerbread was Faye's contribution to the challenge. Was that subliminal approval? He laughed when there was, indeed, a voting slip in the box. Will didn't need to taste them to know himself: he'd vote for Faye, every time.

He lifted one of the deep brown squares with its off-white icing and popped it into his mouth, revelling in the cream cheese with a hint of molasses in the frosting, the mix of ginger, cinnamon, allspice and cloves in the bottom, the sharp hint of heat from the candied ginger on top. Spicy, just like Faye. Will closed the box with the slip between his fingers, dug a pen from his backpack and checked the square next to her creation. Then he snapped a photo of it with his phone and sent it to her. *You win, hands down.* ♥

Hmm. How wrong would it be to propose via text? He was just desperate enough to try, though it could be excruciating waiting for a response.

There was nothing from Faye when they landed. His mom's car was at the Calgary airport, the candy apple red Lexus a giant step up from his rusty Camaro. What else was Julia going to spend money on but her son and nice things?

Julia drove straight to the funeral home, but they didn't spend long there — the details had been pre-arranged long ago, when his grandmother had still been able to make such decisions. Practical people, the women in his life. The service would be at eleven AM tomorrow, and after that, they'd go for lunch — at his mother's friend's restaurant.

From the funeral home, they went to his mother's condo. Though Will had visited before, the contrast between Julia's minimalistic style and the comfort of Faye and Dean's century farmhouse was more glaring this time, somehow. He knew Faye had been self-conscious about his mother staying at the Taylor's home, but Will didn't know how Julia could stand this. It was so stark. Will would go crazy living here. He almost felt like he should sleep on the floor instead of the couch. His mother had turned the second bedroom into her office and reading room instead of a guest room. While she was always pleased to see him when he managed to visit, she didn't constantly pester him to come. It was as if she didn't want anyone to stay for long.

He didn't miss Calgary like Nate seemed to — at least since Nate had come to terms with his past. Being here just reminded Will why he'd wanted to leave: his parents' divorce, the accidental death of his first crush, his grandfather selling the farm Will had loved so much as a kid. He missed the mountains, as he'd confessed to Dean, but that was it. Maybe if he'd grown up in a home like Nate's, he'd feel differently. Will had found his family when he'd started seeing Faye, like his inclusion in that household helped Faye and Dean make up for what they'd lost while filling a void in himself he'd never acknowledged he had. What had made him think he didn't belong? Had it just been in his head? Faye had said it last night, point blank. *I love you and I want you here.* What more did he need than that?

But Faye wouldn't make a scene, cling to him like some distraught heroine in a fifties movie. Take me or leave me, that was Faye. Well — not take me to Calgary. She'd clearly drawn that line.

He checked his phone for messages while his mom retreated to her office. There was the photo and note to Faye, sitting there, unsent. *Idiot.* He couldn't even send a cute text properly. What had seemed endearing at thirty-five thousand feet felt juvenile now. He deleted it, typing — and sending — *At Mom's condo. And yes, it's everything you imagined it to be.* She sent back a laughing emoji.

Then he changed his mind. He found the photo of the ballot slip and added the words. *You win, hands down.* ♥ And this time, he made sure he hit send.

~

THE SERVICE WAS nothing like the last funeral Will had been to in Calgary. It lacked emotion, as if Julia had grieved for her mother long ago and this was merely a formality. Claudia Ackerman had lived a long and full life — to the point she'd outlasted all of her friends — so the only ones present were Will and his mom and some of the staff at the home where Claudia had spent her final year. It made Will think he should have offered to sing to add something personal, like he and Nate had done after Nate's brother- and sister-in-law had died, that service a true celebration of life with tears and singing, a mishmash of souvenirs and sorrow. When the service concluded, Julia introduced Will to the care workers, thanking them, exchanged words with the funeral director, then swept Will off to lunch. All of it seemed too neat and tidy to Will, but that was his mother, wasn't it?

The restaurant's decor was country chic, giving it a warm, rustic feel. *Nice.* Drinks were ordered, then Will scanned the menu, automatically assessing — contemplating both what impressed him and what was missing. *Backroads,* as it was called, boasted farm to table dining, but there was only one vegetarian main course option — something Will was more cognizant of than he used to be since Nate's brother, Tim, didn't eat flesh anymore. Sure, this was Alberta, where beef was king, but these days it was important to have a decent selection of alternatives. People visited Calgary from all over the world.

His mother's friend appeared before their meals arrived, greeting Julia with a brief hug and a kiss on the cheek — so, not a love interest, Will deduced, which had been his first thought. The man was well dressed and trim and wore a wedding band. Will wondered if his mother would ever remarry, or if she was content on her own.

"You must be Will," the man said, thrusting a hand out.

"Malcolm Russell. Enjoy the food, and I'll show you around the place afterward. We'll talk."

Will nodded and sat down after pressing his palm to Malcolm's, feeling like he should tell the man not to go to the trouble, except there was a pleased curl to his mother's lips. The least he could do for her was go along with it for a while. Besides, it would give him time to compose his speech.

The food was good, and they shared a piece of Basque cheesecake for dessert. Will went through the motions during the tour, murmuring appropriate things, thanked Malcolm at the end, and agreed they'd touch base after the holidays. For once, the circumstances worked in Will's favour — Malcolm didn't expect him to decide on the spot — but Will already knew what his answer was. He just felt he owed it to his mother to let her know first, privately.

Will was exhausted, his body still on Toronto time, the big meal making him wish he could take a nap. He forced himself to sit up straighter and drew in a fortifying breath. Julia had thought she was doing the right thing, hooking him up with her restaurant-owner friend. And it was a great place. The owner was a great guy. And Calgary was a great town. It just wasn't his town, anymore.

Julia surprised him by speaking first. "You're not going to take the job, are you?"

Her tone, her face, were not that of his mother, the respected doctor; this was a rare appearance of his mother, the mom. The one who had supplemented his finances when he'd moved cross-country on a path she didn't exactly agree with but refused to get in the way of. The one who gave him too-generous monetary gifts at Christmas and on his birthday — and on other random occasions — just because. The one who, just maybe, harboured a bit of regret, deep down, that she hadn't followed a less conventional road.

"I like the idea," he started. "But that restaurant would never be mine. I want something that's mine. And you know what? I have that already, with Faye — thanks to you, remember? So it's not a fine dining establishment, and I'm not as hands-on as she is. I *have* been coasting. But that's gonna change. I've been thinking about starting a catering business that would complement the café." He glanced over at her cautiously, but her expression showed something like respect — so he went on. "And that whole thing about you getting old and needing me? Come on. We're not there yet."

She laughed. "I'm sorry, that was a little much. But I do wish you were closer."

"I do too, but I am just a five-hour flight away." He thought she almost looked chastised for taking so long to visit him in Ontario. "I'm going back to Toronto, Mom, but if you want to stay here, that's okay. You've met Faye now. I understand if you don't want to be there for Christmas."

Julia pressed her lips together and gripped the wheel. "Of course I'm coming with you. You kids have worked so hard to put this dinner together, and I've already got the time off. If I stay here, they'll just rope me into working somehow, and that's happened quite enough in my career, thank you."

Will grinned, knowing that might be as close to an apology as he got.

CHAPTER
THIRTY-FOUR

How could she go from being overrun with help to this? Faye was not getting out of the café at six today. Emilie was working, Sylvie was out with her boyfriend at some Christmas do, Lucy was tending to her mother, and Faye had chased Liv and Connie away because they'd already done too much. Then there was Will, who wasn't even in the province. All of it left her feeling very sorry for herself.

Just one more day.

Other than letting her know he'd arrived, and that cute comment with the picture of the voting ballot last night, she hadn't heard from Will. She didn't want to read anything into his words — *You win, every time* — and kept from texting him every five minutes like a teenager, even though she wanted to. He needed space to figure things out. The way he'd always talked about Calgary, Faye never would have imagined he'd want to move back. Was he actually considering it? How could he even do that? Maybe that's what stung the most.

Why had it taken *this* for her to realize what she wanted? Now it might be too late.

In the dying hours of the afternoon, people came, dusting fluffy snowflakes from their shoulders and arms. Some were cheery, some grumpy. Most of them were picking up orders, though a few were there for a sugar or caffeine boost. One woman called in to ask if she could come after six to get her order, and Faye had agreed without hesitation. Why not? She'd still be here. At least someone should get what they wanted right now.

Times like these, she wished she had a cot in the back so she could just sleep over. Dean was home, so she didn't have to worry about Gus. She had everything she really needed here — food, coffee, even a toothbrush. All that was missing was a bed. The one at home wasn't as enticing as she'd like at the moment.

Faye forced a smile and exchanged *Merry Christmases* as she passed boxes to the latest patron, then dashed back to the kitchen to make sure the final ones were ready. Earlier than she expected — two minutes before six — the door chimed. She slipped the boxes into a bag to shield them from the snowfall's dampness. Boxboard did not hold up well to moisture.

Faye pushed through the door, looking into the shop, and stopped in her tracks. The customer she was expecting was a regular. It definitely wasn't her.

"Pat?" She set the box next to the cash register, staring at the short, slight man who'd entered, his gaze still taking in the surrounding decorations and artwork before landing on her.

"Hi, Faye. How have you been?"

"Good," she responded, drawing it out. Faye couldn't remember the last time she'd talked to him and kept herself behind the counter so there would be no chance of him trying to hug her. "Yourself?"

Pat shrugged with half a smile. "Okay. This place is nice. I haven't been in here in years, and it looks a lot better than it did back then."

Faye was glad Lucy wasn't around to hear that comment, even if she heard it often enough. "Well, thanks. What inspired your visit today?"

"I was driving by, and thought it was high time I came in."

There had been a time Faye had found Pat Simon more than attractive. Irresistible, even. What was it, eight years ago now? Or seven? She'd lost track. They'd had a lot of fun. He'd played by her rules. Short, sweet; there for a good time, not a long time. He'd been riding a wave of apprentice jockey success and Faye had happily tagged along — then let him go before either of them started thinking it was more than it was. Pat had found someone new to entertain him soon enough, and Faye had felt relief instead of sadness when he'd married that one. She was pretty sure he was on to wife number two now. Or had she heard they'd split up? She wasn't as up on racetrack gossip as she used to be. Either way, each woman had a kid with him. Faye had been *so* young when they'd been together, but thank goodness she'd been smart enough to keep their association safe and brief.

"What are you doing this winter?" she asked, because that was what you asked racetrack people.

He shrugged. "I'm taking a few weeks off. In January I'll go to one of the training centres and leg up horses until the back-stretch opens in February. Can't afford to fall too far out of shape."

Should she offer him a coffee? She didn't want to, in case it meant reliving any of their past. Still, she couldn't just chase him away. This was a bad time of year for some people. "Do you have plans for Christmas?" She hoped he wasn't here because he was hanging by a thread, but if she learned later he was she'd hate herself for not asking.

Pat seemed surprised by her question. "Friends have invited me over. Then I'll get some time with the kids between Christmas and New Year's. What are you doing?"

"Having dinner with Liv and Nate." Not a lie, but the whole truth was too complex to share.

"That'll be nice."

Faye wasn't sure it would be, especially if Will decided to stay in Calgary with his mom after all.

"You okay then?" she asked. If he wasn't, would he tell her? And if he did, what would she do?

"Yeah I am, Faye. Thanks for asking. You?"

She smiled. "Looking forward to a break. This month has been crazy."

The customer she'd been waiting for came through the door before Faye had figured out what to say next — hopefully something that would inspire Pat to go. When the woman left, Faye followed her to the door and paused, fingers curled around the handle. She wanted to lock it so no one else could come in, but needed Pat out first. Glancing out at the parking lot, she didn't see any cars but her own and what she assumed to be his, so she went back to the counter, formed a box, and picked a selection of what was left in the display case.

"It was nice of you to pop in and say hi, Pat, and I'm sorry to push you out the door, but I close at six. Take some treats with you."

His face brightened as she handed him the box. "Thank you. What do I owe you?"

Faye waved him off. She knew he wasn't broke — he still won a decent number of races — but what she'd given him were essentially day-olds. "On the house. Merry Christmas."

"Same to you, Faye. Thanks again."

When he was safely on the other side of the door, she bolted it and turned off the neon "open" sign with a sigh of relief, leaning against the wall. She needed a second to shake off the strangeness of it. That was too weird. Pat's unexpected visit was an unwelcome blast from the past, stirring up memories of her old self. Was this when she reverted to who she was really destined to be — hot spinster, cougar extraordinaire? She shuddered. Will needed to come back to save her from a life of non-relationships.

Faye leapt with a yelp as something tapped against the glass next to her, her pulse shooting through the roof. When she saw it was Nate, peering in with a little wave, she pressed a hand to her chest, willing her heart to settle down. With a click she unlocked the door, but locked it again immediately after he was inside.

"You look like you've seen a ghost," Nate said.

That's two of you, she almost replied. The exes of Christmas past. "Sorry, you spooked me."

"I thought I could pick up some stuff to save time tomorrow."

"Did Liv send you?"

"She said you banished her and my Mom."

Faye gave him a lopsided smile. "That was probably stupid."

Nate shrugged. "Stupidity masked as selflessness. I get it."

"Let's not psychoanalyze me right now, okay?" Some grad student could probably make a project of her.

"Okay," he agreed with a wry smile. "Is there anything else I can do?"

"Not really, but I appreciate you asking. Taking some stuff tonight will make me feel as if we're ahead of the game, so thanks."

He'd brought Liv's Nissan, and they carried out everything

Faye could send with him and set it all in the back. Nate pushed the hatch shut.

"Are you nearly done?" he asked, jamming his hands in his jacket pockets.

"I'm not going to be done until January," she quipped.

"Why don't you close up and go home, Faye? Is there really anything that can't wait till tomorrow?"

She pressed her lips together, a slight tilt to her head as she considered. "I guess not."

"Go, then. I'll wait."

It was a beat before she moved with a nod. She put away everything in the display case that needed to be refrigerated, packed what remained into two boxes, straightened up in the kitchen, then slipped on her coat. When she returned to the parking lot, Nate had knocked the snow off her car.

"Thanks," she said.

"I should have grabbed your keys to start it for you."

"Take these." She handed him one of the boxes then unlocked the car door, setting the one she'd take home to Dean behind the seat.

"He's coming back, Faye," Nate's voice stopped her before she climbed in. "And he'll do the right thing."

One of her eyebrows crept up — because she was, apparently, transparent — and stopped herself from asking how he knew. "Have you heard from him?"

"No. My dad got in today, so I'm dealing with my own special torment." He grinned. "See you tomorrow, I'm sure." He waited until she tucked her legs in and had started the Corolla before swinging the door shut.

Faye huddled behind the wheel as she let the vehicle warm up, peering through the windshield at the Nissan, Nate not moving until she put her car in gear and drove out. She didn't need him to follow her almost all the way home — she'd recovered from the scare — but it was thoughtful.

The old red-brick Northwest farmhouse looked straight off a Christmas card, dressed with snow and coloured bulbs, the windows yellow with the warmth of light from within. Gus gave her his usual welcome and Dean appeared as she set the box of treats on the counter.

"Is that for us to eat now?" he asked, wandering over.

"Help yourself."

After perusing the contents for a moment, he did. "There's some salad in the fridge, and I made a pasta casserole for dinner if you want some."

Faye nodded; she should eat. Her diet had been less than ideal for the past few weeks. The salad was in a plastic container and she dribbled dressing over it, gave it a shake and grabbed a fork, not bothering to put it in a dish as she leaned back against the counter. Gus flopped on the floor between her and Dean.

"When's Will's flight get in tomorrow?" Dean asked, already dipping into the box for another square.

"Afternoon. Three, I think." Faye covered her mouth as she spoke, then kept chewing.

"Maybe his mom won't come back with him," Dean said.

She set the salad aside to pick a glass from the cupboard for water. "That crossed my mind. It doesn't matter either way. The scary part is over." The end of the holiday madness was near. The verdict on her happily ever after was still out there.

"Come here," Dean said, motioning for her to follow.

He dropped into the office chair in front of the desk and extracted what resembled an old cigar box from the bottom drawer, some relic from another time.

Dean handed it to her, saying, "Open it."

Faye accepted it, but hesitated. It felt like Pandora's Box.

Dean's gaze remained steady on her. With a deep inhale, she cracked the lid, the hinges creaking.

Her breath caught in her throat, recognizing the contents. Her parents' wedding rings. The necklace her mother had been wearing when she died. Dean had been the one to pick up their effects. Faye had blocked most of it from her mind — the days, weeks, months, following their deaths foggy with only rare glimpses sharpening into focus. She thought of her mom's engagement ring in the jewellery box on her dresser upstairs and felt the urge to go get it so all these things could be together.

"I just thought," he said. "If you needed a ring. To go with a question. And I'd keep the other one, because who knows, right?"

Faye's mouth opened, then closed again, imagining. "Right. Who knows?"

THIRTY-FIVE

It was still dark when Will's phone woke him up. He squinted at the screen, groggy. Lara, Lemon's owner, had called. The phone pinged a second time with a voicemail notification, then a third time with a text.

Stuck in Seattle. Can you keep Clem? Pls call me.

He pushed himself upright and turned so he was sitting on the couch. Lara was on Pacific Time. Five AM for her was six AM for him — and eight AM for his body. Faye would've already been at the café for a while by now. He hit Lara's number, and she picked up on the second ring.

"Will! I'm so sorry. There's a big snowstorm and my flight is grounded. Christmas Eve, can you believe it?"

He could believe anything this year, but he wasn't going to say. "So you need me to look after Clementine a little longer. That's fine." He didn't tell her that technically Monique was looking after Lemon right now.

"There's more." Lara sighed. "I wanted to talk to you in person. The company wants to transfer me out here. It's an offer I can't refuse but I'm torn about Clementine. I'm worried at her age the flight would be too stressful for her."

Will would take a car cross country if that's what it took to keep Lemon happy — but truth was, that would be stressful, too.

"I've thought a lot about this. I know how much she loves you." Lara's voice was breaking up, and she paused. "Would you consider taking her? Keep her as your own? If you say no, I'll bring her — maybe the vet can give me drugs for her to make it easier — but there's no one I would trust with her except you."

If that was what being driven was about — moving far away and not taking your four-legged companion — Will didn't want any part of it. But he wasn't sure he could judge Lara, either. A selfish voice in his head told him Lemon was content with him. She *was* getting older. She already deserved more consistency than Lara gave her. And darn it, if this thing with Faye was done, at least he'd have someone to comfort him while he got over it.

"I'm honoured you asked me, Lara. And it would be a pleasure to have her. But only if you're sure."

He could hear Lara sniffling on the other end of the line. "Thank you, Will. I know she'll be happy with you."

Will couldn't get back to sleep after that. He switched on his mom's TV and turned the volume low. The storm on the west coast was pummelling both Seattle and Vancouver, places people moved to in order to get away from the cold. *Climate change,* he thought. Emilie would be proud he'd used the right words.

He went to the kitchen and studied his mother's pod-tree of Keurig flavours and selected a dark roast. It was probably better than Dean's black sludge, but couldn't touch Faye's cappuccino. He was sitting on a stool at the island when his mother surfaced. She was an early riser when she wasn't hungover.

She cupped a mug with the hospital's logo on it after making her own coffee. "What's new in the world today?"

"Big snowstorm on the west coast is making a mess for travellers."

Julia nodded. "If that's the biggest news, that's not so bad. Have you checked our flight yet? It could be affected."

He hadn't thought of that, and his heart beat a bit faster. He was so eager to get back to Ontario he'd checked them in online last night and already had the boarding passes.

Nope. No delay. The flight was still scheduled for nine, bringing them into Toronto at just before three in the afternoon. Will exhaled. "Leave for the airport in half an hour?"

There was a knowingness to his mother's smile. "I'll get ready."

CHAPTER
THIRTY-SIX

Faye was beginning to dread the shop door's jangle. It summoned her once more and she grimaced, peeking out from the kitchen before pushing through. She plastered on her best *it's-Christmas-Eve-but-honestly-I'm-not-totally-stressed-out* smile and strode into the front.

A young woman, tall and slender, stood on the mat, eyes darting around the shop as she wiped her feet and pulled off gloves. The long, blonde, hair falling to her shoulders was partially covered with a knit hat, pinks and purples and greens woven into black. Black skinny jeans and a short black jacket made the most of her figure. Pretty face. Probably in her mid-twenties. And something about her was familiar.

"Good morning!" Faye said, hoping her tone matched her smile and not her frame of mind. *Where have I seen her before?*

The woman's smile was less confident — just lips, no teeth. She seemed to reset herself, pulling her shoulders back as she approached the counter.

"Hi. Merry — Happy — Season's Greetings," she said, her lips twisting slightly.

Faye had to laugh. "Thanks. Same to you."

"You're Faye, right?"

Faye tipped her head to the side slightly, imagining the lines forming on her forehead as it tightened. "Yes. Have we met?" she asked, hoping the woman would solve the mystery.

The blonde thrust out a hand. "We have, actually. I'm Monique. I'm a friend of Will's. We met at a Dave Matthews concert a couple of years ago."

Faye nearly slapped her forehead. *Yes. I should have remembered, especially as I've recently cyber-stalked you.* "I knew you looked familiar. What brings you up this way?"

"Will said you're looking for help. I saw the ad on a job site, but I thought, because of the connection, I'd make the drive."

On Christmas Eve? "Don't you live in the city?"

"I'm thinking of relocating."

Faye controlled her expression, feeling she must be missing part of the story. "You know Will through the restaurant business, right?"

"Yes. We worked together at Mysticus and did some of the same catering jobs this year."

Her references would be easy enough to check. But why would someone who worked at a place like Mysticus — and surely, especially because of her looks, made good money in tips — want out of the city? Faye knew from Will that restaurant was toxic, but it wasn't the only fine dining establishment in Toronto. Good servers were hard to find; someone like Monique should be able to get a different job without a problem.

"Can we sit and chat?" Faye asked. "Would you like a cappuccino?"

Monique nodded. "Thank you." She looked around as Faye prepared the machine. "This place is really cute."

"Thanks. Can I tempt you with anything else?"

Monique broke into a genuine smile this time. "The way Will has raved about your butter tarts, I don't think I can leave without trying one."

Faye grinned. "Everything *is* better with butter tarts." She handed Monique a plate once the drinks were ready and led the way to a table in the corner. Her ankle really only felt stiff today so she'd ditched the crutches. "You're serious about moving out here?"

"I've got to be honest," Monique said. "I'm a little displaced right now."

Displaced? That didn't mean homeless, did it? "When could you start?" Faye blurted.

"Really?" Monique said, sitting straighter, hope replacing dejection on her face. "I have a few catering jobs yet between Christmas and New Year's, but come January I'm free and clear."

"Does Will know you're here?"

"I didn't tell him. He'd figure out something was not-right and make a fuss." Monique rolled her eyes. "He's already letting me stay at his place because he said he'd be here with you."

Faye had to smile. He really was too nice a guy for her. "I have to admit, I thought the day at the concert that maybe you two were together. I'd only just met him at that point."

"But you liked him, didn't you?" Monique teased.

From the moment she'd seen him at the Triple Stripe Queen's Plate party, Faye had never denied her attraction to Will, but, "Like is a strong word, or was for me at that stage of things. It was more about lust." A smile tugged at one corner of her mouth. "I was really just hoping for a bit of fun. He totally messed up my plan. Short and sweet was always my go-to before a couple of Calgary boys came along and disrupted my life."

"A couple?"

"Yes. I dated Will's best friend for nine months before that ran its course. He ended up marrying *my* best friend — and we're still best friends — crazy, right?"

Monique grinned. "Should I be heading to Calgary, then? Is that where the good guys are?" Then she dropped her eyes, shoulders slumping. "I'm so tired of the city."

Maybe in time Faye would learn the rest of Monique's story — what had brought her to this point — but all Faye could think right now was that her good guy, her Calgary boy, was still there instead of here.

She glanced at the clock on the wall, needed to wrap this up and get back to work, but she had to ask, "Do you have a place to go for Christmas, Monique?"

Monique looked surprised by the question. "Well, I won't be out on the street, if that's what you mean."

"No, it's not." Okay, it had been, partly. Faye was glad to know that wasn't the case. "You can come hang out with us, if you like. It's going to be a little insane, but if you can deal with that, you're welcome." Faye would run it past Liv, but didn't expect it would be a problem. What was one more, at this point?

Monique hesitated a beat before answering. "I'd like that, thank you."

"That's settled, then. You can stay over so you don't have to drive back to the city, if you don't mind sleeping on the couch. Stick around and help out this afternoon, though we might need traffic lights to keep from bumping into each other in the kitchen. Consider it your trial. If we don't hate each other after that, we'll talk more about the job."

Monique popped to her feet. "Put me to work!"

Faye rose more slowly, envying Monique's burst of energy. "Come with me."

She led the way to the kitchen, Monique producing an elastic and putting up her hair as Faye made introductions.

"This is Monique. She's applying for the job and is going to help out this afternoon." Then Faye gestured toward her mercy crew. "And these are my friends, without whom I'd be crying in a corner right now. They'll all be rooting for you to succeed so they can go back to their respective lives."

Monique dove right in without hesitation. She already knew how to work the point-of-sale and after watching her during a couple of interactions with customers, Faye let her take over. Monique was a natural. She chatted easily, often slipping in an effortless upsell so they spent more money. She knew how to operate the espresso machine and make all the drink variations.

Within an hour, Faye already didn't want to let her go.

THIRTY-SEVEN

He should have known better. Should have checked the flight again before they left the condo. Will compared the information on his phone to the monitor in the terminal, its screen plagued with delays. Outside, Calgary was all blue skies, but things were less friendly in Vancouver, pushing their flight from nine to eleven, which would now put them in Toronto at just before five.

"Do you want to go back to the condo?" Julia asked him.

"I'm fine waiting here if you are." The way things were going, he was terrified that if they left, something random would prevent them from getting back. It was safer to stay right here.

"All right," his mother said.

Will tried calling Faye but wasn't surprised when it went to voicemail. She'd be dealing with all the last minute tasks both for the shop and for dinner tomorrow and he felt badly again he'd deserted her when she needed help the most. His long-winded message was cut off with a rude beep, so he followed it with an equally rambling text relaying the exact same information.

When his phone rang, his heart leapt at the thought of hearing her voice, so he couldn't keep from scowling when he saw the name on the screen.

"Dad. How are you." He didn't frame it as a question or bother offering a seasonal greeting.

"I'm well, son. What are you up to?" his father asked.

I could ask you the same, because you're up to something, aren't you? "I'm with Mom."

His father coughed on the other end of the line. "Oh, that's nice," he said when he recovered. "In Calgary?"

"Yes. Grandma Ackerman passed away. We're here for the funeral."

There was dead air for a beat before his father responded. "I'm sorry to hear that. Pass on my condolences to Julia."

Will almost handed the phone to his mother so his dad could tell her himself. Still passive aggressive, after all these years.

"You're spending Christmas there, then, I assume."

"Actually, she's coming back to Toronto with me." Will didn't bother with the full story. There was no point.

"That answers my question."

"What, Dad?" Will snapped. There was no helping it now.

"We were going to spend Christmas with Ashley's family in Burlington, but they're all down with the flu. I thought I'd call you on the off chance you didn't have big plans."

Was he really suggesting Will invite them to dinner?

"Listen, Dad, I'm getting another call," he lied. "Can I call you back in five?" He disconnected, eyes falling on his mother.

"How is your father?" Julia asked in her best disinterested tone.

Everything right now is a mess, so, hey! Why not make a bigger mess? "I'm going to invite him and Ashley to Christmas dinner. Can you deal with that?"

He didn't miss how her eyes widened before she blinked and looked back at her book "That's fine. But aren't you going to check with Faye?"

He brought up Faye's number and poked the screen, hoping this time she picked up. "That's what I'm doing right now."

It felt like a miracle when she answered. "Hey, what's the latest?" Faye sounded surprisingly upbeat — no pain, no anger, no sadness in her voice. Either she was pretending well — acting because she had people there — or she didn't miss him like he missed her.

"I'm going to ask you something crazy."

Her laugh was light. "Let me have it."

"Can I invite my dad and his wife to dinner?"

The next laugh was almost like a surrender. "The more the merrier, right? Let me just check it's okay with Liv and Nate. We *are* going to be at their house."

"All right. Let me know. See you soon." He clamped his tongue between his teeth to keep from adding *Love you,* then kicked himself for not doing it. Julia remained silent as he waited to hear back. He'd kill to be sitting at the bar with a beer right now. Five beers, and a ticket to Jamaica. Forget freaking Christmas. They could have it without him.

His phone pinged, and he glanced at Faye's text. *Let's do it.* He grinned, letting himself think she was agreeing to Jamaica, not the most insane Christmas he could think of.

"Will?"

He snapped from his phone to his mother's face, and didn't like her expression. "What?"

"The flight's delayed again. They're saying three, now."

Will groaned. Three o'clock in the afternoon? That meant

they wouldn't get to Toronto until nearly nine. And what if the storm found its way over the Rockies and made things worse? He checked the weather app and snow wasn't predicted, but this was Alberta. It could change in a heartbeat.

He started by texting his father to say dinner was okay and felt a twinge of glee at the thought of being stuck in Calgary and missing it — but he couldn't wish that on Faye and his friends. Then he texted Nate to bring him up to speed. Finally, he texted Faye.

Her response came shortly after. *Just get home when you can.*

Home. He liked the sound of that.

CHAPTER
THIRTY-EIGHT

At four o'clock, Connie taped a sign on the door that said SOLD OUT. It wasn't exactly true, but close enough — and it would deter any last-minute shoppers, so Faye wasn't going to argue.

Her phone pinged all afternoon with updates, like Will wanted to reassure her he was trying his hardest to get home when it was completely out of his control. The last one — at four-thirty — had been the most important one. *Boarding!!!*

Which meant, landing at ten-thirty. Faye glanced at the weather app. There was a bit of snow in the forecast, but nothing like was causing the delays out west, so it should be fine. *Please be fine.*

Connie had whipped them all into shape today, as if she needed an outlet for her indignation — which had surfaced upon her husband's arrival. Faye couldn't figure out how Reid Miller could cause anyone that much angst — he was quiet, much like Tim — but after thirty-something years of marriage, maybe a man could get on his wife's nerves just by existing.

It had been Nate's idea to offer free delivery for the outstanding orders, so he'd volunteered to drive around with a hatch full of baked goods for anyone who was willing to send Faye e-transfers to pay. Implementing online ordering was moving to the top of her January to-do list.

At five to six — with Connie's insistence that it was all right smoothing over Faye's reluctance — she locked the door and leaned against it. They'd made it. Faye felt she should break out champagne to thank her wonderful makeshift team, but, besides not having any, everyone was eager to get home. All of them except Sylvie would be at dinner tomorrow, so they'd celebrate then.

"You sure you and Chad don't want to come?" Faye asked. "You'd have to bring Roger and Hélène too, of course." Because what would be four more?

Sylvie laughed. "Thank you, but because my mother feels like we missed Christmas last year when she was so ill, she has a huge day planned, and Chad's parents are coming over tonight for our *Réveillon*."

"Is there anyone you haven't invited?" Nate quipped.

"Yes," Faye said with a smirk. "Pat Simon."

"Was that him who I saw leaving last night?" Nate asked, grinning, like maybe now he understood why she'd looked like she'd seen a ghost.

Faye just nodded. "If there's not going to be champagne, let's all get out of here. You want to follow us, Monique? I have to go to Liv's to drop off some things, then we can head to my place."

Liv's house already felt full, her parents arriving that afternoon from Montreal. Faye had to wait her turn while Connie went straight to them — exchanging hugs without reservation — before Faye had her chance to greet Claude and Anne

Lachance. She introduced Monique to them, then Monique helped with the preparations in the dining room.

Faye wished she didn't have to leave and probably could have solicited an invitation to whatever Liv and Nate had planned tonight — Faye and Dean had always been included in the Lachance family's Christmas Eve *Réveillon,* a lavish meal with seemingly endless food and drink— but Monique looked exhausted. Liv followed them to the car, Monique climbing into the passenger seat.

"Thanks so much for all your help," Faye said, stalling at the prospect of a quiet evening in Will's absence. "And for bringing Connie."

Liv laughed. "Like she would have let me leave her behind."

"I guess I'll see you tomorrow then. By the looks of Monique, she'll probably crash as soon as I get her to the house." Faye reached for the door handle on the driver's side.

"Oh, Faye," Liv said, looking sheepish. "Connie wants to go to church. There's a candlelight service at that one your friend Mallory goes to, and we're going with her. Connie made me ask if you want to come."

Faye snorted. "Made you? Are you twelve?"

Liv's lips twisted. "Sometimes I still feel I am."

"You're going?" Faye asked, her eyebrows peaking.

Liv shrugged. "Sure. It might be nice. The church is pretty and we'll sing carols."

Faye pressed the back of her hand to Liv's forehead. "Are you coming down with something? You can't get sick on us. It's all hands on deck tomorrow."

She gave Faye a wry expression. "I really just want Connie to have a nice time."

Faye's face softened. Connie had proven over and over she was an angel — and Faye had been wishing for an invitation to buffer the disappointment that Will wouldn't be with her on Christmas Eve. "All right. That's good enough for me."

"I'll come pick you up," Liv said, walking toward the house. "Ask Dean, if you want."

Faye wasn't surprised when Dean used the excuse that he had to water off the horses — he always gave Stacy Christmas Day and the night before off. She introduced him to Monique — or reintroduced him, because Dean had been Faye's date for the Dave Matthews concert where they'd initially met — and apologized to Monique again about the couch being the only option. Maybe she should have asked Liv if Monique could stay there. They certainly had the room. Monique didn't seem to mind, though. She made friends with Gus and the two of them were cuddling on the couch in no time. Faye didn't have the heart to tell Monique they didn't normally allow the hairy Golden on the furniture.

Nine seemed late for a church service, but what did Faye know? Liv was picking her up at eight-fifteen — according to Nate, they had to get there early because Christmas Eve services were popular. Faye threw herself in the shower and washed away the residue she always felt she brought home from the café after baking and serving coffee all day. It was more than just the associated food odours; it was tension, physical and emotional. She could let it go for the night, even if it was bound to show up again tomorrow.

When she heard Liv's car, Faye sent a text because she was still standing in front of her closet trying to figure out what to wear. *Come straight in. I'm getting dressed.* In a few minutes, Emilie and Liv appeared at her bedroom door.

"You'll love this," Emilie said. "Our parents are taking Reid and Tim. Nate has my car, and Connie's going with him. I guess the separation extends to vehicles." She rolled her eyes.

"It would have been more efficient for the three of us to go with them, of course..."

"But I thought this way we can get out of there sooner, if we have to," Liv finished.

Sometimes introverted friends were helpful to have. Liv could always be trusted for an escape plan.

"Your parents are going, too?" Faye sized up the sisters; relieved they wore relatively casual clothes. Maybe, like airplanes, people didn't dress up for church anymore.

"My mother is graciously embracing a different tradition instead of judging me for not having a *Réveillon*," Liv said dryly.

Faye laughed, turning back to her closet and deciding on the same outfit she'd worn for the festival of lights — because it wasn't as if anyone she'd see tonight had been there. She checked her reflection in the mirror, and, satisfied, nudged Emilie and Liv out the door.

They tiptoed past the sleeping Monique, Gus in his glory, only the twitch of the tip of his tail acknowledging their movement. Faye had to press her hand to her mouth to keep from laughing. She'd crept into this house in the wee hours more times that she could remember, and here she was sneaking out to go to church.

Snow drifted from the dark sky, and for once she wouldn't complain. It was peaceful in the country, and something indefinable lifted her spirits. When they pulled into the church parking lot, it was nearly full — Nate hadn't been kidding.

He was waiting outside for them. "They grabbed seats," he said, waving Faye and Emilie through the huge wooden doors at the front of the building as he looped his arm around Liv. They huddled together once they were inside, Faye peering around cautiously. Here she was, in a church, twice in one month. Not in her wildest dreams would she have predicted that.

"Faye?"

She glanced around, wondering who could possibly know her here — then she saw Mallory, staring. Mallory quickly snapped her mouth shut and smiled, rushing forward to give Faye a hug. *Guess there's no backing out now.*

Mallory released her, beaming. "Welcome!"

"Everyone, this is Mallory," Faye said. "You've met Liv… this is her husband, Nate, and her sister, Emilie. You probably met the rest of the family without knowing it. They're here already."

The only other time she'd been in this church — not counting the dance, which had been downstairs — had been for a memorial service for the Lachance's old farm manager, Geai Doucet. It had been a sunny June day, light streaming through the stained glass windows while white lilies graced the front — but the mood had been solemn. Tonight those same windows were dark, while the interior was illuminated with white lights and decorated with evergreen boughs and red poinsettias — and the place was filled with a sense of what Faye could only describe as anticipation.

She sang along with the carols as best she could, but quietly, because next to her Connie sounded as if she could be part of the choir. The service wasn't long or complicated, and it wasn't until near the end that the candles were passed out — real candles, even. Then the room darkened before it gradually filled with flickering candlelight as each glim was lit. When everyone sang "Silent Night," Faye just listened. She was even sad when it ended and they extinguished their candles as the lights came back on.

Connie turned and hugged her. "Thank you for coming, Faye."

I owe you didn't seem an appropriate response, so Faye just smiled. Mallory invited everyone for refreshments downstairs, but Liv snagged Faye's eyes, ready for her quick departure. Emilie opted to stay with Tim.

"That was really beautiful, wasn't it?" Faye said once they were in the car. Only then did she realize she'd forgotten to feel lonely for the duration of the service. Liv merely smiled, navigating her car out of the packed lot.

"Come in for a bit?" Faye asked when Liv pulled into the farmhouse.

They went up to Faye's room and as Faye sat on the bed she was reminded of the many times they'd hidden away here as teenagers — except for the bottle of wine Faye brought along.

Liv wandered around the room and stopped in front of the bookcase, laughing softly. "You still have these?"

Faye glanced up. The bouquet was still there, though now she felt as if she'd aged with it; that the promise of love it had stood for a year ago was as fragile as the desiccated petals. "Well, yeah. I can't throw them out."

"Why not? Is that some unspoken rule? If it is, maybe the one-year anniversary means you can let them go. They're looking kind of sad."

"I don't know," Faye disagreed. "I think they're still pretty. It's just a different kind of pretty. Now, would you come drink with me? I'm lonely." Faye jammed her lower lip out in a mock pout.

Liv laughed, and she joined Faye on the bed. "I see church didn't rub off on you too much."

"Connie drinks wine. I don't think it's against the rules," Faye said, handing Liv a glass and tapping hers to it in a silent toast. "So, a year later, do you feel you're in a position to recommend marriage?"

"I'm not sure I have a traditional marriage." Liv's lips twisted into a wry smile.

"What does that even mean anymore? It's not as if most

women these days look to their husband to support them financially. As much as I've thought my life would have been so much easier if I'd found someone who would do that, I've gotta say these last two years with the café have been so much more satisfying than that ever would have been — knowing I can stand on my own two feet."

"You've always been able to do that, Faye," Liv said quietly. "For two people who are so different, you and I are really a lot alike. Neither of us wants to *need* a guy — and we don't. But I think I've finally accepted it's okay to want someone who's going to be there no matter what. It's about emotional support, not financial, now. I'm not your person anymore. Not that I wouldn't do anything for you, but... you don't want that from me. You want it from Will."

And that was exactly it. She and Will were... what was that saying? It was a science thing. Or a math thing. What did she know? Neither had been her strong suit in school, but catchy phrases stuck with her. Something about the sum of two things being greater...

The whole is greater than the sum of its parts.

"Who said that?" Faye said out loud.

Liv laughed. "Who said what?"

"'The whole is greater than the sum of its parts.' It's a math thing, right? You should know."

Liv's brow furrowed, and she pulled out her phone. Google to the rescue. "Aristotle, apparently, though there is some debate over that..."

"Don't get all brainy on me," Faye moaned. "I can't think that hard right now."

Liv shot Faye a grin before her eyes returned to the screen. "It's about synergy. This is maybe more useful: 'it is similar to the acronym TEAM. Together Everyone Achieves More.'"

Faye smiled. "That's us doing Christmas this year."

Her friends had pulled together — and there was no way she was losing the most important member of her team. Faye checked the time. Will should have landed. Where was he? She had things to say.

Liv held out her glass again. "It's the final frontier, Faye. Boldly go."

CHAPTER
THIRTY-NINE

Will couldn't ignore the feeling of relief that came with arriving in Toronto as the 737 descended into the International airport, touching down smoothly. *This is home now.*

Ten forty-five — better late than never. He extracted his phone from his pocket and took it off airplane mode. There was nothing since his last exchange with Faye and he wondered if she was already asleep, her body exhausted after the chaos of the last few weeks. She'd need her rest to handle another hectic day tomorrow, but he'd never hear the end of it if he didn't let her know the flight was in. For now, all he typed was *Landed.* No immediate response. She must've gone to bed. Neither he nor his mother had checked luggage, so they escaped the terminal quickly, paid for parking, and found the car.

"Isn't it time you drove something more...?" Julia paused as Will held the door open for her.

Grown up? Will finished in his head. The theme was getting tired. He swung the door shut and decided to ignore it — she probably wouldn't appreciate that he was thinking of letting the Camaro go so he could buy a truck to pull the espresso trailer. That hinged on how things worked out with Faye, though. A pickup didn't make a great city vehicle.

"I've got to go to my place to pick up a few things," he said, winding his way out of the garage. Will hadn't told his mother about the cat. He needed to check in with Monique and see what her plans were; to be sure Lemon was covered. He hadn't heard from her since he'd left but hoped no news meant everything was fine.

Lazy snowflakes caught in the glow of the streetlamps, promising not to cause trouble. *They'd better not.* He sure didn't want to be stuck in his loft with his mom on Christmas Eve; he wanted to see Faye, to get things back on track. For this to be the best Christmas ever. Not that, with his history, that would be difficult to achieve.

Will knew he was speeding, but Julia didn't comment. The highway was clear, the snow melting as soon as it hit the asphalt, so he wasn't being that unsafe and it was late enough there was little traffic. On the sidestreets, he had no choice but to slow down, and on his street, he crept, looking for a place to park that wasn't too far from his building.

His mother peered around as they walked along the sidewalk. It was a pleasant neighbourhood, so Will wasn't embarrassed to bring her here, but his studio apartment was modest compared to her luxury condo. He tapped on the door before unlocking it, met by darkness on the other side. Was Monique asleep? Will flipped on the light. No Monique. Where was she? He'd trusted that she'd be here to look after the cat.

He heard the thump of Lemon landing on the floor from his bed and she scooted out from behind the curtained-off area. Julia jumped back with an *eek* at the streak of movement. Will laughed. In hindsight, he should have told his mom about the cat.

Julia chuckled, recovering, as Lemon butted her leg. "Hello," she said, stooping to let Lemon sniff her fingers before glancing up at Will. "I didn't know you had a cat."

"I don't," he said. The line had become as comic as a scene from *The Pink Panther*. He sauntered to the kitchen, leaving them to bond, and counted the tins of food. The right number was missing, so Monique had been feeding her. Maybe she'd just gone out for dinner and wasn't back yet. Will sent her a text, then cleaned out Lemon's bowls, gave her fresh water, generously filled the other dish with enough dry food to last a while — and prepared her special Christmas Eve dinner. Because, of course.

While Lemon nibbled delicately, he pulled a small plastic bag from where he'd stashed it in a drawer and crouched to buckle the tiny, sparkly collar around her delicate neck. Will snapped a photo. At least he'd managed to put something shiny on one of his girls.

"*Et voilà! Ma belle.*" He wouldn't dare speak any French in front of Liv and Emilie — they would mock his accent mercilessly — but the cat didn't care.

"Do you speak French now, too?" Julia's eyebrows arched, looking impressed.

"That's the extent of it." He grinned, then dumped the clothes he'd worn on the trip in his laundry hamper and stuffed his bag with clean ones. "Ready to go?"

"What about the kitty?" Julia asked.

His mom was worried about the cat? Had they bonded that quickly? "She'll be fine. Cats are good that way. I'll be back down after I drop you off at the airport on Boxing Day."

He felt guilty leaving Lemon, but he knew she wasn't a fan of the car and an already busy Christmas Day was not the time to find out her opinion on dogs — or a goofy Golden Retriever's opinion on house cats. Spending Christmas alone was probably a cat's fantasy, anyway.

"Do you like cats?" Will asked as he locked the door behind them.

"I had one when I was a girl and took her with me when I left for university. I always wanted another one, but your father was *allergic*." Julia didn't make air quotes, but they were implied.

"Sounds just like Dad," he muttered. Had he really invited his father and new wife to dinner tomorrow? What had he been thinking?

"You're not your father, Will. You're not going to become him. And I mean that as a compliment."

The comment came out of the blue. Will looked over at her, not sure how she'd known how much that had always plagued him — and how much he wanted to be different.

"If you love that girl, marry her. What are you waiting for?"

Will laughed. Everything came in threes, including hearing that phrase. His mother couldn't know he'd stopped waiting, but bad luck had gotten in the way of his plans.

It was well past midnight by the time he drove up the laneway of the Taylors' farm. The house appeared dark but the glowing lights he'd strung around the front door — what seemed like ages ago — made him feel like Faye hadn't given up hope he was coming. When he pulled up next to Dean's pickup, Will thought he saw illumination from the kitchen window, but it was hard to be sure with the back door light on.

Faye was at the kitchen table with a pad of lined paper, making notes, probably obsessing over the details for tomorrow. Gus must've been passed out in front of the fire, because he didn't come scrambling to greet them. Faye smiled and put a finger to her lips in a *shhh* motion. Julia caught it, too, so they remained silent as they removed their shoes and coats.

"We have a houseguest," Faye said in hushed tones, motioning him to the doorway to the living room.

That's where Gus was, curled up cosy as could be with... "Monique?" he whispered, confused.

Faye nodded.

"Good night, you two," his mom said softly, patting him on the arm and brushing past.

"How did she get here?" he asked as Faye led him back into the kitchen.

"She drove."

"Monique doesn't own a car."

Faye shrugged. "She came to the café, in a car. I guess you told her I needed help?"

"Yeah, a while ago." He'd never thought she'd follow up on his suggestion, but a sense of relief washed over him, knowing she was safe under this roof and, he hoped, committed to making a change.

"She helped us out this afternoon, and I invited her to stay," Faye said. "I didn't think you'd mind."

"Um, no. Is she okay?"

"I'll let you and her talk in the morning."

It had never occurred to him that Faye would have seen all the tagged photos of him with Monique but he was sure she must have. She'd never mentioned them, never made catty comments, had never been passive aggressive. He hoped that meant she didn't have concerns about his friendship with Monique, but still, it was generous of her to invite a woman who randomly showed up on her doorstep into her home.

"Thank you," he said, and the way she met his eyes assured him she knew how grateful he was. "Can I help you with anything here?" he asked.

"No. I'm done and heading to bed. I want to hear about your trip, but I'm not sure I can stay awake, sorry."

Will felt extra-bad for deserting her when things had hit their peak. No matter what their future was, they were partners, and friends. He closed his arms around her and she slipped hers around his waist, resting her head on his chest.

As anxious as he was to talk to her — to clear the air — he had to respect her weariness. "Are you ready for tomorrow?"

"It'll be fine," she said, with a calm that surprised him.

CHAPTER

FORTY

It felt like every other morning. Almost.

Faye didn't need to be up this early. She hadn't set an alarm, but her body told her it was time to get up, and when she remembered what day it was, she pushed herself from the warmth of the cosy bed, Will not budging as she tucked the sheets and duvet back around him to keep the heat in. He'd admitted to sleeping on his mom's couch in Calgary, so he was likely due a rest.

The chill in the old farmhouse inspired her to dress quickly, pulling on leggings, then sweats, two pairs of socks, and a wool cardigan over the long-sleeved shirt she'd stolen from Will. It was like combining past, present and future, because the cardigan had been her mother's. Faye could still picture her mom tugging it around herself as she watched her three kids squabbling at the breakfast table.

Faye hadn't been a morning person then, either. But maybe it was time to admit she was becoming one. She grabbed a vest for another layer and slipped from the room, gently closing the door behind her.

Before heading into the kitchen, she nudged the thermostat up and switched on the tree lights. Reds and greens and warm whites cast a soft glow over the room, reflecting off tinsel and ornaments and bathing the few wrapped presents beneath the branches. Monique still lay curled on the couch, her back to the room, but Gus was gone.

Like any other morning, the coffee maker was on and Dean's boots and heavy coat were missing, as was the resident Golden Retriever. Off to feed the horses and set them up with hay, as he often did so Stacy could sleep an extra hour. Even though it was Christmas and Stacy was off today — and Dean always said he was going to leave the stalls, like a lot of farms did on Christmas and New Year's — Faye would bet he was doing a quick job just so they weren't a complete disaster for Stacy tomorrow.

The two cups she pulled from the cupboard were their favourites, and had been for as long as she could remember. Well, at least since Dean abandoned his Masters and came back to the farm. It was some kind of miracle neither mug had broken. Dean's had a racing scene stretched around it. Hers — the volume possibly twice the size of his — only had words. *Better Not Pout.* It was a Christmas mug, sure, but she used it year round as a reminder. Though it hadn't always been an effective one.

The unadulterated bitterness of the black liquid was like a hit of caffeine straight to her brain cells. Later there would be a civilized version from her French press with fresh-ground beans. She savoured the temporary solitude — because this day would be madness.

The crunch of boots on the deck, stomping feet, and a stream of dialogue preceded Dean and Gus's entrance, the two of them arriving with a whoosh of cold air. Gus rushed over to

Faye, his long silky tail waving as clumps of snow fell from his paws.

"Get the horses fed, big guy?" She smiled, removing one hand from the ceramic's warmth to run it over the Golden's head and tug on one of his ears.

Dean left his boots on the tray after hanging his coat, finding slippers before coming over to give her a rare hug.

"Merry Christmas, Faye."

"Merry Christmas," she said, the words muffled as she turned her head so her face didn't get squashed against his chest. When he released her, she turned to pour him a coffee and handed it to him. "Everybody okay?"

Dean nodded, leaning against the counter. "They all agreed, no Christmas emergency calls."

"That's very considerate of them." Faye smiled. There was something to be said for the power of positive thinking.

"So, what's the schedule today?" Dean asked.

She breathed in, resigning herself to thinking about it — when getting up this early had been her reason to escape it.

Before last year, it had always been just her and Dean Christmas morning. She'd slept in while Dean did the horses, clinging to a dream world where their family was still whole, a time when she'd been up before dawn to see what Santa had brought. It was better than remembering the final year they'd all been together, her mother dragging her from bed when breakfast was ready. She'd been such a typical teenager, always a bit uncooperative, bemoaning taking part in the old traditions. How extravagant their celebration was depended on how well her father's horses had done that year. She'd longed to have a normal life, a dad with a regular job — so the holiday didn't make her feel like a character in a movie, some cross between *A Christmas Carol* and *It's A Wonderful Life*. The next year, when they were gone, she'd longed to have that last Christmas back — but there were no do-overs.

"Well," she began, "We'll have breakfast then open presents like normal." Except Julia and Monique were here — what was she going to give them? "Then I'll start packing things up to take to Liv and Nate's, late morning." Crack open a bottle of wine once she didn't have to drive again and get some alcohol in her bloodstream to prepare for the mania to come. "All the cookies and desserts are over there already. The plan is to have a light lunch — finger food, really — and be sitting down at four for the big meal."

"How can I help?" Dean asked.

"Carry stuff, I guess. And entertain Will's mom so I don't feel like I have to?" She didn't care that her tone was pleading. Julia was no Connie; Faye couldn't see her donning an apron and pitching in. "She seems to like you."

He chuckled. "Okay. What about Will's friend?"

"I'm sure she'll help, too. Now, about breakfast..." As she swung around toward the refrigerator, Faye caught sight of Will, standing in the doorway to the living room. He looked as if he didn't know what time zone he was in, but he'd dressed in jeans and a navy hoodie and there was evidence he'd pulled a comb through his hair.

"Why's it so cold in here?" he asked, his voice first-thing-in-the-morning rough.

Faye laughed and skipped over, throwing her arms around him. "Merry Christmas."

Will dropped a sleepy grin on her and when he pressed his lips to hers, Faye regretted she didn't have time to warm him up.

"I'll start a fire." Dean squeezed past.

"Coffee?" Faye asked when Will finally let her go.

"Yeah, thanks." He followed her to the counter. "I only

heard the part about Dean babysitting my mom. What's the rest of the plan?"

Faye returned his crooked smile with a wry grin then repeated what she'd told Dean.

"I'll make breakfast," Will said. "You've got enough to do."

"Thank you. I have one other problem. I don't have a gift for your mom or Monique. Do you think we should skip the presents for now? Dean would understand."

"Got it covered," Will said with a wink. "I buy my mom the same thing every year, and I picked up a box of nice chocolates for Monique to thank her for looking after Lemon. They can be from both of us."

She grabbed fistfuls of his sweatshirt and stretched up on her toes to give him another kiss. "Have I told you lately you're the best thing that's ever happened to me?" she murmured.

Faye wanted to say everything now, before the day ran away with them, but before she could put those thoughts into words, she noticed Will's mother standing in the doorway. A sigh escaped as Faye flattened her feet, and she put on her best smile.

"Good morning, Julia. Merry Christmas."

WILL TOUCHED Faye on the arm and went to his mother, embracing her. "Merry Christmas, Mom. I'm going to check on Monique." After his mother's declaration about Faye last night, he wasn't as worried about leaving the two of them alone.

"I think she's stirring," Julia said as he stepped past.

He grinned when he saw Monique, sitting up on the couch, her clothes and hair rumpled.

"She's alive! Y'know, I'm sure Faye would have found you something to wear if you'd only stayed awake long enough to let her." Gus hopped off the couch as Will sat next to her. Her face was creased and there were crusty bits in the corners of her eyes. "I was worried when I got to my place and you were gone."

Monique frowned, her eyes dropping to her hands, clasped in her lap. "Gerry called me yesterday morning. Somehow he found out where I was staying. I knew you were coming back, so I just bolted. I'm so sorry, Will. I should have texted you."

"Hey, that's okay," he said, putting an arm around her. "You did the right thing. Where'd you get the car, though?"

"I took transit to Vaughan and my friend let me borrow hers. She said I could have it until Boxing Day."

"That's perfect. Once I drop my mom off at the airport tomorrow, I'll come pick you up after you take it back."

Monique draped herself around him, clinging. "Thank you so much, Will. Everyone's been so nice to me. Your friends are amazing."

"Yeah, they are," he agreed. "Now, go have a shower and get dressed. Faye will get you a fresh change of clothes. I need you to keep her busy for about fifteen minutes though, okay?"

Monique grinned. "What have you got up your sleeve?"

"Nothing serious," he said. *Not yet.*

FORTY-ONE

Monique was probably a size zero, so Faye hoped she could deal with roomy clothes.

"Hmm, this wouldn't be too bad," she said, thinking out loud as she pulled an ice blue tunic from her closet. It would look great with Monique's long, blonde hair. "My leggings might be more like capris for you. You can borrow my robe when you shower, if you like, and I'll get you some towels. What size are your feet?"

She left Monique rifling through her small bag, pulling out wrinkled underclothes that looked as if they'd been hastily tossed in. After leaving the towels on the edge of the bathtub, Faye poked her head in the room. Monique sat on the edge of the bed, the robe wrapped around her, hands clasped in her lap.

"All set. I'm going to go help Will with breakfast," Faye said.

"Faye —"

She stopped, turning halfway back with eyebrows raised.

"Thank you," Monique said. "You don't know how much all this means to me."

"You're welcome, but don't thank me yet." Faye grinned. "The real fun is yet to come. And you don't need to stall me anymore." She could hear the generator running outside. "Have your shower and meet us on the driveway when you're ready."

The main floor of the house was empty so Faye tugged on her boots and bundled into her coat, slipping out onto the deck. The serving window of the espresso trailer was open, Will moving around inside while Dean and Julia chatted just in front. Hanging on either side of the window were big, red, velvet bows and under the one on the left, a sign saying *Merry Christmas, Faye. Love, Will.* Faye laughed as she walked toward it.

"I love it!" she said. "But I hope you already know that."

Will grinned. He waited until he had three cups sitting ready to wave them over, and Dean reached up to pass one to Julia, then Faye, before taking the last one for himself. Will made two more, then he joined them, wrapping an arm around Faye and pulling her into him. His lips were warm, and he tasted like coffee.

"Will! This is amazing! Where did you get this?" Monique bounced down the steps from the deck.

"He made it." Faye beamed.

"I'll show you a 'before' picture," Dean offered.

"I had help," Will said. "A lot of help."

"But you were the mastermind behind the creation," Faye insisted. She wasn't going to let him duck well-deserved praise.

Julia looped her arm through Will's. "It's wonderful. Congratulations."

Faye glanced at Julia, then up at Will's face. She was dying to know the outcome of the restaurant visit in Calgary. *Needed* to know.

Will shrugged, handing Monique her cup. "Cheers, every-one. Now let's go inside and eat."

Once he'd closed the trailer back up, he kept Faye tucked under his arm as they walked to the house. "Think I should hook it up and drive it over so we can serve cappuccinos after dinner?" he asked.

"That would be brilliant," she said, then tugged him to a halt. "I can't stand it any longer, Will. What did you think of the restaurant?"

Will dropped his hand to the small of her back and dipped his mouth to her ear. "I'm not going anywhere."

BREAKFAST WAS MADE-TO-ORDER crepes with fruit on the side — Faye could be trusted to stock the fridge for a major holiday, even if she'd probably had to send Dean to the grocery store with a shopping list because she wouldn't have had the time. There wasn't a lot of talking as everyone ate, just murmurs of appreciation, so Will was calling his meal choice a win.

Faye and Monique helped him clean up, then they joined his mother and Dean in the living room. The crackling fire warmed the room, Gus lying so close to it he must be roasting. When Monique sat next to the tree, perched on the edge of a chair looking as if she felt out of place, Gus climbed to his feet and trundled over to her, resting his head on her thigh and looking up at her adoringly like he'd decided it was his job to make her feel welcome. Monique cooed at him and scratched his ears.

"Here you go, Monique," Will said, reaching under the tree and passing her the flat, rectangular box adorned in gold paper and a silver ribbon. He loved it when he could buy things that came already gift-wrapped.

Her eyes lit up when she tore the paper away, and she grinned. "Chocolate is never wrong. Thank you. You shouldn't have."

"See that weird-shaped one, Monique?" Faye said. "That's for Gus."

A tuft of string stuck out the top, so Gus had no trouble using his feet to hold the paper as he drew the multi-coloured tug toy out. He shook it as if he was making sure it was dead, then dropped to the floor and gnawed on it.

Dean laughed when he opened up a new drip coffee maker.

"Will you please get rid of that old thing now?" Will begged.

"My present's better than your present, Dean," Faye teased, beaming at Will. "A coffee machine on wheels. Though it would have been a lot simpler to give me an espresso machine for Christmas, Will." Then she nudged a brightly wrapped oblong box with an enormous bow on it toward him.

Will plucked off the bow and stuck it to the front of his sweatshirt before tearing away the paper. The cardboard was branded with the name of a muck boot company. A crease formed between his eyebrows. Will wasn't sure what he'd expected from Faye, but if this really was a pair of boots... Well, not *that*.

It was. A pair of tall, rubber boots — with a thermal sock stuffed in the shaft of each one. He pulled them out one at a time, holding them up, his lips pressed together.

"Thank you, honey," he said, not bothering to withhold the sarcasm. All she did was give him a wry smile back, enjoying the moment. *Really?*

Monique snorted, palm to her mouth. "Nice boots, country boy."

Was he missing something? Here he was, hoping he'd still find the right moment to pull out the ring, and Faye was giving him rubber boots. Maybe he had it all wrong and he should have bought her a blender. He shuffled over to the tree and retrieved a box with her name on it. It wasn't as expertly wrapped as hers had been, but he'd found an extra-glittery bow for it.

Faye's eyebrows peaked. "I thought the trailer was my gift?"

"There's this, too." Will set the box on her lap and sat on the couch next to her.

The painter's tape lifted easily under her fingers. "Nice touch," she said. "Practical. Scotch tape is so annoying." She was joking and serious at the same time. As soon as she lifted the top from the box, she started laughing. Faye slipped her hands through the handles and held them up, looking as if she was thinking about trying them out.

"Cymbals?" Dean looked confused. "Are you joining the band, Faye?"

Will wondered what was going through his mother's mind — all these gifts probably cost half of what his parents had spent on him as a kid. Gag gifts like the boots and the cymbals were unheard of in the Callaghan's very proper home.

Julia opened her gift demurely, revealing a daytimer with a smooth leather case. "What a surprise," she crooned, her mouth twisting. "Thank you."

"Every year for fifteen years," Will whispered in Faye's ear.

She patted his leg. "I'm doing the shopping next year."

Julia had small gifts for Faye and Dean, and even one for Monique — how, Will had no idea. She gave him a couple of shirts and an envelope, which had replaced the toys and electronics he'd received when he was younger. The cheque wasn't enough to buy a new car, but maybe he'd put it toward the graphics for the trailer.

Faye's phone rang, her brow creasing. "It's Liv. Excuse me. I have to take this." She hopped up as she answered the call and disappeared into the office.

Uh-oh.

~

"HEY," Faye said.

Liv — calling — was never *not* a big deal. A thousand things rushed through her mind. Like maybe the Triple Stripe horses hadn't got Dean's memo about no emergency calls today and one of them was injured or sick and Liv and Nate were on their way to Ontario Veterinary College for treatment — leaving Faye to entertain all the in-laws herself.

"So," Liv began.

"Out with it," Faye snapped.

"Our furnace died. This place is freezing. There's no way it's getting fixed on Christmas Day."

"And you guys don't have a fireplace," Faye realized. "But isn't your house passive solar or something clever like that?"

Liv choked on a laugh. "No, sorry. Besides, have you looked outside? It's not sunny today."

"How many people though? Won't all those bodies produce a lot of heat?" She was grasping at very ridiculous straws.

"With the high ceilings here?"

"Even if I add one more body?" Faye said hopefully.

"Who?"

"Will's friend, Monique, remember?"

"Oh, right. How is she? What did Will say?"

"We haven't really talked yet. She seems fine enough that I can wait till later to find out. Apparently we have a situation." A situation that only had one solution. "We're going to have to have it over here, aren't we?"

"Sorry, Faye. There is good news. We have hydro, so we can cook stuff."

"Too bad you don't have any electric heaters. You can't ask your parents to stand around in a cold house." She sighed. "Give me some time to get organized."

Faye disconnected, counting in her head. Liv, Nate, Em, Tim, Connie, Reid, Claude, Anne...Julia, Dean, Monique... Will would have to call his dad and give him a different address. Had she missed anyone?

Fifteen people, in this tiny house. She took a moment to breathe before going back to the living room and catching Will's eyes before she plastered on a smile. "Change of plans!"

"WHAT DO YOU THINK? Can we fit fifteen people in here?"

Will stood behind Faye as she scanned the long table, the dark wood covered in a layer of dust. He'd never been in this room before and guessed, by the looks of it, it probably hadn't been used since — well — since Dean and Faye's parents and brother had died. He glanced over his shoulder as Dean came up behind them.

"Sure we can," said Dean. "I think the leaves are in the front closet. "Will and I will get them."

The closet looked as if it hadn't seen much use either, full of dated coats and boots. Dean stared at them a beat and said dryly, "You did such an astonishing transformation with the trailer. Any inspired ideas for some old clothes?"

"Sure," Will said. "It's called a thrift store."

Dean chuckled and dove into the back of the closet to slide out two long, flat pieces of wood that matched the table. By the time they got back to the dining room, Faye had dusted the tabletop and was wiping off the chairs and buffet.

"All right, Will. You stand at that end. Hold it, like this." Dean grasped the edges of the table. "Got it? Now pull."

Will grunted. It was tight, but with a couple of good tugs, they got the table apart and slotted the leaves into place — then nudged them together. Now that the surface shone with a soft gloss, he could see what a beautiful piece of furniture it was.

"Liv's going to bring their linens. I hate to think what our old ones smell like," Faye said, yanking open a drawer in the buffet and closing it quickly. "We'll need the kitchen chairs. And a seating plan." She grabbed her pen and drew a large rectangle on her lined pad of paper, then hesitated. "How do I do this?"

"May I?" Will placed a hand on her back. Faye relinquished her pen to him with a look of relief and he bent over the page, marking the position of each seat with an X and scribbling names. Faye pressed close, their arms touching.

"Are you sure you want to put Reid and Connie side by side?" she asked.

"I'm more worried about having Connie and my mom opposite each other, to be honest," Will quipped. "C'mon Faye. It's going to be a circus any way we do it. We've got me next to my mom and Nate next to his, so if war breaks out we'll step in. Besides, my dad and Ashley might steal that show anyway."

Faye snorted. "What have we gotten ourselves into?"

Will turned to her with a grin. "It's going to be great."

She spun toward the living room where Dean and Monique had gathered the kitchen chairs. "They can stay right here for now. We'll space them so people can sit here until we eat. But we need more. I guess I'd better ask Liv and Nate to bring some."

"How about if I grab some of the ones from the shop?

That's probably less hassle than them lugging over their dining room furniture," Will said. "How many do we need?"

"Five. Bring six, just in case."

"You never know who else might show up, eh?"

Faye laughed and hugged him. "I'm so glad you're here."

Will squeezed her, the feeling mutual. "I'll go now. Want to come, Monique? It'll go faster with two of us. Can I borrow the truck, Dean?"

Monique climbed into the passenger seat when Will opened the pickup's doors. It was good to see her smiling and looking rested. He settled behind the wheel and let it run for a minute before heading out the driveway.

"I *love* Faye," Monique gushed. "Oh my goodness, those boots!" She cackled, then started singing, "Thank God I'm A Country Boy."

Will scowled at her. "Yeah. Hilarious."

"It is. Lighten up." She started humming again. "And you'd better still be planning to propose, because if that doesn't say 'marry me,' I don't know what does."

"What? You're going to have to explain."

"Those boots say, 'I want you around. Leave the city, already, will you?' You two aren't just some superficial lovey-dovey couple. You two are partners. You two are hashtag rela-tionship goals."

"You got all that from a pair of rubber boots?" His lips contorted into a crooked smile.

"I'm serious, Will. Do it. Tonight." Monique waved her phone, grinning. "I'll be ready with the camera."

CHAPTER
FORTY-TWO

Faye changed out of her sweats into a long skirt and lightweight sweater because cold was no longer an issue. Once the whole crowd was here, she might wish she'd worn a t-shirt. The rumble of Dean's truck came from outside — that would be Will with the chairs — so she raced down the steps and slipped into the office, closing the door behind her.

It was quiet here. This was likely the last bit of solitude she'd get until much, much later. She found what she'd come for, tucking it into her pocket, and her gaze caught on the largest of her father's numerous win photos hanging on the wall: his best horse, Catch The Joy, after his biggest victory, the Queen's Plate. The whole family was in the winner's circle, Faye and Shawn nestled under each of Ed Taylor's arms; Dean, already tall and lanky, on the other side of their mother, Debbie. They'd had a bountiful Christmas that year. Her cousins from Ottawa had even come, and Faye tried to remember if that was the last time there had been so many people in this house for the holiday.

The sound of another truck distracted her, and she peeked through the blinds to see the navy Triple Stripe pickup back into a spot, Nate and Tim hopping out to unload the plastic totes of desserts. Before they were done, two more cars pulled up. Liv, Emilie and both sets of parents.

All right, Faye. It's go time.

"Merry Christmas, everyone," she said, emerging with her arms wide. The music coming from the stereo was instrumental, a soothing background to the festivities. "Connie and Reid, you both know Julia," she began, biting her lower lip to keep from laughing as the two women exchanged curt nods. "Claude, Anne? This is Will's mother, Julia."

With Gus safely stashed in Dean's bedroom — for the dog's own sanity as much as Faye's — she set the guests up with finger food in the living room then gathered the team of friends in the kitchen to delegate final tasks.

Emilie and Liv put together platters of cookies and squares. Tim set the table. Will and Nate cooked the vegetables, then Nate went back to the house at Triple Stripe for the turkey, which they'd left there to cook. In the flurry of setting up, Faye lost track of time, shocked when a knock came at the door and she realized it was already after three.

"Will!" she summoned him from wherever he'd disappeared to. "Your dad's here!" Just when Faye thought they might've gotten over the Connie/Julia awkwardness.

She was glad for the reminder of their names as Will introduced Ron and Ashley — then it was time to put food on the table. Will and Nate seated everyone like ushers at a wedding.

"No bloodshed yet," Liv whispered in Faye's ear.

"I'm so proud. Everyone seems on their very best behaviour." Faye grinned.

Dean began pouring wine, going around the table, starting with the women. "What will you have, Julia? Red or white?"

"White, please, Dean."

"Connie?" he asked next.

"Red, thank you."

As if they couldn't agree on anything. Faye caught Nate rolling his eyes.

"Ashley?"

Ashley's eyes shifted nervously. It looked to Faye like she grabbed her husband's hand under the table — giving Faye a very bad feeling.

"Oh, none for me, thanks," Ashley said, her voice unnaturally squeaky.

Ron put an arm around the back of her chair and smiled awkwardly.

"Well," Julia broke the silence with a look of comprehension, her tone crisp. "It appears congratulations are in order." She raised her glass and tipped it to her lips, half of it disappearing. It would have shocked Faye if she hadn't already seen how well Julia could toss the stuff back.

An uncomfortable hush settled around the table. Faye forced herself into action. "Yes, congratulations!" she said in her brightest, cheeriest voice. "Tim, I bought a bottle of non-alcoholic wine for you. Would you like a glass of that, Ashley? Where is it, hon?" she turned to Will, feeling as if she was baring her teeth rather than smiling.

Ashley's face was pink, as she looked at Tim. "Are you pregnant, too" she said in a nervous trill.

It might have been funny if Julia hadn't been there. Tim was speechless, his eyes wide, and Emilie's face was so contorted with the laughter she held back Faye thought she might explode.

Will slid Faye a barely-contained look of horror before he squeezed out to the kitchen. Murmured good wishes circulated after he returned and filled Ashley and Tim's glasses, then he rose.

"Anyone except Tim not want turkey?" He scanned faces, then nodded, grinning down at Faye "Stand back and let the professional do this." When he picked up the carving utensils, Faye did lean away from him. Will held the bird steady with the large fork as he sliced with a big, sharp knife.

It felt good to finally just sit and enjoy the food. The table setting was gorgeous, the spread delicious, and the drama smoothed out and was replaced by muted conversation — until Will and Nate started trading stories from their childhood, soon dragging Tim into it. Faye laughed so hard her sides hurt. Dean topped their tales when he shared one of his own about a time he and Shawn had tried to ride their skateboards down the hay elevator when he'd been twelve and Shawn nine, and Shawn had fallen and broken his arm.

"I must've been too young to remember," Faye said. "Or already good at blocking out male stupidity."

"I got in a lot of trouble for that," Dean admitted, grinning. "It's a wonder Shawn wasn't hurt much worse."

"You win, man," Will said, once he stopped laughing, while Nate sang, "Dumb Ways To Die."

Bowls and wine bottles emptied and plates were scraped clean as the candles burned down. Emilie and Tim began collecting dishes and removing them from the table.

"We thought we'd go outside so Will can make us all cappuccinos from our new espresso trailer," Faye announced with a note of pride. "Then we'll come back inside for dessert. But first I'd like to say something." She stood, smiling at Dean. "Most of you know Dean and I lost our family a while ago. It's been a long time since this house has felt like family. But tonight — as unexpected as this was and as awkwardly as it started out —" She focused on Liv and Nate instead of letting her eyes fall to Connie, or Julia, or Ashley. "This feels like family. Thank you, all of you, for bringing family back to this house." Faye took a breath and sip of water, but she wasn't done. "And I'm so happy you're all here to witness this."

She felt warm all over and more sure than she'd ever been in her life as her eyes travelled from face to face, enjoying their slightly confused expressions — before landing on Will.

"Will." She turned to him and reached for his hands, taking them in hers. "When I first met you, I was just looking for another fling. I was pretty miffed you didn't play along. I thought there might be something wrong with you." He laughed, still looking unsure. "But you stuck around. You helped me see the world differently. And now I never want to go back to the way I was before. I can't imagine life without you. But you're not here enough. I want to trip over you. I want to be annoyed that you're always here. I want to complain about you walking across the kitchen in your muddy muck boots. I want you around for the rest of my life." She dropped to her heels, drinking in his champagne eyes, and held up the simple gold band. "Will you marry me?"

"YES!" Emilie shouted, shooting to her feet, then blushed as she settled back into her chair, muttering, "Answer her, you doofus!"

Will gaped down at Faye, his eyes darting from the ring to her face like someone had pulled a fast one on him. He shook his head, slowly.

Was he... actually... going to say *no?* Faye clambered to her feet and almost fell backward, her legs cramping, and she grabbed the back of her chair to steady herself. Her face burned and she stepped away, eyes on the door, but before she could flee, hands closed around her arms, stopping her.

"Faye."

Will stood now, pulling her closer. His finger tipped her

chin up. He was smiling. "My turn." He fumbled with something in his pocket.

The blue velvet box nestled perfectly in his palm, and he opened it, presenting it to her. Faye's mouth dropped open. It was the ring she and Emilie had looked at on their shopping trip what seemed like ages ago —and Faye couldn't help a sly glance at her friend. She should have known it hadn't been innocent. Emilie looked totally self-satisfied. Will's hand on her cheek drew her back.

"Faye, when we met, we were on the same page. But then I started turning pages, and the story got better and better. And it's a long book. I want to savour every word. But I've gotta confess — I peeked at the end. I guarantee you, we live happily ever after."

He grinned at her infuriatingly when she swiped away a tear. *Don't you make me cry, Will Callaghan.*

"Is that the right answer?" Will asked, holding her gaze. "Will you marry me?"

She couldn't stop nodding, cursing the tears now streaming down her cheeks, her vision blurred.

"Say it," he whispered.

She whispered back, "Yes." Faye grasped the lapels of his jacket, drawing his face near. "Your turn."

"Yes," Will said, and the word sent a shiver through her.

She looped her arms around his neck and he lifted her, their lips meeting, everything around them fading away. It was a moment before she realized there was cheering, and a bottle of champagne, and Gus twirling around their legs in excitement.

"How did you get out?" Faye laughed. But she didn't care. Gus was family too.

Will removed the ring from the box, clasping her hand, Faye's fingers trembling as he slipped the beautiful band with its shiny stone onto the appropriate finger. Faye stared at it, let it all soak in — and it felt right.

"Wait— " she said, recovering the ring she'd produced earlier. She held it up, then reached for his hand, guiding it on, and closed her hands around his with a twist of her lips.

Will wrapped his arms around her again, squeezing her tight against him.

Faye grinned up at him. "That was so corny."

"Too corny?" Will asked, a slight tilt to his head, though he didn't look the least bit worried.

She shook her head. "No. It was perfect." And she tugged him down for another kiss.

CHAPTER
FORTY-THREE

The driveway was bathed in light from the spots Dean brought up from the pond, the powerful beams skirting the ground. The steamer squealed, the rich scent of coffee wafting from the trailer. Everyone was bundled in gloves and hats and jackets, half of them with cups, the other half waiting. Monique circulated first with a platter of cookies and squares, then with her phone, showing everyone the video she'd had the presence of mind to capture of the dual proposal. Once they all had coffee, they'd go inside for pie and Christmas pudding.

Faye loitered on the edge of the group with Julia. "Are you going to be a nightmare mother-in-law?"

Julia patted her arm affectionately. "It was a test, sweetie."

Faye almost choked on her cappuccino. "A test? You mean the tough love stance was an act?"

Now Julia squeezed Faye's shoulders in a one-armed hug. "You passed, with flying colours."

"You play a mean game, Dr Mom."

Will's mother raised her eyebrows. "Is that what you call me behind my back?"

"Absolutely." Faye grinned.

Julia shrugged it off, levelling her gaze on Faye. "So, is it too soon to ask when I can expect grandkids?"

"You said you didn't want them!" Faye sputtered.

"It was all part of the performance."

Will finally joined them — just in time to get Faye out of another awkward conversation. He draped an arm over her shoulders and kissed her.

"Were you testing Will, too, then?" Faye asked, eyeing Julia with suspicion.

"Of course. You both needed a push. What better way to convince two people who don't think they're ready to commit to moving forward, than to try to pull them apart? If my little ploys were enough to break you up, you were probably right to walk away from each other. Instead, it drove you together."

Faye wasn't sure she agreed with Julia's logic, but her future mother-in-law's heart was in the right place. Maybe. And it had worked, hadn't it?

"Let me see your ring, Will," Julia said.

It made Faye laugh, but something else bubbled up inside her, too, as Will tugged off his glove and showed his mother the simple gold band. Will hadn't hesitated to wear it. Faye might get him a new ring for the wedding, but the fact that he was ready to freely display their altered status as much as any newly engaged woman, made her heart swell.

"I'm a modern guy," he said with a crooked smile as Julia admired it.

"Oh, by the way, Will — I happen to know your grandmother left you a nice sum of money. Enough, say, for a down payment on a house?" Julia tilted her head, eyebrows peaked.

"Wow," Will said once he found his voice.

A house? Leaving this house? Faye couldn't think that far ahead right now. "Time for dessert, don't you think?" She glanced at Will, who still looked as shell-shocked.

Both of them were exhausted, but once everyone was gone — Dean and Monique in the living room watching a Christmas movie, Julia sitting by the fire reading a book with Gus passed out at her feet — Faye and Will slipped out for a walk. It was a beautiful evening, the sky clear and sparkling with stars, but not uncomfortably cold — although that could've been all the warm fuzzies Faye was feeling.

"Thank goodness Liv contacted Kerrie about using Kerrie's cottage tonight," Faye said. Triple Stripe's farm manager was on vacation, spending the holiday with her parents out west — leaving her home, with functioning furnace, empty. "I was worried we were going to have to have a sleepover."

"That would have been something." Will chuckled. "So, what do you think about Monique?"

"Unless yesterday and today were a fluke, I say if she wants the job, it's hers." Monique's whole-hearted participation in the day's events had only confirmed Faye's feelings.

"She's going to need a place to stay."

"Once your mom goes home, she can stay in the guest room until she finds something permanent." Or maybe they should rent her the room. Faye made a mental note to see what Dean thought about that.

They strolled in silence for a while, then a lone howl pierced the stillness. Faye reflexively snuggled closer to Will, feeling his arm tighten around her.

"Forgot your cymbals, didn't you?" he asked, and Faye laughed.

"Maybe we should go back."

They were quiet again for a few strides, then Will cleared

his throat. "I have a confession. There is something I've been keeping from you."

Faye laughed. "What? I know about the travelling espresso bar, the fact your mother has been playing me, and that you were carrying a ring around with you for two weeks, talking yourself in and out of proposing. I'm not sure you can top any of that."

Will's face became serious. "I'm bringing baggage to this relationship you don't know about, Faye." He hesitated. "There's another woman."

Faye stopped, feeling the chill suddenly. "What are you talking about?"

Will broke into a grin. "Lara asked me to take Clementine. Permanently. She's moving to Seattle and doesn't want to ask Lemon to make the move. She asked if I could keep her, and I couldn't say no. So if I'm moving in, the cat's coming with me. Think we can make it work?"

Faye beamed up at him. "I think we can make anything work, Will Callaghan."

FAYE CAME along when Will took his mom to the airport. He still felt like his head was spinning, but having Faye turn the tables on him last night at least gave him confidence they were on the same page. *You and me. Together, forever.*

They didn't just drop Julia at the curb, instead parking in the short-term lot. Though Julia tried to convince them that would have been fine, Faye wouldn't hear of it. Dr Mom had met her match in Faye Taylor.

"Are you okay with Dad's news?" Will asked as they stood inside the terminal, Will setting Julia's bag down next to her.

"Your father always wanted another child, for some

unknown reason. He could barely deal with the one he had. I just wanted a cat." One side of her mouth tipped up as she met his eyes. "You'll always be my one and only, Will."

She reached for him, enfolding him in a hug, and Will caught the droll twist of Faye's lips.

"But you'll have a little brother or sister," Faye said, grinning at him.

The thought gave Will a weird feeling at first. At his age, he should be getting a niece or nephew, not a sibling. Then he decided he liked the idea. Maybe this would be what smoothed out his relationship with his father. At the very least, he could try to make a point of being part of the kid's life.

"It'll be good practice for your own children." Julia patted him on the arm. Now that she'd given up the ruse, she'd really sunk her teeth into that idea. Then she turned to Faye. "I'll be back. I want to get to know you better. And I don't expect to have to wait too long for those grandkids. Perhaps I'll look at condos in the area."

Julia broke from their hug and gave a little wave as she picked up the handle of her carry-on and headed for the security lineup.

"Does she mean that?" Faye glanced up at Will, her eyebrows nearly meeting as her forehead wrinkled. "Should I be scared?"

"Yes," he said. "Be very, very afraid." Then he slung an arm around her shoulders, rolling her into him, and bent to kiss her. "She's going to be one hell of a grandmother, isn't she?"

Faye laughed, the free warmth of it filling his heart. "I can only imagine."

THANK YOU!

I wrote the first draft of this book (which was really just a glorified outline) before *Horse Of The Year*, then realized I needed to write *Horse Of The Year* first. So I set it aside, wrote and published that one, then came back to this.

And it kind of wrote itself. It was as easy to write as *Horse Of The Year* was hard. I don't know why. What I do know is, it got me through a pretty tough time, as in the midst of it I knew I was going to have to say goodbye to my two senior mares. That's twice now, Faye's helped me through a difficult stretch. I think she's so different from my own character, writing her gets me out of my head! I hope you enjoyed her happily ever after as much as I enjoyed getting her there.

I don't know what's next. I know what should be next, but when I'll get to it, I'm not sure. I hope you'll sign up for my newsletter so that we can keep in touch as I figure it out.

Take care and, as always, thanks for reading.

Linda

PS - You can also join my Patreon to read as I write. While after **Shiny Little Things** I might take a break from publishing, I'll always be writing, and everything new will appear there first. Check it out with a seven-day trial to start, or follow for free. https://www.patreon.com/lindashantz/membership

If you'd like to stay up-to-date on all my writing news and can deal with me sharing pictures of my horses, sign up for my newsletter at www.lindashantz.com/writes

Curious about the music mentioned in the book and what I was listening to as I wrote **Shiny Little Things?** Check out the playlist:

*Scan the QR code for the **Shiny Little Things** playlist.*

FAYE'S SPICY GINGERBREAD SQUARES

I developed all three of these recipes specially for Shiny Little Things. Please give credit if you share!

Faye's Gingerbread Squares

Preheat oven to 350°F.

BASE:

Cream together:

- 1/4 cup butter
- 1/4 cup brown sugar
- 1/4 cup molasses
- 1/4 cup corn syrup

Add and beat together:

- 1 egg

Blend in:

- 1 cup flour
- 2 tsp baking soda
- 1 tbsp ginger
- 1/2 tsp nutmeg

Pour into lightly greased 8 x 8 pan and bake for 20 minutes. Let cool in pan.

ICING:

- 4 oz (125g) cream cheese
- 1/4 cup butter, softened
- 1 1/2 cups icing sugar
- 3 tsp molasses
- 1/4 tsp cinnamon

Beat cream cheese and butter together until creamy. Add vanilla and cinnamon; mix well. Slowly add icing sugar and beat until creamy. Mix molasses into mixture and blend well. Refrigerate for 1 hour and spread over base.

Top with diced candied ginger.

SYLVIE'S MINT REVERSE NANAIMO BARS

Preheat oven to 350°F.

BASE:

Combine in food processor until crumbly:

- 24 crushed Golden Oreos
- 4 tablespoons melted butter

Press into lightly greased 8 x 8 inch pan and bake for 5-10 minutes (until just golden brown). Set aside to cool

FILLING:

In glass bowl :

- 1/2 cup cream
- 2 oz bittersweet chocolate

- 2 oz semi-sweet chocolate (if you prefer something sweeter, use all semi-sweet)

Put chocolate and cream into glass bowl. Microwave for 30 second increments until steaming (I did two 30s increments). Let sit for 5 minutes then stir until blended. If you want it really minty, add 1/8 tsp mint extract.

Spread on first layer and refrigerate for 1 hour.

TOPPING:

Melt:

- 6 ounces white chocolate
- 1 tablespoon butter
- 1/4 tsp mint extract

Combine until smooth and pour and spread over filling. Sprinkle with crushed candy canes. Slice once topping is set, and store in refrigerator.

EMILIE'S VEGAN EGGNOG MOUSSE SQUARES

If you like something a little less sweet, this is the one for you. Also gluten-free!

Preheat oven to 350°F.

BASE:

Mix:

- 1 1/4 cups rolled oats
- 1 cup ground almonds
- 1/4 cup cocoa
- 1 teaspoon cinnamon
- 1 tablespoon maple syrup
- 5 tablespoons melted coconut oil or vegan margarine

Blend together in food processor to form a coarse meal. Press into 8 x 8 baking pan and bake for 20 minutes.

FILLING:

Sweet Cashew Cream*:

- 1 cup soaked cashews
- 1/2 cup water
- 2 tablespoons maple syrup

Blend together with food processor or blender, the fold into one can of coconut whipping cream (I used Cha's Organics).

Spread on first layer and bake for 20 minutes. Let cool, drizzle with melted dark chocolate, then refrigerate overnight before cutting into squares. Keep refrigerated or frozen.

* Sweet Cashew Cream recipe is courtesy of Adeline Halvorson, from her recipe book, "What Do I Cook? Quick and Easy Plant-based Recipes That Are Gluten-free, Dairy-free and Budget-friendly."

ACKNOWLEDGMENTS

Thank you, once again, to my beta readers for taking the time out of your own very busy lives to read. Allison Litfin, Adeline Halvorson, Bev Harvey, Andrea Harrison, June Monteleone, Judi Evans and Ariana Feldberg — I'm so grateful for all of you.

Thanks to my patrons on Patreon! Your support is so wonderful to have, and I hope you had some fun with the little contests.

I'm sure I'm forgetting someone, and I apologize for that. If you're reading this, thank you, too.

I hope you'll consider leaving a review to share your thoughts with other readers. If you're not comfortable with that, even leaving a simple rating helps. I'm so grateful to everyone who takes the time for that show of support. You can also email me at the address below to say hi. I'm always up for talking books and horses!

If you're interested in joining my review team for future books, email me at linda@lindashantz.com

And last but most important, thank you, Lord. You are my only hope.

About the Author

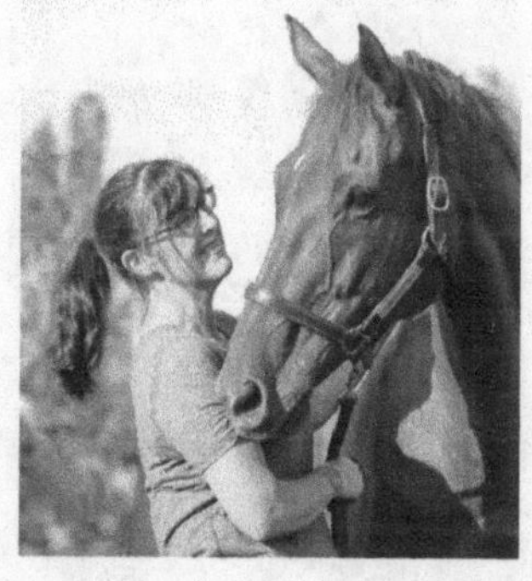

I began working at the racetrack before I finished high school, and after graduating the following January, took a hotwalking job at Payson Park in Florida. Once back at Woodbine, I started grooming and galloping. While the backstretch is exciting, I found I was more at home on the farm — prepping and breaking yearlings, nightwatching and foaling mares. Eventually I started my own small layup/broodmare facility, and in the last few years I've transitioned into retraining and rehoming. Somewhere along the way I did go back to school and get a degree. I should probably dust it off and frame it one day!

I live on a small farm in Ontario, Canada, with my adopted off-track Thoroughbreds and a young Border Collie. If you like my covers, check out my artwork at www.lindashantz.com

Author photo by Kyley Woods Photography, used with permission.